MW01248507

HOW CAN IT BE?

How Can It Be?

KELLI GALYEAN

Copyright © 2024 by Kelli Galyean
All rights reserved. No part of this book may be reproduced in any
manner whatsoever without written permission except in the case of
brief quotations embodied in critical articles and reviews.
First Printing, 2024

For all the women who sometimes need
to be reminded of the truest thing about themselves.
God loves you so deeply. He is real, and nothing is wasted.
Keep going, ladies!

You plead my cause
You right my wrongs
You break my chains
You overcome
You gave your life
to give me mine
You say that I am free
How can it be?
How can it be?

-lyrics by Jason Ingram and Paul Mabury

Chapter 1

The church bells warmed the air with their friendly melody. But nothing could warm the chilly rain drops pelting my face as I ran through the parking lot. I was late.

My foot hit a slick spot and slid sideways into a puddle, splashing muddy water up my shin. Barely catching myself, I groaned. I didn't have time for this! I righted myself and kept running.

Soaking wet, I rushed up the aged front steps of Dallas Christian Church. The thick wooden door opened easily, without a sound. I paused, taking a second to dry my feet on the large entryway mat and to wring the water out of my dress and hair. The smell of rain mixed with the smells of coffee, aging wood, and books.

I hurried through the foyer, running my fingers through my hair, hoping to tame it into some semblance of order. My soaked ballet flats squished water with each step. I passed a small group of the earliest early birds. They visited happily while sipping coffee and eating donuts. My stomach rumbled at the sugary smell wafting through the air, but I ignored my hunger—for now.

When I reached the open sanctuary doors, I knelt, unceremoniously dumping my purse and Bible out of sight behind the door on the right. Nearby, Miss Alma, the greeting coordinator, met my eyes, tiny but formidable. At five-foot-nine, I towered over her shrunken frame, but she was unmistakably the giant in the room. I twisted my face into a look of deep regret and whispered a quick but sincere *sorry* to the fierce older woman. She winked and smiled, my tardiness forgiven. *Whew*!

Relieved, I took a deep, settling breath and straightened to my full height, ready to greet. Pulling the collar of my damp denim jacket back into place, I looked across to the other side, to my friend, Sarah. She looked classically manicured and beautiful in a casual blue dress with white canvas sneakers. It was a simple outfit that somehow screamed, *Trying, but not too hard*. She must have avoided the downpour, I noted grumpily. Her straight, dark hair cascaded down her back like a gorgeous, reliable waterfall.

Ignoring the fact that I looked like a drowned rat, Sarah beamed in greeting and handed me a stack of paper bulletins full of announcements. "Hey, Mia! I was beginning to wonder if you were going to make it," she teased. She knew I hated to be late.

I shook my head in exasperation. "I set my alarm wrong. The stupid AM/PM mistake!" I grumbled. "On top of that, I had hair issues, which is now just a frizzy tragedy, thanks to the rain."

I used my hands to gently scrunch my unruly brown curls. At least I hadn't gone to the trouble to straighten it. That would have been a disaster. With a little guidance, things wouldn't completely devolve into a frizzy mess—maybe.

Just as that positive idea formed in my mind, a cold drop of water landed on the top of my foot, reminding me how truly soaked my dress was. I shook my head and sighed. Maybe today was just not my day.

Sarah looked me over, full of sympathy. She smiled reassuringly. "You'll dry fast, girl! You look great! You know I love a good pink dress!"

I had to admit, it was a cute dress, and it usually dried pretty quickly. Feeling the tiniest bit better, I nodded my thanks. Then I noticed her light application of make-up. *Oh no*. I may very well have rivers of mascara running down my face at the moment. *Good grief*, I thought, wishing for a reset button.

"Do I have mascara all over my face?" I asked, dreading her response.

Sarah squinted, looking carefully. "A little under your left eye, but that's it." It could be worse. I swiped at the area under my left eye and hoped for the best.

"I hate when that happens," she commiserated loyally. Before I could respond, the outer door opened. People began pouring into the foyer. Some were dripping wet, while others held umbrellas. Sarah turned toward the noise and pasted a welcoming smile on her face.

Miss Alma scowled, wielding a damp towel like a sword behind an oblivious man who shook the water off his umbrella, right onto the carpet. People were laughing and greeting one another heartily. I couldn't help but smile.

That reminds me…

I turned to Sarah. We were still handing out bulletins as we welcomed people into the sanctuary, but I was dying to hear about her date the night before. The guy sounded promising online.

"We missed you at the movie last night! How was your date?" I asked. Sarah grimaced, defeated—oh, no. I was really hoping this one would be good!

"It started okay," she said. "He took me to a vegan restaurant. He ordered the "chicken" strips. But then he complained about them, and everything else, for the rest of the meal." She sighed.

I groaned. Another fake vegan. You would think grown men would not be willing to pretend to be vegan to impress a pretty girl. You would be wrong. Sarah rolled her eyes and continued.

"That's not all. When the check came, I offered to go Dutch, but he said he preferred to pay so he could tip the *appropriate* amount for service."

I gasped. She nodded, her eyes wide. "I know! Do I seem like a stingy tipper?"

I shook my head, stunned at the rude implication. I couldn't believe there could be more, but Sarah kept going.

"He said something about waiting tables in college, as if he's the only person who ever waited tables. Then he complained to the server about the prices, saying plant-based meat should not be as expensive as actual meat! He was all over the place. It was just weird."

Sarah blushed, re-living the embarrassment. She put her hand over her eyes, as if it gave her a headache, and shook her head. "I should have gone out with you girls instead. I would have had more fun, for sure." Her shoulders slumped. "I think it's time to take a break from online dating. I'm just going to enjoy my life for a little bit."

I couldn't blame her after such a disappointing evening. I laughed at the ridiculousness, but I could tell Sarah was discouraged. It was rough out there.

"Don't give up," I tried to encourage her.

I sensed someone moving in close to me, but before I could turn to see, a warm, male voice rumbled in my ear.

"Well, well, well, if it isn't the prettiest girl in the whole church." It was such a cheesy thing to say, but I couldn't help but smile at my new boyfriend, Preston. In one move, he slid out of the way of the foot traffic and wrapped his arm around my waist, giving me a squeeze.

Sarah smiled knowingly. "Hey, Preston!"

He smiled back at Sarah. "Good morning to you, Sarah. How's it going?"

Sarah shrugged. "Pretty good so far."

Preston turned toward me and saucily waved a finger around in front of his left eye. "You trying something new there, Mia?"

Sarah chuckled.

"Ha ha," I grumbled. I looked around. I could swear I felt Miss Alma looking at me. She didn't like dalliers, and Preston was dallying. We were skating on thin ice. I angled slightly away from him, so he released me. I glanced at him and realized he didn't have a drop of rain on him—even his hair was perfectly styled.

"Where are all your rain stains?" I asked jealously.

"On my umbrella, babe. Always be prepared," he answered. I briefly stiffened at being called *babe*. Ew. I *really* did not like that nickname. But Preston didn't notice. He smirked confidently, leaning in closer to me. "I could have shared with you if you'd let me drive you to church," he pointed out, his nose grazing my temple.

I looked at the floor, feeling self-conscious. Preston and I hadn't been dating long, only about three weeks. I was still getting used to being close with him at all, much less being affectionate in public.

"Have y'all tried that new climbing gym in Oak Lawn yet?"

I could hug Sarah for interrupting the awkward moment. Preston looked over and shook his head. "Not yet, but I heard it's nice. I want to take Mia soon. Would you like to come with us when we go?"

I softened and leaned into him in spite of myself. It was things like this that made me give dating Preston a chance. He was fun, open, and generous. Everyone was welcome. Since I became a Christian, dating wasn't a great experience for me. I'd given up after a while. But Preston slowly wore me down over the last few months with his openness and (sometimes overwhelming) enthusiasm.

He reached for my hand, entwining his fingers through mine. I tried to relax and just enjoy the moment. Miss Alma was talking to someone, distracted for now. But our luck wouldn't last. I turned toward Preston and changed the subject.

"Hey, would you mind saving our seats?" I asked, squeezing his hand.

Preston took the hint and released me with a perceptive smile. My heart melted a little bit.

"Sure I will, even though you're trying to get rid of me. I see Miss Alma over there. She's cute, but that scowl could peel the skin off a banana." Preston looked into my eyes, wiggled his eyebrows, and turned to walk through the double doors into the sanctuary.

Sarah mockingly wiggled her eyebrows as he walked away, cracking up at the exchange.

"You've still got mascara on your cheek, *babe*." She chuckled. "He is so nice, Mia."

"Yup, he's great," I agreed. I feverishly rubbed my cheek, trying to de-smudge myself.

I looked around the room. People continued to mill around, still a little damp but content and enjoying seeing their friends. Greeting at church was one of my favorite things to do. It was a good way to catch up with people, and I liked getting to see all the faces of the congregation. Warmth and gratitude welled up in my heart. I loved my church.

Traffic picked up the last couple of minutes before church began. The sanctuary was filling up so much we couldn't see the stage. The bulletins seemed to fly from my hands. I greeted friends, acquaintances, and students I knew from serving at the youth camp last summer. When I ran out of bulletins, I reached for another stack from the box behind the doors and kept going.

Our friend Maddie arrived. She wrestled through the crowd to hug both Sarah and me, totally unfazed by Miss Alma's glare.

"Today's the day, ladies! Time to meet the new worship minister," Maddie announced.

"Ooh, I forgot today is his first day!" Sarah perked up.

The church leadership made the announcement last week, but I was in Atlanta, visiting my parents, so I missed it. I didn't know much about the new guy.

I smiled, playing along. "Tell us all the things, Maddie."

Maddie wiggled her eyebrows and ticked the items off on her fingers. "He's single. I've heard he's super nice. He knows The Martins, and he is apparently extremely cute too. It's too bad the church website has been down, so they couldn't post a picture."

I nodded. "Yeah, too bad. He could be the man of Sarah's dreams."

Sarah shook her head, holding up her hands. "Too soon."

We all laughed. Maddie adjusted her hair.

"Wish me luck, ladies. I'm going in," she said comically.

"Preston is in there. He saved seats already," Sarah told her. "We'll be in, in just a minute."

Maddie nodded and walked into the sanctuary just as the music began to play. I recognized the opening notes of "All Creatures of Our God and King."

The flow of people slowed down. I took a second to look at the bulletin myself. I skimmed the baby announcements and prayer requests before checking out the song list. Since it was the new guy's first day, I was curious to see what songs he'd chosen. "Great Is Thy Faithfulness" was on the list, after communion. I couldn't help but smile. Two old hymns in one service? I liked that.

The leader's deep, smooth voice joined the instruments.

All creatures of our God and King
Lift up your voice and ever sing,
Oh praise Him, Alleluia!

My heart swelled. I loved this song. The voice sounded pleasant and vaguely familiar. Where could I have heard it before? I didn't know many worship leaders—just our former one, Donnie, and one other, from the youth camp, but I couldn't remember that guy's name.

The music continued. Sarah and I put our remaining bulletins in a box and gathered our things. My hair and dress were still slightly damp, but I was distracted by the sound of all the people singing in the sanctuary. Who could worry about hair when people were singing at the top of their lungs?

Praise, praise the Father, Praise the Son
And praise the Spirit, three in one
Oh praise Him, Oh praise Him

The people were singing extra loud this morning, the joy palpable, even out in the foyer. I could tell from the energy in the room and the sound coming from the speakers that this new worship leader was talented. Like everyone else, I was curious.

His name was Ryan Lyles, which was all I knew about him. Unfortunately, I couldn't look him up on Facebook or anything. My parents were extremely anxious about image management—always had been. My dad was a State Senator in Georgia, which (according to my parents) meant our family needed to look as perfect as possible at all times. Unflattering pictures on social media would not do. It was easier for me to avoid it and keep peace with them. I didn't miss it, except for times like this.

I followed Sarah into the sanctuary, singing along, looking toward our usual pew. Our friends waited with saved seats for us. I turned my head for a second to look up at the stage.

Everything stopped.

Sound. Movement. My lungs. My feet planted on the carpet like it was quicksand. I was sinking. In an instant, time darted ten years to the past and back to the present. Everything hurt. My hands began to shake. My throat clenched like I was going to be sick, but I stood, frozen, unable to look away. I could not believe my eyes.

Ryan Blackstone?

I forced myself to blink and looked again. It was him. In a second, I took in everything that was different ten years ago and everything that was the same.

Tidy, short hair? Different.
Eyes the color of an October sky? The same.
Tall, beautiful, confident, talented? The same.
Standing in a church, wearing a soft, broken-in leather jacket, looking older and clean-cut, singing a worship song about God into the microphone while playing a guitar? Different. All of it.

I couldn't think in fully formed thoughts, except for one that pushed through the fog:

But Ryan Blackstone was a drummer.

Completely shaken, I looked down, grounding myself. *Breathe. In and out. Again. Breathe, Mia!*

I blinked and lifted my head to look around. Everyone was still standing, singing at the top of their lungs. Sarah was waiting for me in the pew by our friends. By Preston. I couldn't stay here. I turned and walked back up the aisle, hands shaking, head pounding. *Breathe.*

My mind spun like a tornado. *How did he get here? After all this time? That's not his name? He plays the guitar now? What am I going to do?* I put my head down, picked up one foot, and put it in front of the other, all the way out of the sanctuary.

I kept going, plodding through the foyer, picking up speed once I hit fresh air. The dwindling rain felt cold on my face as I rushed down the steps and ran to my car. My hand unlocked the door by memory. Shivering with cold, I sat in the driver's seat.

The panic crested. Hot tears overflowed. *How? Why? God?* I couldn't hold onto any one thought. Flashback images and memories stormed across my field of vision.

It was all Ryan. Blips I hadn't thought about in years: playing drums in the flashing light of the club. Eating waffles at the diner. Holding my hand as we walked up the stairs to my college apartment. Wrapping his arms around me. Laughing together. The phone calls and *I love yous*.

I knew what was coming next, and I was powerless to stop it. I tried to focus on my breathing, but the images shifted.

Two lines on a plastic pregnancy test.

The tidal wave of panic. The look on my mother's face. The pain. The long, winding darkness. Many, many tears.

Chapter 2

I opened my eyes. I was still sitting in the church parking lot. I grasped the steering wheel of the parked car as if I was desperate to keep the car going somewhere straight ahead. My knuckles were white. The adrenaline was fading a little, and my body felt drained of energy, as if I could pass out at any moment. I was still breathing fast, but my vision was clear.

The rain skated down the windshield, drops racing downward like tears. Lots and lots of tears. Everything good about my life seemed far away, like I was looking at it through the wrong end of a telescope.

What am I going to do? How is he here? Why is this happening now?

A knock on my window startled me. I jumped and turned, looking up into a very confused, handsome face. Apparently, Preston followed me. *Oh no.*

"Babe? Are you okay? What happened?" he yelled through the window, clutching his umbrella. His hair was still perfect.

I motioned for him to get in. I wasn't ready for this, but I couldn't just leave him out there in the rain. I tried to breathe, to stop crying. I scraped my fingers under my eyes, trying to remove any streaks of mascara.

Preston got in on the passenger side, collapsed his umbrella, and tucked it between his feet on the rubber floor mat my best friend's husband, Gage, insisted I needed when I bought this Honda Accord. He was right, it *was* helpful. I'd have to thank him for that. Preston turned his body toward me, looking at me earnestly. A single drop of rain traveled down his temple.

"Babe, you look like you've seen a ghost," he said, looking me over. "Are you okay? Should I go get someone to help?"

My eyes filled all over again. A ghost was putting it mildly. I shook my head.

"I'm fine," I mumbled through the tears. "I just had something unexpected happen. I wasn't prepared, and I'm freaking out a little bit. But I'm okay."

I knew from therapy that Preston's emotional state wasn't my responsibility at this moment, but I tried to be reassuring. It was a good distraction from the dynamite that was just planted in the middle of my life. I couldn't know when it would explode.

Ryan is on the stage at my church. Right now.

I shook my head, trying to get through the next breath.

"Preston, I don't talk about this a lot, but I have some things in my past I'm not proud of."

He smiled kindly. Clearly relieved, he shook his head and said, "You and everyone else, babe. That's okay. It's part of growing up."

I sighed. He really was sweet. I tried to explain. "I had a relationship in college that didn't go well. I saw the guy from afar at church today. It was a shock. I just panicked and left. Sorry if I scared you. I'm fine now."

Yes, fine. *Breathe.*

"Babe. Lots of people have bad exes. You should see a couple of mine." He mimed an explosion with his hands while making the accompanying noise all middle school boys excel at making.

"Do you want me to beat him up?" he asked so sweetly I hugged him right there.

"No, I'm sure Miss Alma would frown upon that. You could be banned for life." I found the strength to joke back. But my heart was sinking.

My friends knew about my past, and I was glad God used my story to encourage the women at the pregnancy center, but telling men about it hadn't gone well—ever. If Preston liked me as much as he seemed to, I would eventually have to tell him. I could wait, but I'd rather know. I tried to think on the bright side: *maybe this time will be different*. I took a deep breath.

"There's more." The best way was just to say it. I kept going. "I was nineteen. I got pregnant and had an abortion."

Whew. Saying those words never got any easier. I looked at Preston. He looked stricken. He sat silent, one hand resting in mine on the center console, the other in his lap.

"Wow." He said nothing else for a few seconds. He took a breath, looking outside, then down, anywhere but at me. He patted my hand absentmindedly.

"Thank you for telling me," he said gently, stroking my hand with his thumb. "I'm sorry seeing him was so upsetting. He's in there right now?"

I nodded. "I haven't seen him in ten years. He doesn't know about that part of it."

"Wow," Preston said again.

I could tell he was not sure what to do with all this. I didn't blame him. I wasn't always sure either.

I was exhausted. I told Preston I was going to head home. He offered to come with me, but I could tell he was a little discombobulated and clearly felt dazed from this new information.

I didn't have the energy to have a big discussion right then, so I told him no thanks. I'd rather have some time alone, and I'd talk to him later. He accepted that. He kissed my cheek and got out of the car, umbrella in hand, still protecting his hair like a fortress. I watched him walk toward his car. He didn't look back.

I couldn't worry about Preston right now. I needed to get away from here. I glanced up at the steeple of the aged building, the only church home I'd ever known. Six years ago, Maddie invited me to a Bible study, and I met the Lord. Dallas Christian Church had quickly become one of my favorite places, a refuge from the world, from ugliness and weariness. Now Ryan was literally standing on the stage inside. I felt totally overwhelmed. *God, why?* I prayed over and over as I drove away. I didn't have any other words.

Once I was home, I answered Sarah's and Maddie's baffled texts, told them I wasn't feeling well, then turned off the ringer. I changed out of my (now twice-soaked) dress and into my oldest, comfiest sweatpants. They were baggy, soft, and pilling. They were the coziest pants I owned. I pulled a sweatshirt over my head and crawled under the covers.

Anna and Gage were out of town for one of his co-workers' weddings, so I couldn't call her to warm up a frozen pizza and turn on an episode of *Friends*, like the old days. We weren't kids anymore. *I am a grown woman,* I told myself. *And I'm not alone.*

I reminded myself of one of my favorite scriptures: *God set me free for* freedom, *not for the prison of my own shame.* I would figure this out. I just needed some time to wrap my head around this, then I could make some decisions. I had options. There were other churches out there. I could leave and go to church somewhere else.

If I did, it would mean leaving my community, friends who were now my family, friends who knew about my story but might still be shocked to find out my drummer was now a guitar-playing worship leader. Ryan must be a Christian now too. Wow.

God sure does have a sense of humor, I thought. Maybe one day I would laugh at this situation. Not today. Today I felt completely exhausted. I rolled over, falling asleep quickly, escaping the chaos.

Chapter 3

When I awoke, the rain had stopped. The clouds were gone, and it was still light out, but I could tell the sun was going down on the other side of my apartment building. I looked at the clock display on my nightstand: five o'clock. Wow. I must have slept the day away.

My phone had lots of text messages from friends checking on me. Both Maddie and Sarah sent texts to check on me. I told them both I was fine. Anna and Gage landed at the airport then invited me out for wings and a drink on their way home. I declined, saying I had some things to do, but I'd talk to her tomorrow.

What would I say?

Remember my drummer? The beginning of my life's most shameful decision? Well, funny story…

Yeah, right.

This conversation could absolutely wait until tomorrow. I got up and wrestled my hair into a bun on top of my head. I walked down the short hallway into the kitchen and poured a bowl of cereal—the dinner of champions.

I felt a little more clear-headed. I considered the situation as I ate. No one knew who Ryan was to me except for Anna. Not even Preston knew. *Oh no. Preston.*

I wondered how he was doing this evening. Now that I thought about it, he wasn't one of my missed calls or texts. Maybe he needed a nap too. Or maybe since finding out, he thought I was an evil succubus. He wouldn't be the first.

I went into the living room and settled in on the squashy leather sofa. It was beautiful, mahogany brown. I loved it. The sofa was an exciting "grown up" purchase when I moved into this apartment a couple of weeks before Anna and Gage got married. Gage sweetly offered for me to live with them, but it was time to live on my own.

I was happy to discover I enjoyed living alone. I was rarely lonesome. A house full of girls from church lived about two blocks away, and Maddie lived in my neighborhood too. Being home alone was still kind of a luxury. I turned on the TV while I ate my cereal to watch an old rerun of *The Office*. It felt refreshing to laugh on such a flustering day.

I couldn't help but reflect on the morning. It seemed like weeks ago instead of just hours. The shock was wearing off a bit. I had tried to forget Ryan and the whole experience, but I could never fully forget. I thought about young Mia, just nineteen years old, naive and innocent.

At the time, meeting Ryan was a huge thrill. Our weekend together felt like a dream. I fell for him so fast, and I fully believed we were in love. Finding out I was pregnant was such a shock, and then everything that happened afterward was awful. Healing was a long process. In some ways, I never fully recovered. It was still heavy, even ten years later.

Giving everything to God was one of the hardest parts of embracing faith. God's forgiveness and forgiving myself were two different things. But I wasn't that girl anymore. I was a new creation. Meeting Jesus changed everything for me. I would never stop marveling at the love and freedom I'd found in Him.

I could hear my therapist, Brooke's voice in my head: *we can do hard things*. It *was* hard, but I did it, over and over again. God's grace was real and sufficient to cover my sins. And nothing was wasted; everything had purpose. I would remind myself of that as many times as it took.

Most days it was enough. The month of November was still tender and tricky, but that was understandable. My relationship with my parents never fully recovered, but I accepted that, and we did our best. In all of it, I embraced the truth of grace as well as God's sovereignty and omniscience. God knows everything, yet He still saw fit for me to hear His truth and believe in Jesus. I did not take that for granted.

I reminded myself that Ryan was a minister now. He must have found Jesus too. I was glad for him, even as I wondered about him—where he'd been, what he'd done. I was twenty-nine, so he would be in his early thirties now. Had he ever married? He could be divorced or even a widower. He could have children!

I reflected on the last ten years. There were ups and downs, but I had a happy, fulfilling life. I loved being a nurse, and I had wonderful friends and community. My life didn't necessarily fit a traditional mold with a husband and children, but I was grateful to have so much goodness and joy.

When I was young, I assumed I would have a traditional life. In fact, my parents insisted I would. Until sophomore year. After everything happened, I was a mess for a long time. Dating got complicated.

Becoming a Christian hadn't made it any simpler. I'd tried, but so far, those guys didn't want a woman with a past like mine. It happened every time, so after a while, I pretty much gave up on the idea and focused on enjoying the life I actually had. Preston was the only guy I'd dated in over a year. Then, just when I thought I was making progress—*bam*. Ryan.

I pictured him from earlier in the day. I only caught a quick glance, but I would know him anywhere, even with his hair short and clean-cut. Those eyes would haunt me forever. Did he know how to play guitar back then too? We'd only spent a couple of days together, and I hadn't asked. He could be a musical prodigy, for all I knew.

I shook myself, coming out of my reverie. The show was over. I turned off the TV, set my bowl on the coffee table, and turned on the lamp by the sofa. I pulled my Bible into my lap, opening it. In the book of Joshua, I found the story of Rahab. It was the lesson the first time Maddie invited me to Bible study—the beginning of my faith journey. I was shocked by the story that first night. I never dreamed a woman like Rahab would be in the Bible at all. Over time, I learned that there were a lot of surprising people in there. I'd gone back to read Rahab's story many times since that first night, and it encouraged me every time.

I was always amazed at Rahab's simple, true faith being counted to her as righteousness. I needed the reminder myself. She didn't have anyone else around her to encourage her. She just believed God. I admired Rahab for her faith and for her courage—to have hidden the spies, protected them, confessed her faith to them, and asked them to spare her and her family when they took the city.

All of this took tremendous courage and trust in God. Because of her faith, Rahab and her family were safe when the city fell. Afterward, she joined the family of God, eventually marrying Salmon. Rahab was the mother of Boaz, the great-grandfather of David. Rahab, a vulnerable Canaanite woman with a past, was part of the genetic line of Christ and was even written about in the Great Cloud of Witnesses. God's out-of-the-ordinary redemption of this woman was a favorite story of mine.

Thinking about Rahab's story reminded me that God can save anyone. Even me. Remembering the goodness of God lifted my gaze every time. I took a deep breath, refusing to cry any more, and just prayed, thanking God He was not surprised by this day. I asked Him for guidance, for wisdom, and to please help me along the way. I certainly didn't know what else to do, but He would. He always did.

What a gift, to be free to trust God with our cares and burdens, to be able to give them over to Him. I still wasn't over it, even after six years of knowing Him. I reminded myself that whatever happened, it would be okay in the end.

Lord, what are you doing? I prayed. *A heads-up might have been helpful*. I closed the Bible, laying it back on the table.

I stood up then grabbed my cereal bowl. Walking to the kitchen, I contemplated what to do next. Should I call Preston? I could call Anna, but she would just freak out. I couldn't handle more emotions today. I rinsed the bowl and decided it was probably best to keep it simple. I'd take a hot shower, go to bed, and sleep some more. Work was waiting in the morning, and tomorrow would certainly have enough trouble for itself. Tonight, I needed rest. Tomorrow, I would face whatever came.

Chapter 4

Monday morning came and, with it, the fervor of a new week. The hospital was hopping all weekend, and Monday was no different. The ER was full when I arrived. I focused on helping my patients, and the day flew by.

My phone was pretty much off during the workday, so when I left the hospital, there were a few texts waiting for me, all of them asking if I was feeling better. I felt deeply grateful for this community of women. They were a gift. Preston sent me a text too, asking if we could get coffee tomorrow. I accepted, then told him I would text him tomorrow to decide a time and place. Anna was waiting for me, and I needed to focus on her.

When I got home around eight in the evening, Anna was already there, waiting at the top of the stairs, seated next to a bag of Thai takeout. This was our Monday night ritual since she and Gage got married a couple of years ago. She'd changed out of her corporate tiger lady suit, into comfy clothes, and she was ready to watch our weekly helping of reality television and catch up.

"Hey!" I hugged her hello. She opened a bottle of wine and loaded up our plates while I quickly showered, then we sat down in the living room, ready to feast and catch up from the weekend. We dug fragrant noodles out of the deceptively small white boxes and crunched on spring rolls. Anna went first, describing in detail the gorgeous, over-the-top wedding they attended. It sounded beautiful, though a little overwhelming.

Having to sit still through the couple singing an old Celine Dion song to each other during the reception, complete with choreography, wasn't my idea of fun, but Anna and Gage enjoyed a great time in Napa. I was glad. They both worked so hard, and telling a relaxed Anna about my weekend shock would probably go a little better than telling a stressed-out Anna.

When she was finished sharing, I decided it would be better to just rip off the Band-Aid.

"Do you remember that drummer I met in college? Ryan Blackstone?" I asked. She startled, then nodded. Of course she remembered him. My weekend with him impacted both of our lives monumentally. I took a deep breath, forcing myself to look Anna in the eye.

"Well, apparently, he also goes by the name Ryan Lyles, and he's the new worship leader at church."

Anna sat still for a second, eyes wide. I waited for the news to sink in. It took a few seconds. It was only us in my apartment, so it was a little funny when she whispered, "Ryan is *here*? What in the world? A minister? A different *name*? Are you okay?"

I nodded, powerless in the rolling wave of shock and memories. My eyes filled with tears all over again. So did hers. Anna leaned over to wrap her arms around me. Nothing else needed to be said.

She hugged me so tight I was sure she was going to leave a bruise, but I didn't care. I just hugged her back, this dear friend who was closer than a sister.

Anna was a better friend than I could have ever deserved. She was with me when I met Ryan at that club. Then she stayed with me that day, after my mom kissed me goodbye and left for the airport as if nothing ever happened. Anna helped me through the darkness. When I couldn't stop crying, Anna made an appointment and made me go to counseling. When I sought comfort in self-destructive choices, she threatened to find a new roommate, so I stopped. For me, a messed-up kid in pain, Anna was a miracle.

We were roommates, from our freshmen dorm in California to our grown-up apartment in Dallas, until she and Gage got married. Anna and Gage both came with me to church when I first started to believe in God six years ago. Anna grew up going to church, so she was more comfortable there than me at first. Over the past twelve years, Anna had truly become my family.

We pulled apart, drying our eyes.

"Thank you for understanding," I said. "You are the best."

"Mia, of course! This is a big deal," Anna exclaimed. She looked me in the eye, prodding. "Are you really okay?"

I nodded again. She looked skeptical.

"I am," I insisted.

Anna nodded, satisfied. "I haven't thought of him in years. I have so many questions! Number one: what's the deal with the name change?"

I laughed. "Exactly! I don't know. My best guess is the witness protection program."

Anna laughed, getting fired up now. "That's as good a guess as any. Okay, question two: How does a drummer from a punk band in California end up leading worship at a church in Dallas?"

I shrugged. I knew it was by way of Nashville, but no other details.

"But I guess if God can bring *me* here, He can bring anyone?" I suggested.

Now it was Anna's turn to shrug. "Very true. I guess we'll find out eventually," she said.

The name thing remained a mystery. Most of our theories on that were theatrical in nature and improbable at best.

Now that Anna knew, my mind was freed up to ask more questions. What had Ryan been doing for the last ten years? Would he remember me? Doubtful. Actually, that was a hopeful thought. I latched onto it.

"He may not even remember me. I mean, he probably had a girl in every town along the 101," I speculated.

I looked at Anna. *Oh no.* It was the wrong thing to say. Her eyebrows were raised, and her brown eyes were huge. She squared her shoulders.

"He will *absolutely* remember you! You are unforgettable, Mia!" She was indignant.

"It would be easier if he didn't," I pointed out.

"No chance, *amiga*."

Classic Anna. She was too good to me.

"Well, I'm going to hold out hope," I decided. I changed the subject. "I told Preston about my past. When I saw Ryan, I panicked and ran to the car. Preston followed me, and I explained what happened."

"Wow. How did that go?" Anna asked supportively. She knew sharing about my past had been the kiss of death for more than one dating relationship.

"Well, he hasn't called," I pointed out with a shrug.

Anna's shoulders slumped. She shook her head. "Oh man. Maybe he's just processing. Or maybe he's not even thinking about that. He's been really busy at work, right? Maybe he has to work late."

I shrugged. "Yeah, maybe. But he wouldn't be the first guy to hear this news and break up with me immediately."

Anna shook her head, determined. "Don't think like that, Mia. Positivity!"

"Honestly, I'm okay either way. It's nice to have someone to spend time with and go out on dates, and he really is nice and fun. But I don't feel that...that *connection* with Preston," I admitted guiltily.

Anna nodded, her face scrunched up with understanding. "I can't pretend I didn't see that coming."

"What do you mean?" I asked.

She shrugged. "I just mean, I have seen you when you were really into a guy. And I can tell you tried hard to like Preston, but that…" She searched for the right word. "That *excitement* just isn't there."

She was right. I sighed, regretful. Prior to Sunday morning, dating Preston was going well, but I could already tell this was not "it" for me. Something was missing. *Why am I like this?* I thought.

Anna put her hand on my shoulder. "Mia Browning, don't you dare feel guilty about this. You've tried! You put yourself out there! That is super brave! I'm proud of you! It's not your fault he's not a perfect match."

Anna was right. I nodded in agreement.

"Thank you for encouraging me," I said, stretching. "Okay, roomie. I'm kicking you out. It's getting late, and we both have work in the morning."

Anna nodded and gathered up the remains of dinner. We took everything to the kitchen, and I walked her to the door. I told her to say hi to Gage for me and locked up behind her.

I was washing the wine glasses in the kitchen sink when a knock on my door startled me. I frowned at the door, alert. It was late for an unexpected visitor. A muffled voice came through the door.

"Mia? It's Preston. Can we talk?"

I went to the door and looked through the peephole. It sure was Preston, and he looked terrible. His hair was a mess. This couldn't be good. I opened the door, and he walked in quietly.

"Sorry for dropping by without texting first. I knew you'd be up, though, because of *Mondays with Anna*." He smiled. We both laughed awkwardly at the joke. He'd asked me out for a Monday once, but I told him no because Mondays were reserved for Anna.

Up close, his hair was even messier than I thought. Considering Preston's vanity, this was concerning. I'd never seen him like this.

"Are you okay? Come on in and sit down." I gestured to the couch. Preston walked over and collapsed onto the closest seat, looking somber. It all came out in a rush.

"Mia, I'm sorry I didn't handle your news very well yesterday. I really like you. You are beautiful and smart. You're important to me." He paused, then took a big breath. "I'm sorry, but I just can't marry someone who would do that."

Wow. I stood there, trying to process. Of course this wasn't unexpected. Hadn't I just told Anna he wasn't the one for me? But it still hurt.

Someone who would do that. The sting of those words was sharp, even after all this time. It was a cut-off. He didn't want to know more, didn't want to consider the person who lived the choice, and everything before and after it.

It was painful and disappointing, but I immediately rejected the idea of snapping back at him. I understood. I had said much uglier things to myself over the years. Furthermore, I couldn't help but note that relief was already oozing through my muscles.

"I understand," I said quietly.

Silence. I looked up, meeting his eyes.

"That's it?" Preston asked, clearly miffed. I wasn't sure what he meant. I raised my eyebrows, puzzled.

"You're not going to say anything to try to change my mind? You're not going to ask questions about how I feel or how I got here?" he demanded.

Wow. He seemed genuinely hurt, but hadn't *he* just dumped *me*? *I* had now hurt *his* feelings? Bewildered irritation blazed up my spine. I sighed, tamping it down.

All doubts were erased—Preston was not the guy for me. I took a breath, swallowing down everything I felt tempted to say in defense. More than anything, I just wanted this moment to be over. I looked at him, pulling my lips into what I hoped was a gentle smile.

"I'm grateful you let me know, Preston. Thank you for coming to talk to me in person." I was still standing by the door. I reached over and turned the doorknob, opening it expectantly.

Preston huffed, still indignant. Was he expecting me to cry or beg? I didn't consider myself an overly prideful person, but in a moment like this, I was glad to have already cried the day's available tears.

But I didn't like burning bridges. I reminded myself that we were friends. I didn't want things to be awkward at church, no matter how annoyed I was at the moment. I reached out to hug him.

"Your friendship is important to me, Preston. I appreciate you taking me out and being so sweet these last few weeks. You are a really fun guy."

He warmed up to the compliment and hugged me back. He kissed the top of my head.

"Thank you for understanding my convictions," he said sincerely.

I repeat, *wow*. Finally, he walked out. As I shut and locked the door, I sighed a prayer of relief. Nothing about these last couple of days had gone the way I expected, but I felt lighter, somehow.

I turned to walk toward the kitchen. I finished the previously interrupted cleanup, started the dishwasher, and went to bed.

Chapter 5

The week passed with more spring showers, plus one tornado watch—typical spring weather in Texas. I was afraid they might have to cancel evening Bible study, but the rain let up in the afternoon. Anna came to Bible study that night. It was great to see her this much in a single week. Sarah was there too. She asked if I was feeling better since Sunday, and I told her yes.

I shared the news of my breakup with the girls, but I didn't offer any details. I just told them Preston and I weren't a good fit, and we both realized it. They all looked indignant at the idea that Preston would dump me.

I appreciated the loyalty, but these girls were single, and one of them may very well be a great match for Preston, so I made sure to add that we kept the relationship very casual and had not dated long at all.

Singles-group dynamics can get a little weird around dating. Maybe the damage control was just my parents rubbing off on me, but I was not about to let Preston Holden cost me a friendship.

After Bible study ended, some girls were hanging out, finishing off the snacks, when someone brought up Ryan. I had carefully avoided the topic all evening, mostly out of self-preservation.

"Okay, ladies, what did we think of the new worship guy?" Emma asked. I turned to leave the kitchen, but I was too late. The way was blocked. I'd have to squeeze by three girls to get to the living room. Everyone chimed in with their opinions on how talented he was, how much they enjoyed the service, etc.

Avery piped up first. "Have you ever seen such beautiful eyes on a man?" It wasn't unexpected; I'd certainly thought it myself enough times ten years ago. All the girls giggled.

Of course, I didn't blame them. Even now, I couldn't help but agree. Ryan had aged well, filling out into an even more attractive man. I acknowledged it. I just preferred to think carefully about separating my Skittles into color groups instead. Yellow, green, purple, red.

"Apparently, he was roommates with Jamie Martin," Jenny reported. Around the room, eyebrows raised, mine included. Breaths caught. Everyone sighed sympathetically. Jamie Martin, Pam and John's son, was deeply missed. He was killed in a rock-climbing accident shortly after I met them a few years ago. He'd been thirty years old.

"Yeah," Avery agreed. "Jamie was the first person to share about Jesus with him. Apparently, Ryan was living a pretty wild life before they met, then once they became friends, things changed a lot."

So that was his story—or part of it. I could only imagine what his grief was like. I thought of Maddie, who was such a special friend, and a huge part of my life. I would always be grateful she invited me to Bible study during lunch in the cafeteria at work, six years ago. I couldn't fathom losing her.

I was actually planning to go to the Martins' the following evening for dinner. Pam and John had become something like mentors to me over the last couple of years. Come to think of it, I was surprised Pam and John had not mentioned the Ryan thing, but it made sense. I usually ate dinner at their house every other Thursday, but we hadn't been able to connect as much lately. They had gone on a two-week cruise, and I filled in for someone at work the week before their trip, so I hadn't seen them in over a month.

Pam and John still talked about Jamie all the time. They were incredibly proud of their son, and they missed him constantly. Pam had recently shared with me that, in some ways, grief brought her and John closer. They felt safe to grieve with each other, to be sad, and also to celebrate the good—to enjoy the things they could enjoy. They grieved with hope, holding tight to one another in it. And they had never grieved alone; the whole church loved Jamie and grieved with them.

I found their hope and faithfulness beautiful. It was overwhelming at first. Jamie's death gave me my first glimpse of grief as a Christian. He was young and living to the fullest, and in his death, I had seen his parents grieve to the fullest extent. But I also saw their hope for eternity, and their encouragement to keep going, to keep really *living*. It made me ask myself, *was I really living as fully as I could?*

After so much counseling in college, I assumed I was healed. But watching the Martins suffer unlocked a deeper grief in my own heart, and I started counseling again. I needed to grieve with hope in Jesus and the promise of eternity.

Going back to counseling was incredibly helpful to me. Brooke was a wonderful licensed therapist, and she was a Christian. A few months into the process, she suggested I attend a grief program at a local pregnancy center. It was more helpful than I could have ever expected. Brooke also worked with me to stop holding back out of fear of messing up and embrace the chance to live my life. I was a work in progress on that front, but I'd come a long way.

Later that night, I left Bible study thinking about Ryan and Jamie Martin. I thought about Maddie and Anna and how God gave us all exactly who we needed in order to hear the truth, to believe. I missed out on knowing Jamie Martin, but he was the catalyst for a huge part of my healing journey. Because of him, I'd embraced my life, choosing to get out of my comfort zone, to pursue goodness, and even to serve others, at church and at the pregnancy center. I would always be grateful for him.

I laughed at the irony of the other girls checking out Ryan. He was a beautiful man. It was undeniable. He was tall with broad shoulders. He had dark-blond hair, a gorgeous smile, those October sky eyes. But all that was just a distraction.

I prayed for God to give me wisdom to know what I needed to do in the moments to come. I had no idea what it was going to be like to see Ryan on the stage Sunday morning, but I was glad to have some time to prepare. I didn't want to go running out of church every Sunday. It wasn't out of the question, but it wasn't reasonable either.

I considered ripping off the Band-Aid. I could march up to him, say, '*Welcome,*' then shake his hand like nothing ever happened. I reminded myself he might not even remember me. That would be ideal.

Whatever happened, I needed to be gentle with myself. This wasn't urgent. If I didn't feel ready, I could wait. I didn't sing with the band or anything. I wouldn't have a reason to interact with him.

Sitting at home, I sighed. Worrying about this was not going to do me any good. I prayed for God to hold my fears in His hand and help me trust Him with all of it. I learned quickly that the power of God to carry our burdens was a wonderful, peaceful help in times of trouble. I was glad to know it now, in a moment of need. The song was true:

What a Friend we have in Jesus
All our sins and griefs to bear
What a privilege to carry everything to God in prayer

The following evening after work, I drove over to the Martins' house.

Pam knew my story, but of course she would never guess I would have a connection to Ryan. I was hopeful I might get to gain some perspective, but it may not be the right time. I would need to wait and see. Grief made Pam's heart extra tender, and she still had hard days sometimes.

If Jamie had known Ryan, and Ryan was here now, it stood to reason she would love him like another son. It felt important to remember and honor that. I wasn't sure if I should ask her advice or not. But if I was going to seek wisdom from anyone in this matter, it would be her or my therapist. I would see how the evening went, then if there was time, I could bring it up. If not, I'd wait.

Pam and John ran a business together. They served in the church in different roles too. On top of that, she was a talented decorator and an excellent cook. I was extra grateful for her gifts on a day like today, when I hadn't had time for lunch. Absolutely starving, I parked my car and hurried up the sidewalk to their front door. I rang the bell, and the door opened almost immediately.

John Martin was a tall, broad man. He filled the doorway, enveloping me in a big bear hug. He was a kind soul. I was always glad to see him, and the feeling was mutual.

"Mia! It's great to see you," he bellowed. John was an enthusiastic person, who didn't seem to have a *whisper* setting on his vocal cords. Pam always joked that the whole neighborhood always knew their business because John was so loud. We walked inside together, John immediately asking me about the grossest thing I'd seen that day.

John owned a contracting business, which was totally disconnected from the medical field. But he loved surgical documentaries and *ER* reruns on TV. He was fascinated by stories of wounds, injuries, and blood clots. I didn't talk about those parts of my job with most people, so I usually tried to embellish the stories really well to make them as gruesome as possible, which he loved.

I told him, fortunately-but-unfortunately, it had been a pretty chill day in the ER. Only a couple of broken bones, spring allergy-induced asthma attacks, and a woman who didn't know she was pregnant until she was in labor. A busy day, but nothing truly gross. I assured him the full moon would hit next week, and I'd have a doozy for him next time. John shrugged good naturedly then moved on.

"Are you going to the summer camp again this year?" John asked as we walked through the sunny entryway into the living room. It was a large room with welcoming butter-yellow walls and beautiful decor. I nodded as I turned to put my purse down by the sofa.

"Yes, I'm super excited! I can't wait! It will be great to get away and be at camp again," I gushed. I really loved it there, so I was glad the youth minister asked me to be the camp nurse again this year. We were only about six weeks out from going. Spring was passing quickly. I made a mental note to check the schedule at work to make certain I was off the whole week.

I followed John through the living room as well as the dining room of the sprawling, ranch-style house. We entered the bright, cheerful kitchen. Pam and John updated it the year before as a project to do together in their grief. It was a beautiful, cozy room, with a feeling of welcome that took over the second you walked in.

I loved Pam's kitchen. The sun was already set, but the dusky sky was still on display through the large windows. I could see they had turned on the string of lights zig-zagging across the patio, and the table outside was set with flowers. Inside, the Shins' playful *ooohs* flowed quietly through expertly concealed speakers. Pam washed an overflowing colander of salad greens at the large sink. She smiled when I walked into the room then began drying her hands so she could wrap me in a warm hug.

"Hi, honey," Pam drawled in her pretty Alabama accent. She wrapped her arms around me. Pam was a great friend, but she also loved me like a daughter, which was very special to me.

Sometimes people talked about having a *Church Mother*, someone who loved and mentored younger people in the church as they grew spiritually. Pam was a Church Mother for me, no doubt. I was humbled she and John would want to spend time with me. They faithfully asked me to dinner every other Thursday, and I couldn't help but say yes. They were always kind enough to study with me and answer my questions, or even just listen. Their gentleness and knowledge was a happy surprise for this new Christian. I learned a lot from them.

Pam squeezed me tight then pulled back to look me over, a Southern habit leftover from growing up in Alabama. Having grown up in Georgia, it felt like home to me. My heart warmed, even as she tsk-ed.

"You look a little worn, hon. Here, have some of these apples while I get dinner on the table." She turned her head toward the living room. "Johnny, can you pour the tea please, love?"

Her use of his nickname made me smile, as it always did. Only Pam called John "Johnny." All of us from church thought it was adorable. They'd been married thirty-five years, and they still obviously enjoyed each other. The Martins had gone through a lot, but they chose to cling to the Lord and to each other through all of it. I couldn't think of a better example of strong, loving commitment.

Pam pushed a plate of apple slices toward me. I obediently shoved a piece of apple in my mouth. My stomach had been growling since I smelled the chicken spaghetti, still steaming from the oven. It was cooling on an iron trivet on the stone countertop. Browned cheese bubbled with creamy sauce and promise. It was all I could do not to grab a fork and dig in.

Pam stuffed her hands into two oven mitts then took hold of the hot dish, asking me to get the door. We'd be eating outside on their beautiful backyard patio. I grabbed the salad bowl then held the door for Pam as she muscled the heavy casserole dish across the patio and over to the table. She set it down on a metal trivet with a thump and removed the oven mitts with a sigh.

"There. Let's eat!" Pam pulled out the chair to her right and settled in, placing her napkin in her lap.

I was fully intending to ask about their cruise, but as I pulled out a chair, I noticed an extra place setting, identical to the other three. A chill ran down my spine. *Oh no.*

"Are y'all expecting someone else tonight?" I asked lightly, in a voice I hoped in no way reflected the dread quickly pooling in my stomach.

Pam was dishing out chicken spaghetti onto her plate, but she paused. "Oh, yes, Jamie's friend Ryan, the new worship minister, may stop by after the band practice tonight. I didn't want to not have a spot ready for him if practice ends early."

I swallowed, reaching for my glass of tea. I took a breath.

"Have y'all been spending a lot of time with him since he came to town?" It would make sense. The Martins were wonderful, and if he had known Jamie, they would want to spend time with him. And they were busy people. I hadn't been to their house in a few weeks.

"Yes," Pam replied with a smile. "He's been a real sweetheart through everything. He was Jamie's roommate, you know. He was there when Jamie fell, rock climbing with a couple of other friends. He's been a godsend. I think it's been good for him to have us too. Did you know Jamie was the one who first told Ryan about Jesus?"

My eyes widened, taking all this in. I already knew about most of those details, though I didn't realize Ryan was there when Jamie fell. I was processing a mile a second.

Jamie ultimately died of a head injury, in the hospital, shortly after transport. Ryan would have been one of the people with him in the mountains, waiting for the helicopter, stabilizing his friend as best he could. Those final moments would have been terrifying for anyone. Now he was here, at our church.

It must be a wonderful blessing and comfort for my sweet, grieving friends to have this man live so close. I felt horribly selfish. I reminded myself that God had saved me. I needed to follow *Him*, not be worried about seeing someone from my past or wasting time worrying about experiencing pain. I wanted to move on, as he undoubtedly had. But I also had a feeling of strong curiosity. I wanted to know more.

"Were y'all close with Ryan before he moved here? Or are you still getting to know him?" I asked.

"Here, Mia, hand your plate over here, and I'll dish this out for you. It's too hot to pass," Pam offered. I passed my plate, waiting as she heaped it high with delicious goodness then passed it back to me. I was so hungry moments ago, but now anxiety was building in my stomach, crowding out the hunger pangs, replacing them with a rolling acidity. Pam took a sip of tea and began to answer my question.

"We've known Ryan for years now. He used to come down when Jamie would come to visit. And we'd go up to Nashville to see them too. They were best friends for…oh, I guess about six years. They'd been roommates for four years when Jamie passed. Ryan was a studio musician. He and Jamie worked for the same company. That was how they met."

"When we found out Donnie was leaving for a bigger congregation, we asked Ryan to put his name in the hat and come to the interview. The elders and staff loved him because he's *precious*, and he moved down a couple months later. His mom, Stella, moved too, so she's here. She has a hard time sometimes with her health. He takes good care of her. He's a great guy."

"Have you had the chance to meet Ryan yet, Mia?" John piped up, wiping his mouth with a napkin.

I had just taken a bite of food, so I used the chewing as a chance to gather my thoughts. My head was spinning. I was momentarily saved from answering by Pam interrupting.

"Oh, John, I just remembered—sorry, Mia—remind me to take those sweaters to Stella tomorrow. I don't want to forget." Pam's interjection saved me. I had time to take another bite. If I just kept shoving food in my mouth, I might be able to avoid furthering this conversation. I wanted time to think, to process all this new information.

"Stella has some cabinetry she needs fixed, so we're going over to-morrow. We'll fix the cabinets and take her to lunch," Pam explained. My plate was empty, and my mind was spinning, on high alert. If I didn't get out of there soon, I might be re-meeting Ryan Blackstone/Lyles this very evening. I could feel tension slowly tightening up my neck, bringing my shoulders up ever so slightly around my ears. A headache was on the way.

"Thank y'all both for having me," I said, rubbing my neck. "I think I have a headache brewing. Maybe it's the pollen count or something." I shrugged and scooted back in my chair. "I'm sorry, but I probably need to get home before it gets any worse."

Pam blanched. "Oh, I didn't think about the pollen! I'm sorry, Mia! Here, let me make you a takeaway, and we'll get you home." She bustled inside to get a Tupperware container then came back out and piled it high.

"Do you need John to drive you home?" Pam asked.

John nodded. "I'd be glad to."

I shook my head. "Oh no, I can make it just fine. Thank y'all so much. I'm sorry I can't stay longer."

I hugged them both goodbye, took my Tupperware full of delicious-ness, and hurried to my car. I buckled my seatbelt then put the car in gear. I felt bad. I hadn't exactly lied, but this was avoidance. I couldn't do this forever. I was going to have to face this sooner rather than later, and my main mentor may not be the best person to talk with about it.

I made a mental note to call my therapist the next day to get an ap-pointment ASAP. Maybe she could help me process through all this so I could get to a good place before I saw Ryan again. I couldn't avoid him forever, and I didn't want to leave my church. This felt overwhelming and complicated. I understood my response was normal and okay, but anyone could see there were difficulties ahead that had to be dealt with before things could get easier.

I prayed the whole way home, begging God to help me and give me wisdom.

Chapter 6

Friday was my errand day. My therapist had a cancellation that afternoon, so I took the appointment and went for a run. Running always helped to clear my head and organize my thoughts. Three miles later, the order of issues to discuss was decided in my head, ready to go for the afternoon. I drank a green smoothie while I spent time with the Lord, reading my Bible and praying.

I read the story of Abigail, admiring her great courage and wisdom. I prayed for the same kind of courage to handle my circumstances with wisdom and humility and for God to bless whatever came next. My mind began to wander. I needed to start my packing list for camp, which was coming up in three weeks. I couldn't believe it was almost here! I truly couldn't wait.

For some reason, thinking of camp made me think of Anna. I texted her to check in and see what they were up to over the weekend. Maybe we could have coffee or see a movie.

Me: Hey! What are you up to over the weekend? Want to do something?

Anna: Definitely! Want to come over for lunch after church on Sunday?

Me: Sure, that sounds great! What can I bring?

Anna: Fair warning, Gage bought a new grill this week, and he's excited to use it. He's going to grill burgers for lunch. We'll be his guinea pigs.

Me: I'm in! I'll bring dessert.

Anna: Great! Thanks for being brave, haha! I'm still praying for you. Any updates?

Me: Nothing, thank goodness.

Anna: It will be okay, amiga! Keep me posted, got to get to my next meeting! xo

Me: xo

I looked around. My apartment needed some attention. I cleaned my bathroom, picked up, dusted, then vacuumed, and it was time for my appointment.

I started seeing Brooke for counseling almost three years ago. I did not know she was a believer when I started seeing her. She was just a regular, licensed counselor. When I told her I was a Christian, she told me she was too. I was glad to have another person in my life I trusted who held the same beliefs. I appreciated the perspective she could offer when it came to overwhelming situations.

Brooke was a huge part of my grief recovery and healing. She and I met monthly now, usually just to check in. We didn't see each other outside our sessions, but she was an important support and help in my life. I sat down in her cozy office then started in immediately.

"The guy who got me pregnant ten years ago is our new worship minister at church."

Man, I was getting really good at ripping off the Band-Aid. I patted myself on the back. Saying those words left me feeling a little queasy, so I promised myself I would never say that sentence again. Who could handle hearing that?

To her credit, Brooke only flinched a little bit. Her eyebrows shot up, and her mouth dropped open.

"Wow," she responded. "I knew something must have happened, but wow."

Yeah.

"Okay. Let's do this." Brooke nodded. She settled deeper into her chair and took a big breath. I knew she wanted me to breathe too. We did co-regulation techniques a lot. I exhaled slowly then told her my update. I told her about seeing Ryan and being triggered so hard I could barely see. I told her about Preston dumping me. The Martins loving Ryan. How I dodged the dinner bullet.

I told her everything. She didn't interrupt, just listened. Then we talked through scenarios, grounding, even what to do if I was triggered again. Brooke reassured me it was going to be okay.

Time was almost up. I uttered my deepest fear, something I barely let myself consider at all because it was so painful: *What if Ryan hated me, then everyone at church turned against me?*

Brooke understood.

"I don't think that will happen. Let's wait and cross that bridge if we come to it. Your job right now is to keep living your life then to get through the first meeting, whenever it occurs. I'm happy to be here for you, if you want. We can book some sessions closer together so you don't have to wait weeks to talk."

I was instantly rejoicing that God had given me Brooke, on top of everything else. We scheduled a session each week for the next three weeks, plus one the week after camp. Thinking about escaping to camp again was a great way to calm down from the chaos of my current circumstances.

I was certain Brooke would call it avoidance or escapism, but I didn't care. I just wanted camp. I wanted to spend time outside, no work, no miserable summer heat, no Ryan. I laughed at myself while I was driving home. If you'd told me, five years ago, I would be excited to spend a week with a bunch of rowdy teenagers, hiking in the woods, with no cell service, I would have laughed in your face. But, here I was, ready and waiting. Life was funny like that.

I woke up the following Sunday morning filled with a calm acceptance. It felt better than dread. I would take it. I was determined not to let it occupy my mind entirely.

I sat down to spend some time with the Lord, directing my mind to Him. I read the 23rd Psalm, trying to meditate on the idea of God's perfect plan. When it was all said and done, I wouldn't want anything else. I was glad to have a place to cast my burdens.

I could acknowledge the facts. All of this was happening because of my regrettable choices years ago, *and* I was grateful to have the Lord, a gracious Friend to go with me, parenting me and loving me perfectly through it. I wasn't alone.

That comfort gave me strength to stand up and head to church. Whatever happened, God would be with me. I was still holding onto hope that Ryan would not even remember or recognize me at all.

I walked into the old, steepled building and was immediately comforted by the sounds, smells, and people. Light flowed and danced through the foyer, softened by the filter of the stained-glass windows. Taking a deep breath, I moved forward, took a bulletin from the smiling teenager at the door, and made my way to sit with my friends.

Sarah was already there, along with Maddie and some other girls. Preston came to chat with us for a moment but went to sit with other people in a different area. It was still a little awkward with him. It might take some time, but whatever wound was there would certainly heal quickly. I hoped we would be able to get back to being friends again soon.

The room continued to fill. At 8:59, the band walked onto the stage then picked up their instruments. Ryan swung his guitar strap over his head, onto his shoulder, as he leaned into the microphone, greeting us. The band started playing, and everyone in the congregation rose to sing.

Take my life and let it be consecrated, Lord, to thee.
Take my moments and my days, let them flow in ceaseless praise.
Take my hands and let them move at the impulse of Thy love.
Take my feet and let them be swift and beautiful for Thee.

I loved this song. I laughed to myself. It felt ironic that I enjoyed Ryan's choices in songs so much. I wondered why the hymns were special to him. They weren't popular with everyone, because they were old, but I loved them. They made me feel firm on the foundation of Christ and connected to the generations of Christians who had lived before me. I sang along, trying to focus on the words to the hymn.

Church eventually ended, then I headed out to join Anna and Gage for lunch, as we'd planned. I did not see Ryan after church, and I made it to my car with no tears. I relished the win, even remembering to pick up dessert on the way to Anna and Gage's new house. The storm door clattered as I walked up the sidewalk to their vintage bungalow. Gage stood in the doorway and yelled into the house, "Honey, she's home!"

When they got married, Gage was very sweet to me about taking my roommate away. He helped me move to a smaller place, and he even tolerated a couple of girls-only sleepovers each year. He jokingly threatened to put our bras in the freezer, but he also went to buy us a bunch of junk food at the store. Gage had two sisters of his own, and it showed.

I hugged Gage warmly then handed him the grocery store bag. He eagerly looked inside.

"Chocolate pudding cups! Yes!" He reached inside the bag.

I swatted his hand with a severe look. "They're for after lunch!"

Gage burst out laughing and stepped aside with a smile and said, "Yes ma'am! Come on in. Anna's changing."

I walked inside their bright, adorable, extremely dated home. This little fixer upper needed some serious love, but Anna and Gage insisted she had great bones. They positively adored the house, and I was happy for them to have it. The avocado-green kitchen tiles shone with welcome.

We might laugh at the hideous tile, but it was kept with loving care and would be a distant memory soon enough. Anna and Gage were meeting with a contractor soon to finalize the tile and paint. Anna begged me to help her choose a backsplash a few weeks ago. It was stressful, considering a backsplash was supposed to last years, but it was fun to see all the beautiful tile and stone.

I unpacked the pudding cups, placing them in the fridge. Gage went outside to see to the grill. Anna came in from the other room, freshly changed into comfy clothes.

Anna and Gage went to the same church as me, but since getting married, they sat with Gage's man-friends and their wives, so I didn't see them as much. I thought it was good for both of them. It wasn't easy to find community as a couple. We would be friends no matter what, but I didn't have a male counterpart. I thought it was important for them to cast a wider friend net and find some great couple friends.

"Hey, roomie," she greeted me with a smile. We hugged, holding on for a minute. Living as roommates for so long, we were basically sisters by now with a symbiotic routine and shorthand.

"What did you think of church?" Anna asked as she grabbed my pony-tail and started sniffing my hair. "Did you get new hair stuff? You smell good!"

I yelped then pushed her away.

"Surely you are not so grossed out living with a boy that you need to smell my hair!" I laughed and straightened my ponytail.

"Gage smells great for a dude, but it's not the same," Anna said mat-ter-of-factly.

I'd certainly encountered my share of dude-stench over the years in the ER. Anna was lucky; Gage could smell much worse.

"To answer your question, church was better than expected, and I did not make contact," I reported with a sigh of relief. I wouldn't ever feel ready for that moment. I wasn't in denial; of course it was unavoidable. But I was okay putting it off a while longer.

Anna and I chatted while she sliced tomatoes and lettuce. I got out the pickles and condiments. Gage popped his head inside to ask for the sliced cheese, then we were ready. Gage came in with the burgers a minute later, and we began to fill our plates. We sat at the kitchen table with glasses of iced tea, the delicious burgers, chips, and some fruit.

"Okay, I'm ready to hear this story," Gage announced, holding his burger. A pickle fell out, hitting his plate with a *thwap*. I wanted to change the subject, but I reasoned with myself that it might get easier over time. Telling other parts of my story certainly had.

"You know most of it," I said, grabbing a chip off my plate and hold-ing it. "Sophomore year, I had a crazy weekend with a drummer and got pregnant. I had an abortion a few weeks later."

"Yeah, because your parents are terrible people," Gage stated.

Anna rolled her eyes at him. "Unhelpful, baby."

I was used to it. "It's okay." I shrugged. "It was terrible, and as you both know, it has certainly not been easy since. But I have tried to move on, and now there's more to the story."

Gage took a bite of his burger and motioned for me to go on.

"Last week, I walked into church and realized the new worship minister is The Guy." I said it all in a rush. My breath whooshed out. My heart was pounding, just saying it aloud to Gage.

It was frustrating. I had done so much therapy and counseling. I'd come a long way. But even after all this work, seeing Ryan was overwhelming.

Gage put his burger down. He looked me in the eye. "Are you serious?"

"Yeah. I thought Anna told you," I answered.

"She did. But still. That's…" Gage searched for a word.

"Messed up?" Anna suggested.

"I was gonna say wild," Gage said, looking between us.

"That's putting it mildly," I murmured, taking a sip of iced tea.

"I'm so sorry, Mia. That would be totally overwhelming," Gage said. With no warning, my eyes filled with tears. Gage was always fun, like a silly big brother. Now he was being a sweet teddy bear.

"Thanks, Gage." I sniffed. "I appreciate your empathy."

"Do we need to go to church somewhere else for a while or something?" he asked.

I blinked, surprised. I looked over at Anna. She met my eyes, unflinching. Obviously, they were the very best, but I hadn't realized how supportive they were prepared to be. I almost broke down at the offer. My eyes filled, but I blinked away the tears.

I appreciated the love and support, for sure. But leaving was the absolute last resort. I didn't have a husband to be my community. My church community was a huge part of my life. It was a huge part of their lives, too. They still attended the men's and women's Bible studies, and we all loved our sweet church. I would rather endure a little awkwardness and keep my church community than avoid it and have to start all over, *thankyouverymuch*.

"No," I replied, strengthened even more by their love. "It's going to be fine. It might be a little awkward, but it's not like I actually knew him well or anything." I blushed. I knew better than to stew in shame over my past, but I still hardly recognized the version of myself who'd basically had a two-night stand with a stranger. That sort of behavior hadn't been typical for me then, and now, I was not interested in anything like it ever again.

"I will move past this. It's going to be fine," I assured both Anna and Gage as well as myself. I would. I didn't know how. I honestly didn't feel strong enough, but at some point soon, I would have to be. God had not brought me through everything else to leave me now, I reminded myself. I took a breath, held it, and then let it out slowly. It helped.

We chatted about other things while we finished our food. Then we all giggled as Anna and Gage told me stories while I looked through all the photos from their trip. By the end of the camera roll, a vacation to Napa was starting to sound good to me too.

Gage went outside to clean the grill while Anna and I worked on clearing the table and doing the dishes. The lemony smell of dish soap filled the air, and the sprayer shot a fine mist of water everywhere as Anna handled the dishes. I was in charge of putting away leftovers.

I was zipping the remaining lettuce into a plastic bag when Anna stopped, turning to me.

"Are you truly okay with staying and seeing him every week? You don't have to be strong here, Mia."

I sighed. I had asked myself the same question plenty of times over the last couple weeks. I answered her honestly.

"I think so. I'm not necessarily looking forward to it. I think the hardest part will just be meeting him again. But honestly, Anna, it may not be a big deal. If he doesn't recognize me, I'll just act like we've never met before and move on. No one knows it was Ryan who got me pregnant, except you and Gage. No one else would even guess."

"Okay," she said. "You know we'll support you, full stop. I just want to be sure we are doing the best right thing."

I smiled. Anna was a big fan of the phrase *the best right thing*, as she believed sometimes there was not only one right thing to do. She used the phrase at work a lot, but it translated well enough into regular life to show up frequently. It was endearing and very much an Anna phrase in my life.

Anna and Gage loved me and would do anything to support me and look out for me. I didn't need them to leave their church home to do that, but I appreciated the loyalty and love.

"Honestly, I think it will be fine. I mean, if he's a professional worship leader now, I'm guessing he's probably a new person too. We can probably just acknowledge one another then give each other space," I speculated.

Anna nodded. "That makes sense. Does he look different to you? I don't think he's changed much, but I didn't spend a lot of time with him. I just remember those dreamy eyes. Dang." She fanned herself with her dish glove-covered hand.

I rolled my eyes. "Oh, Lordy. Do *not* start with that please." I took a breath and blew it out. "He looks...recognizable but a little different. I only looked at his eyes once—the first time I saw him on stage."

I'm not a masochist. I was absolutely not interested in checking Ryan out. I remembered exactly how easily I responded to his pretty eyes ten years ago. It was *not* something I was interested in re-living.

I'd given so much time and effort in therapy, working through it all. It was a long road to forgive myself and my parents. I even forgave Ryan, who had no clue. I worked hard to stand on my own two feet, to have a good, happy life. I wasn't interested in going backward. I was reminded of a phrase Brooke used to say: *My life lay ahead of me, not behind me.*

Anna and I finished cleaning up, then Gage came in, and we all watched a show together, like old times. I headed home with a bag full of leftovers. Anna was adorably proud to pack it for me. Yes, we were almost thirty, and we were still discovering some of the cuter parts of adulting. I hugged them both then headed home to prepare for the coming week. My hours were a little strange for the week. I was scheduled to work late on the day of Bible study. I hated when my work schedule interfered with my actual life, but sometimes it couldn't be helped.

I got home and put away the food. I checked my scrubs and threw a load of laundry in the washer. I reflected on my afternoon with Anna and Gage. My heart was full! Anna and I could still have fun doing anything or doing nothing. She was my family. She was always there for me, no matter what. And Gage was part of the mix for so long that he understood we were a two-for-one.

I figured it would all be fine, of course, but a small part of me had wondered how it would go once they were married. Two years in, it was great. I was glad we were still "us." I read for a bit and ended up praying, thanking God for His steadfast love and all He'd done for me. How could I fear anything when I had all this goodness? With gratitude in my heart, I went to bed and slept.

Chapter 7

The week started with a bang—literally. I was driving to work when I heard a loud noise, and my car started listing roughly to the right. When I pulled over and got out to check, the tire was completely flat with a nail sticking out of the tread. Looking around at the side street I'd turned onto, I was glad I was on a neighborhood road and not on the nonexistent shoulder of a fast freeway. Dallas was a big place with lots of freeways. I took a calming breath and called a tow truck. They showed up almost an hour later, so I was late to work, and the day went downhill as it progressed.

No one likes vomit, but it's just an extra-bad day when it lands on your shoes. After I got cleaned up from that, a gunshot victim came in. Those situations were always scary, with a lot of moving parts and a ton of paperwork, but he lived as far as I knew. Later that afternoon, I worked in to share the load to do chest compressions on an older man who had a heart attack. He died later that day. Working in the ER, I was always aware that anything could happen—we all were. But I would never get used to losing patients.

After a Monday like that, I was a little afraid of what the rest of the week would hold. Luckily, I only worked half a shift on Tuesday, and life seemed to behave itself.

On Wednesday, I was processing patients then administering the necessary items as fast as I could. I finished up with a patient in one room, walked into the next, and found myself face to face with John Martin. He looked haggard, completely overwhelmed, and he'd been crying. Pam was lying on the gurney, looking pale, but she perked up when she noticed me.

"Mia! Boy am I glad to see you! You can tell my sweet man he is overreacting." She rolled her eyes in John's general direction. I rushed to the bedside, looking her over.

"What in the world are y'all doing here? What happened?" I asked.

John sounded near panic. "Pammy fainted, Mia! We were standing in the living room at the Paulsen house, where we have a project going. One minute we were looking at blueprints, discussing the light fixture, and the next she was lightheaded, then she fainted!" His chest heaved. He was scared out of his wits.

Pam broke in then. "I came to almost immediately. It was just a hot flash, Johnny." Her tone softened at the end. She was annoyed to be there, but she knew he was truly scared. They had been through a lot, and some wounds left us tender for the rest of our days.

I stood tall, in what I hoped was a reassuring pose. Having been a nurse for a while now, I had enough experience with anxious family members to know this was not the time to engage in a discussion about what actually happened, nor the possibilities thereof. I nodded my head briskly and got to work.

"Well, let's get started with your vitals, and we'll go from there. It's been a busy day, but we'll get the doctor in as soon as we can," I told them as I busied myself taking Pam's temperature and blood pressure. I noted her blood pressure was mildly elevated. This was not rare when people came to the ER, because they were usually scared, in a lot of pain, or really sick.

I was unwrapping the cuff from her upper arm when the door opened. A deep voice said, "John? How are you? Any update?" I turned as a tall man with dark-blond hair walked through the doorway. That was my only warning, if you could call it one. A lead weight dropped right through my abdomen. I was frozen in place for a second.

"Ryan!" John turned his broad shoulders in the tiny space, sweeping by me and the vitals tower with surprising grace. He took the younger man in his arms, wrapping him in a big hug. The men embraced for a second, and Ryan quickly looked at Pam.

"Are you okay, Pam? What happened?" His voice had matured and deepened ever so slightly. I hadn't noticed on Sunday. I busied myself with wrapping up the blood pressure cuff so I could get out of there.

Pam held up her hand and said, "I'm fine, Ryan. Just a little hot flash is all. I'm fit as a fiddle! This is just a precaution."

Ryan looked at me then, asking, "Has the doctor been in yet?"

Recognition dawned. He froze. I was stuck, unable to speak. His eyes held me. It wasn't fair. *I should be immune to those eyes*, I thought, trying to calm my heart rate.

His voice broke into my thoughts. He sounded like he could barely breathe when he said my name.

"Mia?"

He remembered me. That was inconvenient. I didn't know what to say. We both just stood there, suspended in time, trapped. *Words?* I drew a blank. My tongue wouldn't work. Tearing my eyes away with superhuman strength, I looked over at the vitals screen, running my hand along the edge like I was hunting for the right button.

Pam could still talk just fine. "You know our Mia, Ryan? How wonderful! I hoped to introduce you sooner, but you know each other! How fun! When did y'all meet?"

Curious to see what he would say, I looked at Ryan. He was still looking at me, confounded. His neck began to turn red. I stood there, fascinated, just staring at the blotchy redness.

It was Ryan's turn to search for words. "Um..." He looked down, rubbing the side of his neck with his hand, then looked over at Pam. Freed from the pull of him, I turned to her and answered.

"We knew each other back in college, a long time ago. Nice to see you, Ryan." I nodded in his direction, avoiding eye contact. I moved toward the door—the gateway to freedom from this extremely awkward moment. I babbled what I hoped sounded like the words of a seasoned professional.

"I have other patients to assess. Pam, I'll come check on you in a little bit. Please don't hesitate to ask if y'all need anything at all." I was so flustered all I could think of was getting out. But I remembered at the last second that I really loved these people, and they were more nervous than me right now. I paused, patting John's shoulder. "We'll take good care of her."

In the next breath, I was on the other side of the door, quietly closing it then walking around the corner. My whole body slumped against the wall for support, as if I had just run a marathon. *Whew. That could have gone worse*, I thought to myself. I took slow, deep breaths, assessing myself. I was still in one piece.

It was finally done, and I'd survived. After the emotional upheaval of the last couple weeks of discovery, remembering, processing, and waiting, the heavy burden of anticipation lifted off my shoulders and disappeared. A tiny beam of light pierced my soul. I was proud of myself for staying strong through the moment and not falling apart. *Wow*, I thought. God really does meet us where we are.

The collision of the past and the present left me feeling alive in an unexpected way. I felt like standing tall, throwing my hands in the air. At the same time, I wanted to lie down to sleep for ten hours. Neither option was available to me right then, so I took a deep breath, gave myself a hug, whispered a quick prayer of thanks, and moved into the next room to assess my patient.

I checked in on Pam a while later. Ryan was nowhere to be found. Pam and John were alone in the room, both agitated. The doctor wanted to run a couple of tests and draw some blood. Pam was sure the tests were a waste of time, but John was anxious.

I had dealt with enough families in the ER to know telling them not to worry was just as big a waste of time as the actual worrying. But these people were like family to me. I was concerned too. I did my best to reassure all three of us. I told them I was glad the doctor was being thorough, and I'd let them know any updates as soon as I could.

I took my time fluffing Pam's pillows then bringing her a fresh blanket from the warmer. When the phlebotomist came to draw blood, John looked terrified enough to faint, so I stayed in the room and held Pam's hand. I was in and out of their room the rest of the afternoon, checking in or sometimes playing referee when Pam grew tired of waiting. Finally, the doctor came in, saying she was satisfied with all the test results. Pam was free to go with instructions to follow up with her primary care doctor in a week or sooner if the symptoms persisted.

"I told you I was fine, John Martin!" Pam huffed. I could tell she was relieved too. Pam pushed the blankets off and sat up, swinging her legs off the side of the bed. She turned to John and blustered.

"Now take me home, sir. You promised me an ice cream if I let that man take my blood, and I'm holding you to it."

John beamed at her and stood, as happy to be leaving as Pam. The whole interaction made me smile. I found Pam's sass completely charming, even when she was mad as a wet hen. She looked at John pointedly while sliding her feet into the shoes I'd set up on the floor by the bedside. Pam stood up slowly, but I didn't dare try to help. Once she was up and walking, I hugged them both, thankful Pam was okay.

When Pam hugged me, she said, "I am exhausted right now, but let's find time to chat sometime this week. Thank you for taking good care of us, honey." I walked them to the door of the ER and went to finish up my paperwork for the shift. I hadn't been this ready to go home in a long time.

Chapter 8

The rest of the week passed without event, so I was able to take some time to recover. I had a great therapy session with Brooke and left encouraged after sharing with her how God was maturing me. I told her about encountering Ryan. We talked through it a little bit. We were both proud of me but glad it was done.

My homework was to think about other things. I accepted the assignment gladly. Dwelling on this situation wouldn't be good, for me or anyone. My power had not changed. I could do my best, and that was it. Wise boundaries protected me from so much. I prayed for the wisdom to always value boundaries, to continue growing.

I checked on Pam each day. She seemed to be doing well. I reminded her to check in with her doctor, and we agreed I'd come to dinner the following week.

Saturday arrived, and I met up with Anna at the farmer's market. I already told her earlier in the week about coming face to face with Ryan. She knew I didn't want to dwell on it. We roamed the different booths, choosing fresh veggies and bread. We grabbed a coffee and a pastry then sat at a little iron table under an umbrella for a bit before we each went home.

"Do you remember the time I tried to cook spaghetti sauce from scratch in college?" Anna asked, looking suspiciously nonchalant.

"Which time?" I replied. "The time the paramedics came because you set off the fire alarm in our building?"

"No, the other one," Anna said pointedly.

I took a beat then nodded sagely. "Ahh, the good one?! You made The Good Sauce?"

Anna smiled like a Cheshire cat. "And it turned out!" she squealed, shimmying her shoulders.

This was a big deal. We high-fived.

"Way to go, Chef!" I said enthusiastically.

The Good Sauce was this super-complicated recipe for Bolognese with lots of ingredients, including three kinds of meat. It took forever to cook. Anna made it successfully exactly one time, so we called that specific iteration The Good Sauce. We tried not to speak of the other attempts—too many memories of charred pans, burned tomatoes, or over-cooked meat. Suffice it to say, it went badly every other time.

Once, the tomatoes caught fire while roasting in the oven. The visit from the firefighters actually ended in Anna going on a date with one of them (it didn't work out, obviously). After several tries, Anna gave up on the sauce, calling it her *nemesauce*, a few years ago.

"Gage has been begging me to try it since we got an enameled cast iron Dutch oven at our wedding shower. When it turned out, he straight up called it the Sauce of Redemption," Anna said, beaming. "I'm so glad it turned out! I was a little curious myself. I told Gage I would give it exactly one shot. We made homemade pasta for it and everything! It was great!"

"They say good equipment covers a multitude of sins," I pointed out.

We continued chatting until it was time to head home. I had things to do, and Anna and Gage were headed to her parents' house for the after-noon.

"Give your folks a big hug for me," I told her before I left. Anna promised she would and said she would bring me a bag of leftovers—this was the best promise she could ever make. I could positively drink her mom's homemade salsa. Looking forward to it and laughing at the mem-ories of all the versions of Bolognese I witnessed over the years, I headed home.

I cleaned my apartment then ate a fresh tomato sandwich for lunch. While I ate, I looked over the packing list for camp. Only one more week! I couldn't wait to get away. It was going to be fantastic.

Saturday night, I went out to dinner with some girls from Bible study, which was a lot of fun. We ate fondue. Eating cheese for three hours wasn't my usual way to spend a Saturday night. I regretted nothing, though I slept terribly from being so full. Sunday morning came early.

Chapter 9

I was right on time Sunday morning, but the glower on Ms. Alma's face said, *On time is five minutes late*. Unfortunately, she'd undergone cataract surgery the week before, and she was sporting a huge black patch over her right eye. Glowering with only half of one's face is way less effective and is honestly more hilarious than scary.

Between the glower and the pirate jokes Ms. Alma would *not* appreciate, I couldn't trust myself to speak. I clamped my mouth into a straight line, took a deep breath, and took my post without a word. Avoiding Sarah's hysterical glance, I shook my head, trying not to smile. Ms. Alma inspected us shrewdly for a moment then turned away, taking her glower with her.

For the next several minutes, I stood at the doors with Sarah, handing out bulletins and greeting people as they came in. When the music started playing, I realized this would be the third Sunday Ryan was here. I wasn't giving him nearly as much thought now that I'd survived our first meeting.

Sarah and I were standing in the doorway, chatting between handing out bulletins. She was as excited to head to camp the next weekend as I was. We were discussing our packing lists and making a small bet on who would be thrown in the lake first. Sarah thought it would be one of the senior girls, Emily.

I could see that happening; Emily was very sweet and outgoing, and the boys flocked to her. My guess was the youth minister, Chris, but it might have been wishful thinking. He'd already started talking trash about winning Capture the Flag again this year.

Capture the Flag was played the last night at camp, boys vs. girls. I was still a little salty about the game last year. Our team carried the flag across the finish line in a beautiful victory. We had thought we won, and all of us were celebrating. But upon further inspection, the flag was a decoy—an over-the-top (in my opinion) prank by the youth minister and some of the senior boys, who crossed the line just a couple minutes after us. On the grounds of this technicality, we lost the game.

I am not usually competitive, but that particular loss stung. It was so unfair and mean. It may have been an overreaction, but I still held Chris responsible. He'd gone too far. I was hoping for a revenge-win for the girls. If victory turned out to be unattainable, I was willing to (secretly and solely) settle for planting an open can of tuna fish inside a very specific *youth-minister-mobile*. Texas grew very hot in the summer. It wouldn't be pretty. With any luck, the smell would last at least a year.

Chris was a nice enough guy. He hung out with my friend group from time to time. In fact, he and Maddie had gone on a couple of dates once upon a time. Unfortunately, he randomly stopped calling her, which then made her feel awkward at church for a while. Not okay. Even a couple years after the fact, I still felt protective of my friend. I would never tell anyone my plan, of course, so they could not be implicated.

Sarah laughed innocently at my projection and probably the look on my face as I silently plotted. She reached back to fish more bulletins out of the box behind her.

The music started in the sanctuary behind us. I was finishing up passing out my remaining bulletins. My foot was already tapping to the beat of the drums as the singing began.

> *My hope is built on nothing less*
> *Than Jesus' blood and righteousness.*
> *I dare not trust the sweetest frame,*
> *But wholly trust in Jesus' name.*
>
> *Christ alone, Cornerstone*
> *Weak, made strong in the Savior's love,*
> *Through the storm, He is Lord,*
> *Lord of all.*

I had to hand it to Ryan, he had a talent for picking good songs. I was excited to go into worship this morning. Wednesday's win felt so good I hadn't worried much about him the rest of the week.

I gave myself a pep talk the entire time in the car on the way over, just in case. I could do this. He was just another guy now. It was going to be fine. He wasn't interested in me, and I wasn't interested in him. We could co-exist at church, no problem. We would probably never see each other or need to talk to each other. It was going to be fine!

Sarah waved, getting my attention. She was out of bulletins, and I only had a couple left. Once again, we'd fulfilled our promise to Ms. Alma and her glowering eagle eye. We gathered our purses then stepped into the sanctuary, walking quickly down the aisle to a row in the middle. We shuffled down the pew to our seats then put our purses down. Settled, I looked up, ready to join the singing.

My eyes were drawn to Ryan. He was singing into the microphone, strumming his guitar, and looking directly at me. Taken aback, I looked away immediately. My mouth went dry. I took a deep breath, looking down at the floor, counting to ten. Maybe I wasn't ready for this. My armpits were suddenly sweating. *Great.* My favorite light-blue linen wrap dress was going to be in shambles if I kept this up.

I took one more deep breath, then reminded myself of the truest thing about me: I am a child of God. I am loved by God, saved by the blood of Jesus, fully, freely, forever forgiven in Christ. I belonged here, because the invitation of Christ was for ALL. *Breathe, Mia!*

I looked up as I exhaled. Ryan was looking somewhere else now, thank goodness. The band started the next song during my mini-melt-down, and they reached the chorus.

Jesus paid it all, all to Him I owe
Sin had left a crimson stain,
He washed it white as snow.

I listened to the song and read the words on the screen above the band. I let the truth wash over me, reminding myself this was why I came to church: to spend time with my Lord, to be with my church family. I prayed. *Lord, help me focus. Help me worship you with my whole heart, mind, soul, and strength. You have given me life to the fullest. You have set me free from my past. Help me move forward.*

The song ended, then we all sat down, settling in to listen to the Bible reading and preaching. My heart swelled with love for my sweet church as I looked around the room. From my spot in the middle, I could see several of my friends, including Anna and Gage across the room. Anna smiled at me and winked. Pam and John Martin were sitting in the third pew from the front. Miss Alma was seated with some older ladies over to the right, and youth group kids filled three pews toward the front on the left side.

It was Senior Sunday, so part of the service was going to be used to recognize the kids who were graduating high school. It was sweet, getting to reflect on how much they'd grown over the years and taking time to pray for their future.

Seeing the youth group reminded me about camp. We would leave for camp the following Saturday. I had a lot to do before then. I was reminded I had everything to be grateful for. I was loved. I belonged. My story wasn't a secret; it was just part of my testimony. I wasn't in a prison of fear anymore. God set me free to a new life. It was going to be okay. I flipped over to Psalm 23 and quietly read it.

The Lord is my shepherd,
I shall not want.

I thought of Brooke and the goal we set—to be able to see Ryan at church without worrying or overthinking it. I remembered the breath work she introduced me to over the years. I could do hard things. I had done hard things before. I could do this. I told myself it would get easier. God was with me. I wasn't alone. He'd given me a family in Anna and Gage, in the Martins, and in my friends.

I could keep breathing and resting in the truth as much as I needed to in the moment. I told myself I could stay present. I struggled to concentrate on the sermon, but I did my best.

Chapter 10

After church, some of us went out to lunch at a pizza place nearby. We were seated at a big, long table, ten of us squished in together. It was loud and refreshing. The smell of garlic bread wafted tantalizingly through the room. I was seated between Sarah and Maddie.

Maddie was sharing some major news: she'd adopted a dog and named him Kevin. Sarah and I congratulated her then had lots of questions. We were interrupted by the server.

I'd just ordered a salad with a slice of Hawaiian pizza when one of the guys at the end of the table perked up and called loudly, "Ryan! Over here!"

For a split second, everything went still. I blinked a couple times, turned to look, and sighed quietly. Sure enough, Ryan stepped up to the table, dressed in the same jeans and button-down shirt he was wearing on stage today. He must have driven over right after the band finished cleaning up from the service. Those blue eyes met mine for a split second, and I immediately looked down at the plastic checkered tablecloth. *Wasn't church enough?* I groaned inwardly. I thought I was home free! What was he doing here?

I could feel the impact he made, settling into the crowded table as everyone shifted to make room. The guys all welcomed him, introducing themselves. Jenny sat across from me. "It's not fair for anyone to be that good-looking," she whispered to Emma. I silently agreed. Even the air felt different with him here.

I took a deep breath and tried to think reasonably. A convicting thought rose up in my mind: I was making this all about me. *Ugh.* It was true. Ryan did nothing wrong by coming to lunch. He was new, probably looking for friends and community—*which is totally normal and good to do,* I chided myself. I felt a twinge of embarrassment, seeing my selfishness bubble up to the surface so quickly.

The server came back, and I heard Ryan's low voice join the cacophony around me as he ordered. I reminded myself I wanted good things for others, including Ryan. What had he done to me? Nothing. He deserved the benefit of the doubt, even if he was a trigger for bad memories that made me feel panicky and sad. Even if those blue eyes haunted me and put me in some kind of trance. No. It was a long time ago. *I'm not that person anymore*, I said firmly to myself.

Refocusing, I turned to Maddie and asked her how it was going, getting used to living with a dog. The Friday before was pick-up day, but I hadn't met him yet. I asked to see pictures, and she pulled out her phone. I was trying very hard to pay attention to my friend and the ball of gray-and-black fluff on the screen, but it was a struggle. I was extremely aware of Ryan's presence at the other end of the table. I could hear the rumble of his low voice, making the temptation to lean closer to hear more overwhelming.

I was starving when we arrived, but now I was too flustered to eat much. Maddie was deep-diving into the dog thing. She went on about training methods and stuff. I tried to follow for the most part. Kevin sounded like a handful but very sweet. I could tell Maddie was enjoying him, and I was glad. She invited me to go for a walk with them that evening, and I accepted. She invited Sarah to come too, but Sarah blushed and said she had a date.

"Ooh, who's the lucky vegan?" Maddie wanted to know. I was curious myself. I straightened in my chair.

"Do y'all remember my friend Ben, from work?" Sarah asked a little self-consciously. *Did we?* Maddie and I exchanged a look. This was huge news. I could feel my eyes popping wide open, my smile reaching from ear to ear.

"YES!" I pumped my fist and did a mini-shimmy of celebration.

"Finally," Maddie squealed, shimmying with me. We had been waiting forever for Sarah to go out with Ben! Every now and then, Ben joined our group for different activities. He was tall and quiet with glasses and a beard. He was funny, sweet, and good at bowling. He was also vegan! Multiple times over the last two years, Sarah absolutely swore Ben was just a friend. But the way he looked at her…I could tell friendship was not his goal. This felt like great progress. I was happy for my friend.

"Tell us everything," Maddie demanded.

Sarah shrugged. "I'm not sure where to begin. You know I went out with the fake-vegan guy a few weeks ago, and it was awful. I decided to take a break from the dating scene, just enjoy my family, my job at the firm, and take some time for *me*."

We nodded, motioning for her to get to the good stuff.

"Well, Ben and I had an...encounter last week. Everyone from the office went to this warehouse for a group team-building thing. We got a little competitive at dodgeball, and the trash talk got a little flirty. I noticed because Ben doesn't flirt with me—ever."

At this, Maddie and I both rolled our eyes. Sarah was just oblivious. And maybe Ben was a little too subtle. Sarah kept going.

"Anyway, I didn't think about it after that because work is busy, so I got distracted. On Tuesday, I was out running at White Rock Lake after work. Ben was there to run too. He changed his route to run with me, and we chatted and laughed the whole time. We ended up getting a smoothie at the Smoothie King by the parking area for dinner. I didn't think anything of it until he just told me outright that he really enjoys our friendship, and he doesn't want to make things weird, but he'd be interested in going out sometime if I would like to. And I said okay."

She seemed a little unsure. She desperately looked back and forth between us.

"Do you think it's a mistake? Am I ruining a good friendship with a great guy?"

Maddie shook her head. "Of course not! There's nothing wrong with dating to see where it could lead, and why *not* start with friendship? Are you interested in Ben in a dating way?"

Sarah sighed. "I'm not sure. He's been a good friend to me. I like working with him. I am attracted to him. But honestly, hanging out with him is easy! We always laugh together, and we actually have a lot in common. I love our friendship. Honestly, y'all, I've dated so much. I'm tired of the runaround, all the rigmarole. I just want to hang out, enjoy a man, and see if something can grow."

I sighed. I liked the sound of that. In a world where every date was either an unrealistic fairy tale or a dumpster fire, something simple sounded really special.

I patted Sarah on the shoulder.

"You're both worth trying for," I assured her. "You know we think Ben is great, and we LOVE you! Be brave! Go for it!"

Sarah let out a nervous sigh, nodding her head with determination. Maddie agreed. Then she wiggled her eyebrows.

"I'm excited to hear how it goes, Lady Risk-taker. Let the shimmy resume!"

We all laughed and shimmied with her. It felt good to laugh. Everything seemed a little more intense lately. Maybe I was more weighed down than I thought. I wanted to move. Maybe go for a run in the early summer heat. I looked around for the server. She was handing out checks to everyone.

My eyes fell on Ryan for a second. He was smiling, talking to a guy named Luke. I was tempted to let myself observe him out in the wild like this. Those blue eyes were a constant reminder. *Nope*, I told myself firmly. I looked past him.

Ryan could weigh on my mind endlessly if I let him. I needed to move on, to let go of my past and the ties binding me to this man, a stranger. I was a new person. So was he. I couldn't keep letting memories drag me backward. Something needed to change. *Wow*, I thought, *maybe Sarah's bravery is contagious.*

Everyone was finishing up, so we all paid our checks. I told Maddie I was going to go for a run, then I'd be over around six to meet Kevin and go for a walk. I slung my purse over my shoulder as I stood up with everyone. We all pushed in our chairs and turned toward the door at the same time. We shuffled along, chatting and making small talk as we headed out. I waved to Sarah, giving her a thumbs-up as I walked to my car. I was opening the door when a deep voice called out, "Hey, Mia! Wait up!"

Chapter 11

My heart rate picked up, a flutter in my chest. I considered ignoring him, but he was already there, by the trunk. I sighed. *Here we go,* I thought. I pasted a small smile on my face and braced for impact, lifting my eyes to his.

Boom. There he was. His blue eyes, his stubbled chin. His dark-blond hair was shorter now, but otherwise he hadn't changed much. I could practically feel him *existing.* My skin hummed.

I would be puzzled later when I thought about this moment. How could I go years and never feel much of anything for any of the guys I'd dated, but put me within twenty feet of Ryan Blackstone, and everything in me awakened, fully alert. *It's not fair. It's been ten years,* I thought. *Whatever. Just breathe.*

"What's up?" I asked. I hoped I looked friendly and nonchalant instead of hunted and panicked.

"Hi," he said, then he paused, looking at me. I raised my eyebrows, waiting for him to speak.

"Uh…" he trailed off. The moment stretched out, softened. *Maybe he feels a little unsure too,* I thought.

He tried again.

"Um. Hi," he repeated. He shuffled his feet, pushing his fingers through his hair self-consciously.

"Hi," I replied softly. His awkwardness was a relief. I was glad I wasn't the only one struggling through the moment.

"I'm very surprised to see you…here in Texas," he finally said.

I raised my eyebrows in question, not sure how to respond to those words. He explained further.

"I just mean, I am surprised to see you at all. It's…it's GOOD to see you." He swallowed and looked up at the sky, visibly frustrated with himself. He squeezed his eyes shut for a second then opened them, looking at me with sincerity.

"I…it's wild to see you after all this time. I have questions. I don't want it to be weird. I hope we can be friends." He blew out a breath. I felt my eyebrows raise of their own accord.

Wow, I thought. *Friends*. Friendship honestly hadn't occurred to me. He was waiting for a response. I shook myself.

"Um, okay, Ryan *Lyles,*" I emphasized, raising my eyebrows at him. It was a small detail, but I wanted to know his explanation for having a different last name.

He cocked his head, clearly confused at the emphasis on his last name. I took a steadying breath and looked at him. *Keep it simple*, I thought to myself.

"You had a different last name. Before."

His eyes lit with recognition. He knew what I was asking.

"Ah. Blackstone is my middle name. It's my mother's maiden name," he said. "My full name is Ryan Blackstone Lyles. I used Blackstone as a stage name. Still do."

He shook his head and smiled self-deprecatingly. When I didn't respond, he tried again.

"I can show you my driver's license if you like," he offered, eyebrows raised.

I absorbed the information and shook my head. I was a little frustrated with his simple-but-satisfying explanation.

"I guess that makes sense. It's good you're not a creepy identity thief or something," I said and moved to get into the car.

He laughed at my dry humor until he realized I was leaving.

"Wait," he started and came around to the driver's side. He stood back several feet, holding out his hands like I was a wild animal he'd just startled in the woods or something.

I straightened, waiting.

"Could we maybe meet up for coffee? Maybe we could catch up? I'm curious about you. It's been a long time. And now we're both going to church. I'd love to hear about how you came to be part of the church. I ended up in church too, obviously. I'm a worship minister now—which you also already know." He paused, closing his eyes for a second.

His awkward babbling was a little funny, even endearing. It was so far removed from the confident rock star I pictured in my mind from years ago. But I couldn't look away from him. Fascinated, I just kept staring at him, wondering what was coming next. He went on.

"I wasn't a Christian when I met you, and now I am. Seeing you is this blast from the past, and I am totally overwhelmed by it. Seeing you with the Martins at the hospital the other day was a shock, then John told me you go to the church. I've wondered about you every now and then over the years, prayed for you, and now you're here! It's so surprising, seeing you."

He took a breath, swallowed, and ran a hand through his hair. He looked almost desperate to get to the point, but I wasn't sure how to help him. I just kept listening.

He rambled on. "I'm not that guy anymore. It's been a long time. Not that I expect you to know that—or care. I don't expect anything from you. But I saw you look at me like I'm a ghost, so I think it might be strange for you to see me too. And I want to know... How are you? Are you okay?" He took a small step forward and stopped, heaving a big breath.

Wow. I hadn't expected such...word vomit. He looked worn out. He smiled sheepishly. I huffed a small laugh. I wasn't sure what to say to such a deluge of words.

"Um, wow. Thank you for sharing...all of that."

He slapped his hand over his eyes.

"Sorry for the word vomit. I'm usually a better communicator than this," he chuckled, shaking his head. He ran his hands through his hair again. "I'm a little flustered."

I shrugged.

"It's fine. I'm glad you told me." I paused. "I guess it's my turn," I told him. I searched the sky, looking for the best place to begin.

"I'll work backward. Yes, I'm okay. It has been very strange for me too, seeing you here, seeing you at church. I'm glad to see you at church, though. I'm glad you met the Lord. He's changed a lot of things for me—well, everything..." I trailed off. I couldn't remember the rest.

Ryan nodded but kept watching me.

"I'm glad," he finally said.

We stood there a minute, staring at each other, nodding. Then I remembered Ryan had experienced pain of his own. My hand came up to my chest.

"I'm sorry for your loss of Jamie Martin. I didn't know him, but I love his parents. They are important to me. I know he was wonderful."

Ryan's sad smile broke my heart a little. I started to worry he might start to cry or something. He swallowed. Oh no. *Please don't cry*, I silently begged, mostly out of self-preservation. I was not ready to hug Ryan, but if he started crying, I would have to hug him. Talking to him was one thing. Touching him was out of the question.

"Thank you," he said softly. He cleared his throat. "Jamie was my roommate in Nashville. He was the one who told me about Jesus. He was my best friend."

"I heard. Pam and John have told me a little about you. They really love you. They seem very glad you are here," I said, hoping to send us back to safer territory.

"Yeah, they're great. They're the ones who invited me down here to apply for this job. I've never been a minister before. I led worship at my church in Nashville for a while, but that's all the experience I have. I was a studio musician for a long time. I quit the band a year or so after, um…meeting you, and I moved to Nashville."

More word vomit, but it felt less emotionally charged. It was sort of nice to be chatting with him, connecting some of the dots. I nodded.

"Studio musician-ing sounds serious. How many instruments do you play?" I asked.

He looked like he was calming down a little too. Work was a safe subject. This exchange was starting to feel more conversational than awkward, now that we were both breathing a little easier.

"Yeah, it paid the bills. It's a fun job. Every week is different. I play several instruments. I mostly play guitar now, but my love is the drums."

I blushed, remembering. He kept talking.

"I played drums, guitar, and bass a lot in the studio. I can pick my way through on piano pretty well and also on the harmonica. But I am terrible with a bow, so no fiddle or anything. Also I sing, which I guess is a different type of instrument, technically. How about you?" he asked, turning the tables. I shook my head.

"Oh, I don't play any instruments."

He huffed a laugh, nodding.

"Good to know. What about work for you? You're an ER nurse?" He trailed off again, encouraging me to speak. I leaned against the car.

"Yeah, I'm a nurse. I've been working at the hospital since I moved here about seven years ago. Maddie—she was here today—we work together at the hospital. She invited me to a Bible study about six years ago. I started going to church a few weeks later, and here I am."

Now it was my turn to heave a breath, releasing some of the tension. We were doing this, talking like normal people who did not have a past together that was totally overwhelming. It was…well, it was okay. I was breathing normally. I was not shaking or triggered. I was just chatting. I gave myself a mental high five, thanking God for therapy.

The pause lengthened. It was time to wrap up and get out of there.

"Okay," I started speaking at the same time as him.

"Would you—"

We both stopped, our words hanging in the air. He went ahead.

"I was hoping maybe we could have coffee sometime," he said.

He quickly read my face, and suddenly, we were back to scared animal hands.

"Sorry!" He paused. He shook his head, took a breath. This was so awkward.

"I'm sorry," he said again. "I just meant, could we have coffee, maybe talk? It's been a long time. We could catch up?"

I looked down.

"I don't think so." I felt bad rejecting him immediately, but it was important to be honest. I could not let this moment be something I romanticized.

He looked down too, disappointed. But he cleared his throat then gave a small nod.

"Totally understand. No problem!" He nodded reassuringly. *Like a minister*, I thought. *Man, God really does have plans greater than we can imagine.*

"Well, I better go," I told him, grabbing the door handle of my car.

"Okay," he agreed and began to slowly walk backward. "Thanks for talking to me, Mia. It's good to see you again. Have a great week!"

He turned and walked over to his car, a silver SUV. He didn't look back.

Whew! My adrenaline was pumping, but it was slowing down. I was relieved I made it through the whole conversation with him. Also, strangely, I felt bereft. It was a little sad to see him walk away.

I assured myself that saying no to coffee was the right thing to do. I wasn't ready to spend time with Ryan. But it was a good conversation—certainly better than I had anticipated. I was grateful and hopeful. Maybe he and I could be friends one day. *God can do anything*, I reminded myself as I slipped into my car, shut the door, and put the key in the ignition.

Chapter 12

Monday came, and with it, a summer rainstorm. The rain kept on all week. By the time the sunshine returned on Thursday, everyone and everything was a soggy mess.

Maddie sent me pictures of poor Kevin, covered up to his floppy ears in mud. I laughed, glad it wasn't my job to clean up after him. He was super sweet, but mud is mud. Cleaning up people was part of my job. I loved serving them, but it was nice to be able to go home and have a break.

I did some shopping Thursday evening to replenish the first aid kits and the big nurse's trunk for camp. I needed to focus on getting myself packed Friday evening without the distraction of all the nurse stuff in addition to everything else. Anna came over to keep me company. She arrived with sushi for her and noodles for me. I was starving.

"What's Gage up to tonight?" I asked, shutting the door.

"He joined the church softball team. They have practice tonight." Anna rolled her eyes in a way that said, *He's a dork but he's my dork.*

I was loading the food onto paper plates and pouring us each a glass of wine in the kitchen while she picked a movie.

"Aw," I replied. "How fun! Can we go to the games and cheer for them?"

Anna nodded excitedly, putting the remote down. She took a few steps toward the kitchen.

"There are a bunch of them on the team. They have team shirts with matching socks for what Gage calls 'a team vibe.' He says I wouldn't understand." She scoffed, rolling her eyes.

I was with Gage on this one, but I didn't say so. Anna hadn't played team sports growing up, so she didn't understand things like how socks could matter for team spirit. However, Anna *did* have a fear of missing out, which made her want to experience everything, even sometimes pointless, silly things, like matching socks with a bunch of dudes.

"I'll wear matching socks with you," I offered. "It will be great! Who all is playing on the team?"

Anna counted them on her fingers. "Gage, Ben, Bryan, Luke, Hunter, Youth Guy Chris, Teague, Stupid Preston, and Ryan Blackstone Lyles."

She held up her fingers in air quotes when she recited Ryan's name, which was funny, but I laughed aloud at the way she curled her lip in disgust when she used the new nickname she'd given Preston. Anna's loyalty truly knew no bounds. It didn't matter to her that we hadn't dated long or that I was totally okay with him ending the relationship. To Anna, Preston committed the unforgivable in dumping me.

I did pity him a little, having made such a fearsome enemy without even realizing it. But what could I say? I would do the same thing for Anna if the situation were reversed.

I ignored the rest of the names. I just wanted to enjoy this evening and laugh with my best friend, but Anna would have none of it. She dove right in.

"You told me about the name situation, but what else happened when you talked to Ryan? I can't believe you made me wait this long!"

I rolled my eyes at her. "I've been busy! And it wasn't a big deal. We just chatted about work for a minute. It turns out he plays a lot of instruments. At the end, he asked if we could have coffee and catch up."

Anna's eyes were like saucers. "What did you say?"

"No, of course!" I said, surprised she even needed to ask. "I'm not interested in hanging out with Ryan, no matter what his last name is now. I don't have time, and it's not like we'll see each other a lot or anything. It was a nice conversation, and I am happy to leave it at that."

Anna just stared at me, eyebrows raised. I tilted my head, begging her.

"Anna, please, can we drop it? I can't deal with that right now. I'm leaving for camp tomorrow, and I just want to hang out with my best friend and eat something fabulous before I have camp food for a week."

Her shoulders fell, and with a final, knowing look, she nodded and picked up her plate.

"Works for me," she conceded, tapping her wine glass to the one in my hand. "Cheers."

"Thank you," I sighed. Holding my wine glass, I picked up my plate of noodles and walked toward the sofa in the living room. Setting it all on the coffee table, I settled down into the cool leather.

"Okay, what movie are we watching while I pack for camp?" I asked. My suitcase was sitting open on the floor in front of the coffee table. An unruly pile of clothes, toiletries, and snacks sat next to it, awaiting some semblance of order.

Anna set her plate, towering with sushi, next to mine. Then she held her glass of wine aloft, did a drumroll thing with her mouth, then using an extremely nasally voice, announced, "The unmatched, classic artistry of Steven Spielberg: *Jaws*!"

I nodded with appreciation. *Jaws* was a classic. It was in no way about camping, former flames, hospital life, or anything else I might want a break from thinking about in the next week. I held up my wine glass. "Cheers, to an excellent choice!"

Anna clinked her glass with mine. "I'll drink to that," she agreed victoriously.

We settled in on my squashy sofa, and dug in. The movie played, keeping us entertained for quite a while. Eventually, I moved to the floor to begin packing in earnest. By the time Hooper surfaced and paddled through all the shark guts, heading back to Amity Island with Chief Brody, my suitcase was full and zipped, ready to go. The bus would be heading out bright and early the next morning. We both stood up to stretch, sleepy from sitting for so long.

Anna gave me a huge hug, saying she would be praying for a great week. I thanked her, walked her to the door, and locked up behind her.

I put away the dishes, washed the wine glasses, and got ready for bed. I was excited for camp, but tomorrow was going to start early. I prayed God would help me to be a blessing to the people there in the coming week and for Him to reveal more of Himself to me while there. Snuggled down in bed, I fell asleep in record time, filled with hope and excitement for the week to come.

Chapter 13

S aturday morning came very early indeed. I arrived at the church parking lot a few minutes before 6am, bleary-eyed but excited. I unloaded
my suitcase and the trunk of medical supplies then added it all to the
still-small pile of suitcases. Two of the dads were crouched down under
the huge charter bus, helping the driver get everything loaded. I had my
backpack full of road trip gear on my back, and I was holding my pillow.

One of the moms brought coffee and set it up for anyone who wanted
it. *Praise God.* I thanked her when she handed me the cardboard cup. I
balanced the coffee carefully on my way up the steps into the bus. The
second row was empty, so I stepped in to put my stuff down.

Bringing my coffee with me, I went down the steps and walked over
to a chair with a big lockbox next to it. A sign on the box read *Nurse Station*. As kids arrived, I would check in the medications and secure them in
the box. There were only a few kids who took medicine, but I organized it
all meticulously.

Once the last medical form was filled out, I walked across the parking
lot, the relentless humidity and diesel smell clinging to me as I moved.
As I climbed the steps into the bus, the relief of the air conditioning took
over more with every step, releasing me from the dense humidity of the
air outside. Looking around, I breathed in with anticipation. Between the
heat and fifty teenagers, this was probably the best the bus was going to
smell for the whole trip. Honestly, I didn't even care.

I looked around the bus before I sat down. Sleepy teenagers filled the
scratchy gray seats, most of them wearing headphones. The majority of
them were looking at phones, and some of them were chatting softly. A
couple were dozing, their heads pressed against the glass. I smiled. This
was going to be tiring, stinky, and so much fun. I was super excited.

A noise caught my attention. I turned to see who was coming up the
stairs behind me. It was Youth Guy Chris. I smiled in greeting, partly because of manners and partly because I had a can of tuna fish in my suitcase
with his name on it. After consideration, I decided to give him a chance to

redeem himself. If he was kind, fun, and showed personal growth, great. If he was a jerk during Capture the Flag again, well, he'd had his chance.

"Hi Mia. Thanks for coming this week," he said with way too much energy for this time of day. I just nodded and smiled. I hadn't consumed quite enough coffee to want to chat yet. He handed me a folder.

"Here is the schedule for the week, meal plan, anything I thought might have potential for a nurse. I noticed the medical trunk under the bus. I assume you packed it up with everything?"

I nodded, impressed at the organization of it all.

"Great. Thank you for taking good care of us. We'll get going soon." With that, he turned to walk back down the steps. Several more teens boarded the bus, then Sarah showed up. Maddie wasn't going this year because Kevin was still too new and too young to be boarded.

Sarah put her stuff next to mine in the narrow leg space, then we both carefully sat down, our legs curled underneath us in our seats. The coffee was slowly taking effect. I was able to chat with Sarah, who was, of course, a morning person with or without coffee. She wore a sunny smile, truly excited to be there, even this early.

"I'm so excited," Sarah exclaimed. "Did you bring good snacks?"

I scoffed, almost insulted. "Of course I did," I retorted. Snacks were not something to take lightly, especially if one was going away to a remote location for a whole week. I packed a stash of snacks for the whole week in my suitcase. My road trip snacks were carefully stuffed in my backpack, along with a couple of books, a sudoku puzzle book, headphones, and charging cord for my phone.

I was just about to open my backpack to show Sarah what we had to work with when Youth Guy Chris came up the steps with Ryan trailing behind him.

Chapter 14

I was taken aback.

"What are you doing here?" I asked him abruptly.

Ryan hesitated. Sarah turned to me, a shocked expression on her face. Even Chris' eyes widened. I blushed.

"I'm sorry, how rude of me. I haven't finished my coffee yet."

"No problem." Ryan shrugged it off graciously.

I closed my eyes and pinched the bridge of my nose, embarrassed. When I opened them, Chris was shuffling into the row across the aisle from Sarah and me. Ryan was putting his stuff in the row in front of us. He wore an old, soft-looking t-shirt with the orange Tennessee T emblazoned on the front and jeans.

The other adult sponsors, mostly parent volunteers, were stationed throughout the bus. Sarah began asking Chris about the weather forecast. It was supposed to rain on Wednesday, the day of the long hike. Chris told her he didn't trust the weather forecast for a second. The bus door closed, and we began to move, pulling out of the parking lot.

I began to dig around my backpack for my water bottle. I needed a minute to breathe, and while I had the opportunity, I talked to myself. *This is a surprise, but it doesn't have to be a bad one. I can handle having Ryan at camp. We will hardly see each other. There probably won't be any time for interaction anyway. Camp is a busy place. Every day has a full schedule. I can just avoid him if I need to. It's fine. Breathe, Mia!*

My thoughts were interrupted by a quiet, low voice just in front of me.

"I'm sorry."

I looked up into the crack between the seats. His eyes were waiting for me. My chest immediately grew warm. What was it about this man and his eyes? It was so frustrating. I took a breath, forcing myself to look away for a second, to recover.

"No, Ryan, *I'm* sorry. Please forgive my rudeness. I don't feel the way I sounded. I was just surprised. It's going to be a great week at camp. I hope you enjoy it." I managed a small smile. Then…there! My hand finally closed around the handle of my water bottle. I settled back, opened it, and took a drink of water.

But Ryan wasn't done. He shifted around in his seat until he was facing me.

"Thanks for tolerating my presence," he intoned pleasantly, his deep voice filled with irony. I wasn't sure what to say in return. Was Ryan being funny or sarcastic? Were his feelings hurt? This was too much for Morning Mia.

Just when the awkwardness was starting to make my scalp tingle, Sarah moved in my peripheral vision. Sarah! I was saved! No one could feel awkward with Sarah. It wasn't possible. I turned to her. "Sarah, have you met Ryan yet? He's the new worship minister at the church."

Sarah smiled widely, full of welcome. "I haven't yet. Hi, Ryan! We're glad to have you here. I'm Sarah."

She reached across the back of the seats and shook his hand eagerly. Ryan smiled politely and said, "Nice to meet you, Sarah. It's good to be here. This is my first time going to camp. Is it yours?"

Sarah answered him, then they were off to the races. Satisfied, I stretched then scrunched down, trying to get more comfortable in the seat. My work here was done. Sarah loved camp even more than I did, and she was super outgoing. She and Ryan could talk the whole five-hour bus ride, meaning I would be free to just observe or do my own thing—or so I thought.

"Mia, how many years have you gone to camp with us?" Sarah asked, expecting me to participate.

I sat up, startled to be brought back into the conversation this quickly.

"Just one. Last year was my first year," I told her.

"What's your favorite part?" Ryan asked.

I took a moment to think about my answer.

"Probably hiking. It's beautiful there, and I like being outside."

Ryan nodded. "Me too."

"The hiking is great, but my favorite part is worshiping around the campfire in the evenings," Sarah remarked. "I guess that's where you come in, Ryan." He nodded agreeably then looked back at me.

"I guess you're going to be the camp nurse? Your title sounds very official." He cracked a smile.

Inwardly, I rolled my eyes. Why was he trying to keep me in this conversation? *Fine,* I thought grumpily, *I'll talk to you.*

"Yes, I will be at the nurse station some. I'll also go on the big hike, and I'll hand out meds at meals…that kind of thing. Usually, if there is a large group activity going on, I'll be there with everybody—just in case."

Sarah spoke up, changing the subject. "Ryan, are you a hiker?"

He looked at her, shifting in his seat. "I don't get to go as often as I'd like lately, but yes, I like being outside. How about you?"

Sarah nodded. "Definitely. I just got a new mountain bike last year. I've only taken it out a couple times. I love outdoor sports."

They talked about mountain biking a little bit. Dallas had a surprising number of trails in the area. I had nothing to contribute, and I hadn't eaten breakfast yet, so I dug into my snack stash. I pulled out a box of chocolate Teddy Grahams and opened them, the wrapping crinkling loudly. I had a handful of the bears in my hand and was mid-chew, when I looked up and noticed Ryan staring at the box, his face carefully blank. I was about to offer him some when I remembered. *Oh.*

I'd eaten Teddy Grahams with Ryan before. I took a breath and talked to myself. *I could freak out about this, or I could stay calm. They're just Teddy Grahams. This doesn't have to be overwhelmingly weird.* I decided to breathe and keep going, to try to let this moment pass without overreacting.

Sarah, bless her, provided the perfect distraction. She asked if either of us had seen the latest action movie in theaters yet. She and Ben had gone the night before. I couldn't help myself. I wiggled my eyebrows, sing-songing, "Oooh, a night out with Ben!"

She smiled excitedly and held out her hand for some Teddy Grahams. I opened the box to pour several into her hand. Then, in the name of manners and personal growth, I offered the box to Ryan. He held out his hand and thanked me as I poured out a handful. *Whew*! The moment had passed. I said a quick prayer of thanks. We were going to get through this.

"How was the movie?" I asked, back on track. Sarah lit up from the inside, telling us all about her date with Ben. I was really happy for both of them. I snuck a look at Ryan. He was smiling too. Sarah told us about going out to dinner and the movie. She left out the juicier details, which was understandable. But Ryan, it turned out, was kind of a sucker for a love story. He wanted to know more.

Was this their first date? How did they know each other? Did she put "the moves" on Ben at the movies? Sarah blushed at his questions but told us Ben held her hand during the movie, and afterward, he walked her to the door and kissed her good night. Ryan gave her a high five. Sarah and I shimmied in our seats. I wished Maddie and Anna could have been there to hear this with us. It was so fun to celebrate this very good date for my friend. Finally!

I was so busy being happy for Sarah I almost forgot to notice how easy it was chatting with Ryan there. I didn't know if it was because Sarah was so personable or what, but somehow it *was* easy. I was glad for this gift. I breathed a sigh of relief. The sigh died on my lips when Sarah turned to Ryan.

"Do you have a girlfriend, Ryan?"

I held my breath. It was involuntary.

My mind began to spin, suddenly curious about that part of his life. Ten years was a long time. Back then, I convinced myself he kept girlfriends in every town. But here, now, it felt odd to consider it. Ryan could be engaged, or he might date around, or he may even have been married.

My lungs constricted weirdly at the awkwardness of the moment. I shouldn't engage with him about this. But like an accident on the side of the road, I couldn't look away. Here, in this moment, I wanted to be anywhere else, but I also really wanted to know.

He cleared his throat. "No, no girlfriend. I was engaged before, in Nashville. It ended about a year ago. She broke it off."

Wow. Engaged. Committed. *Ryan was going to marry someone.* Questions immediately filled my mind. Who was the girl? What was she like? How long were they together? What was Ryan like back in Nashville?

I gathered my courage to look at him. He wasn't hiding. His eyes were clear, looking Sarah in the face, open and honest. Sarah started to ask more questions but was interrupted by Youth Guy Chris speaking over the intercom. Everyone jumped at the loud greeting.

"Rise and shine, folks! We are on our way to the best week of the summer! We'll stop for the bathroom in two hours. Do not ask any sooner. Who's ready to play?" With that, he held up a rubber chicken. He launched it toward the back of the bus. One of the boys rose up to catch it. This began an intense game of keepaway in these very close quarters. Youth Guy Chris possessed a special gift for riling people up at the most inopportune times.

I shook my head. The antics were starting a little too early for my taste. But I reminded myself I wasn't in charge. I was there to serve. Time to put on the big-girl panties and have some fun! I turned in my seat to look just in time to see the chicken hurtling through the air, straight toward me. I had no time to react. I was about to be hit with a rubber chicken at 6:30 in the morning.

But a hand passed in front of my face, moving faster than the chicken. It caught the chicken right before I would have been stabbed in the eye with the red beak. The chicken disappeared over my head. I turned to see Ryan rearing back to throw the chicken toward the back of the bus. The yellow-and-red missile was lost from sight in the mass of flailing arms.

I sat back in my seat, still processing what just happened in the last 1.5 seconds.

"Thanks," I muttered quietly to Ryan. His blue eyes smiled at me.

"No problem," he replied.

"Ooh, that was hero stuff, Ryan! I'm glad you're here,"' Sarah gushed with a laugh. She shook her head. "Leave it to Chris to start something way too crazy in a tiny space."

I laughed in agreement. Chris leaned across the aisle toward us then.

"Thanks for being here, you guys," he said. "It's nice to have some young adults along. All the other grownups are parents. They get tired too easily."

I'd hate to break it to him, but I felt pretty tired myself. Chris was a good guy, and he was a great youth minister, meeting the kids where they were. He was good at holding out the beauty of God's Word to them. He was just also sort of obnoxious.

Chris asked Ryan, "Who are your sports teams, bro?"

Ryan answered, "The Titans, obviously, for football. Other sports, I'll support the local team, so the Rangers and the Mavericks."

Chris nodded then started talking about some statistics for some team and their defense. I was not against sports, but I didn't find them interesting either. Sarah usually felt the same way, so I was surprised when she said, "Ben and I are planning to go to a Rangers game when I get back. Have you been to a game lately?"

I told her I hadn't, but I was excited for her to go. We dug into my snack stash, each taking a Twizzler from the package. We spent the next little bit chatting about Sarah's excitement about getting to know Ben better then sharing our predictions for the Young Adults Retreat.

It was coming up on Labor Day weekend, still a long way off. Sarah was on the planning committee, so she wanted to hear my opinion on the activities she was planning.

We were laughing at the idea of dress-up races as an icebreaker activity. I was taking a sip of water when Sarah leaned in close to me so I could hear her over the rumble of the bus. She said quietly, "I can't help but notice Ryan is VERY cute, and he seems VERY interested in getting to know YOU, my friend."

I was so startled I inhaled right as some water was going down my throat. Immediately drowning, I coughed violently. Sarah pounded on my back as I coughed. Ryan looked over, concerned. Row by row, everyone turned to look at the commotion. Youth Guy Chris took the opportunity to yell obnoxiously.

"No peeing your pants on the bus, Mia!"

He received a few laughs, but it didn't last long. Everyone went about their business once the storm passed, and I drew in slow breaths, coughing intermittently. I gasped, "I'm fine. Sorry."

Sarah leaned in, her eyes huge. "Wow." She tilted her head. "I didn't expect you to react like *that*. Are you okay?"

I looked at her, askance. "I'm fine. But that's not what is happening."

She pulled back from my abrupt tone, eyebrows raised in surprise. My heart plummeted.

"I'm sorry. I totally overreacted," I apologized, sighing. Sarah looked at me questioningly. She knew me well enough to know I did not usually respond to innocent statements like one would respond to news of an accusation of murder. I had to tell her something. I took a breath.

"We've met before, back in college, in California. He's not the person for me." There. I'd explained and kept it simple. But Sarah's eyebrows drew together in a way that filled me with dread.

"Oh. How did y'all know each other?"

I paused before answering. It was an innocent question. I was tempted to overreact again, but what would that solve? I was on this bus, headed to camp, with him here, and we had just lived through the Teddy Grahams thing. Also, Sarah was a close friend. I decided to answer her honestly.

"He was in a band. We met at one of his gigs."

Sarah wanted more details. "So, you were friends?"

When would this end?

"We were more like acquaintances, but we didn't stay in touch," I said, begging God to send a bird into the windshield or something to distract my friend from this line of questioning. I wasn't sure what would come next.

Sarah looked to the row ahead of us, where Ryan finished his conversation with Youth Guy Chris. He was reading in his seat. She perked up when she realized what he was reading.

"Ooh, *Pilgrim's Progress*! Such a great book!"

Ryan looked back at us. I silently offered him the pack of Twizzlers. He took one, nodding thanks. He responded to Sarah.

"Yeah, I'm working through it slowly. I like it so far."

Sarah looked at him curiously. "Are you new to professional ministry?"

Ryan nodded. "Very. This is my first ministry job."

Youth Guy Chris interjected. "Yeah, but not your last, bro. You're doing great. And if you need tips, I can help you."

Ryan looked at him sincerely. "Thank you, Chris. I appreciate your encouragement."

Sarah smiled at me. She could appreciate a sweet "bro moment" as well as anyone. I took another bite of the Twizzler in my hand and chewed slowly.

I took a moment to reflect. This was exhausting, but I was surprised to be enjoying myself. It hadn't occurred to me that our paths might cross very often, yet here we were. Learning how to be around Ryan was going to take time. It would help a lot if he could quit popping up out of nowhere and startling me. But we went to the same church. We were in similar stages of life. It would be wise to assume he was going to be at activities from now on.

Chapter 15

The bus driver signaled as we exited the highway. It was time to get off the bus, stretch, and use the facilities. Youth Guy Chris took the opportunity to use the intercom to tell everyone we would be leaving again in fifteen minutes. He moved to the side, motioning for us to begin the exodus. Ryan went out and down the stairs first, then Sarah, then me.

I was almost down the steps, but something went wrong. I missed the actual step and toppled forward. It happened so fast. One second, I was falling, watching the pavement get closer and closer. The next, an arm wrapped around me in mid-air, then pulled me up, securing me against a firm torso.

Bewildered, I turned my head, finding myself inches away from Ryan's stubbled jaw. He bent his head toward me, meeting my eyes, but said nothing. He set me down gently, making sure I was solid on both feet before he let me go. My mind was blank. My body jolted to life as if I'd been shocked. *What just happened?*

Sarah's voice shattered the moment.

"Mia, are you okay? Oh my gosh, that was close! Ryan, amazing catch! I can't believe you moved that fast!"

My brain came to life again as I stepped away from Ryan's warmth.

"Thanks," I breathed in his direction, and walked quickly toward the convenience store of a massive truck stop. I could hear his deep voice chatting with Sarah right behind me, but I just kept moving.

I wasn't ready for this. I felt embarrassed and overstimulated by such close contact with Ryan. My skin may as well have been flashing neon: OVERWHELMED. I didn't want to call any more attention to myself. I walked through the convenience store doors then turned right and headed toward the ladies' bathroom.

Twice in one day, I thought. *First the chicken, now the step. Geez, what next?* I could feel his phantom warmth on all the places on my body where we made contact. I took a breath.

This was just strange. Why was I so *aware* of him? I sighed with frustration, knowing deep down I knew the answer to that. But still. Ryan was invading my life! How was I supposed to process all this in the moment, with him *right there*?

In fairness, I was probably invading his life too. I shut myself in a stall to do some grounding exercises I learned in therapy. The breathing helped. I didn't know what else to do, so I prayed. *What are you doing? Help me, Lord. I trust you.* I repeated the simple prayer over and over, breathing in and out, until I felt calmer.

The fact was, we were both on this trip. Knowing the rhythm of camp, it was almost a certainty we would be spending more time together. I needed to accept this fact and find a way to be around him without feeling anxious, or trying to run away, or generally overreacting. I didn't know how I would do it, but I needed to figure it out.

The week before, Brooke and I worked on unclouding the waters, keeping the main thing the main thing. What did I want my main thing to be? I wanted to be walking with God, moving closer to Him. I wanted to shine His Light wherever I went, including camp.

I began to pray, clearing my head of the cobwebs, focusing on the main thing. *Help me serve these kids with joy. Help me keep my eyes on you, without getting distracted*, I prayed.

A verse came to mind. *You will keep in perfect peace, all who trust in you, whose thoughts are fixed on you!* I didn't know where it was in Isaiah, but I often noticed it on a table in Pam and John's study, part of a little collection of inspirational tchotchkes. Thinking of Pam and John made me remember how much they loved Ryan. He seemed to love them back. Ryan wasn't my enemy. He was a neutral party.

I walked out of the bathroom with new resolve then nearly ran right into Ryan. Because of course I did. I jumped back at the very last second.

"Whoa! Sorry about that," I said.

"No problem," Ryan assured me.

I gathered myself and looked into his eyes.

"Thank you for catching me when I fell off the bus," I told him. "And for stopping the rubber chicken from putting out my eye."

He smiled, his teeth so white and straight it was distracting. *Why couldn't he have some spinach between his teeth or something, just once?* I wondered savagely.

"Glad I could help," he said. He swallowed, his Adam's apple moving down his neck, then continued sincerely. "I'm sorry again, about invading your space."

I shook my head, pleasantly surprised he understood. "It's okay. I'm glad you're here. It's going to be a great week."

He cocked his head at me then, with a bemused look in his eyes. "You don't seem glad. You seem tense and frustrated. I don't understand. You're the one who—" He was interrupted by Youth Guy Chris, who walked up to us, holding a huge turkey leg in one hand.

Standing close enough for us to smell the smoked meat, Chris took a huge bite out of it and then, with his mouth full, asked, "You guys almost ready to go?"

"Yup," I replied, thankful for a way out of the conversation. I walked over to the cash register to pick out some gum. The bell above the door sounded every time someone came in or out. I focused on counting the rings of the bell as the teenagers trickled out to the parking lot.

I was walking to the bus when Sarah caught up with me in the parking lot.

"Hey, girl! I lost you for a minute," she said.

"Here I am," I told her with a smile. She hooked her arm in mine and leaned her head close to me so we were temple to temple.

"You okay, friend? Seems like you've got a lot going on in that mind of yours today."

I nodded. "Oh yeah, I'm good. Definitely dreading sharing the bus with Youth Guy Chris and his turkey leg, but I guess it's not much different than smelling a bunch of teens' feet," I quipped, smiling.

"Gosh, I can't believe Maddie went out with him. He's obnoxious. But the kids seem to love him," she pointed out. Chris was being chased by two sophomore boys, both of whom seemed intent on dumping their icy drinks over his head. This wasn't Chris' first rodeo. He side-stepped them easily then ran up the steps to the bus, turkey leg undisturbed.

I had to hand it to him; he was excellent at all the silliest parts of his job. Maybe Maddie observed something special at some point? I still wasn't sure what made her say yes to a date with him. I trusted she had her reasons.

I looked around, soaking in the moment. It was going to be a great week. We climbed the steps to the bus. I checked the time. We would arrive at camp right around lunch time, and the first dose of meds was due for a few of the kids.

Having taken care of business, we were all tucked back into our bus seats, counted by one of the parent sponsors to make certain we left no one behind, ready to finish up the last couple of hours of the road trip to camp. I was about to pull out my book to read for a little while when Youth Guy Chris leaned across the aisle and, trying to be heard over the rumble of the bus, loudly said, "Hey, bro, thank you for sharing your testimony to kick us off tonight. I appreciate it."

Ryan looked over and just said, "It's no problem. I'm glad to share."

His testimony? Wow. That was something I'd be very interested to hear. As if he heard my thoughts out loud, Ryan turned around to look at me. He asked, "Have you shared your testimony before?"

I nodded, thinking of the families at the pregnancy center. "Yes, a few times."

Sarah piped up. "Ryan, I'm glad you're sharing your testimony! It will be a good chance to get to know you better, since you're so new."

I nodded quietly, afraid of where this was going. I was not prepared to share my testimony right there on the bus, especially with this audience. Ryan just shrugged. "Thanks, Sarah. My testimony is a little bit grimy. I didn't start out in a Christian home, like a lot of these kids."

Sarah nodded with understanding. "We all have twists and turns, don't we? No one is perfect, or we wouldn't need Jesus. I'm excited to hear how you found Him!"

Just when I was afraid Ryan was going to ask about my story, Youth Guy Chris changed the subject.

"Guys, you know those boys who tried to dump their sodas on my head? How about we prank them this week? I brought a rubber snake and some firecrackers." I could have hugged him for saving the moment. Maybe I wouldn't need to prank him after all. Then he opened his mouth again.

"Hey, Mia, remember my great prank last year?"

There it was: the other side of the coin. *Ugh.* I rolled my eyes but somehow managed to keep my mouth shut. I wasn't about to dignify that with a response.

I comforted myself, knowing I still had the can of tuna. I could put it in his car as soon as we got home. Or maybe I'd just throw caution to the wind and toss all his shoes into the lake at camp. My vengeful daydreams were interrupted when Sarah leaned onto me.

"I can't believe I forgot to ask you. Did you know Preston brought a new girl to church last Sunday?"

I raised my eyebrows. I hadn't known, but I wasn't surprised. I took a second to check in with myself. I was fine and not bothered at all. Poor Preston. I hoped this new girl liked him a lot—to make up for me being lukewarm. It wasn't his fault I was a mess.

"No, I must have missed seeing them," I replied.

Sarah sighed. "He's an idiot, Mia. I can't believe he dumped you in the first place. Now he's already showing up with someone new!"

I appreciated her loyalty. Sarah was a good friend. I hadn't told her about the reason he broke up with me, and I didn't intend to tell anyone but Anna. I did not want to stir the pot.

"Oh, it's no big deal, Sarah. We were not compatible. Truly, I hope he finds someone great. Preston is a good guy; he's just not for me. Honestly, I was relieved he ended it," I insisted.

"You're a better woman than me." Sarah shook her head. "I always want to be the dumper, no matter what. You handled it well, though. I don't know many people who could be so gracious about it."

Ryan poked his head over the seats. "Hey, do either of you have a charging cord I could use to plug in my phone? There's a jack here, but my cord is down in my luggage."

Sarah dug through her bag then handed him hers. She lifted her chin and asked, "Ryan, what do you think? Is it better to be dumped or be the dumper?"

He took a second to think. "Hmm. I don't know," he answered. "I guess it depends on the situation."

"I'm guessing you were upset when that girl broke off your engagement," Sarah said pointedly. I wanted to fold myself into the seat cushion and disappear. I did not want to continue the previous conversation with Ryan. He nodded at Sarah.

"Yeah, I was. But she was right to do it," he said matter-of-factly.

"Do you mind me asking what happened?" Sarah asked. She was so open and kind. Who could resist her? I was curious about Ryan's fiancée too, but it felt awkward. Apparently, it only felt awkward for me, though. Ryan opened right up.

"We were engaged for about a year. It was kind of a difficult relationship from the beginning, personality-wise, but we loved each other, and we wanted to make it work. Then my best friend passed away, and grief just…swallowed me for a while.

"Lindsey and I drifted apart. We couldn't find our way back to each other afterward. We tried for a while, but we just couldn't get there. She gave me back the ring and started dating a guy from work a few weeks later. It was tough, going through it, but now I can see it was the best thing for both of us. They're married now. I think they're really happy."

Sarah nodded, full of compassion. "I'm so sorry that happened."

Ryan shrugged, smiling softly. "Thank you."

I just looked at him. I didn't have any words. All I could think was, *Wow*, over and over. Losing his best friend. Losing his fiancée. Moving multiple states away from his life. Changing careers. All of it combined was a *lot*. The more I learned about this man, the more questions I had. Pam had not mentioned anything about a fiancée. I looked up, processing everything I'd just heard. His eyes met mine.

"I'm sorry too," I said.

He nodded. "Thanks. It's okay. God's been faithful in all of it. He'll get me where He wants me to go."

I blinked, truly seeing for the first time. Ryan was not a figment of my imagination, the unreasonably beautiful, self-assured, charismatic musician I held onto in my mind all these years. That was a story I told myself, based on forty-eight hours together, over a decade ago.

To be fair, he *was* unreasonably beautiful, but more than all of it, he was an actual, real person with a story and value. With gifts. Convicted, I felt humbled, sorry I had judged him. Who was *I* to judge anybody?

I considered him. Who was this man, so full of experiences, life, and truth? I was curious but more than a little bit scared to try to find out. Ryan interrupted my thoughts.

"How about you, Mia? Are you in a relationship?"

Heat climbed up my neck. It felt weird to share something like that with Ryan. I kept it simple. "Freshly dumped."

Ryan's eyebrows lifted. "Ouch! Are you doing okay?" he asked.

Sarah piped up proudly. "Oh, she's fine. She didn't like him much anyway." I groaned inwardly, looking out the window at the thick trees. I appreciated Sarah's loyalty, but she didn't make me sound very nice.

"Mia's a heartbreaker, alright," Ryan murmured. That got my attention. I snapped my eyes to him, indignant. *What did he mean?*

Ryan didn't say anything else. He just sat down and picked up his book, like nothing happened. Sarah dug around for more Twizzlers, like she hadn't noticed. *Did I dream that?* I wondered.

Just then, the bus lurched, making a wide turn into the entrance to camp. I hadn't realized we were this close. All the kids cheered. I got to work gathering my stuff so I could get the meds set up right away. It was almost lunchtime.

Chapter 16

The bus pulled up at the Hub, where we would eat all our meals. The Hub was the middle building at camp with other buildings surrounding it in a circular configuration. We had the girls' dorms at the opposite end from the guys' dorms, the craft barn, the equipment shed, the volunteers' dorm, and down closer to the lake was the firepit, which was surrounded by log benches.

Everyone gathered their things then filed noisily off the bus. A few of the guys pitched in and started unloading the cargo area underneath the bus. The teens and sponsors headed to their respective dorms, including Sarah.

Meanwhile, Youth Guy Chris began assigning rooms in the volunteer dorm to the rest of us. The volunteer dorm was two-story with suites of four rooms that all shared a bathroom.

Since I was the nurse and I was in charge of all the medical gear, I got the biggest room on the bottom floor—a single with its own bathroom. I wasn't about to argue with that, so here I was, given a spacious room and even privacy. I was very grateful to have the space to myself, especially now, with Ryan being a surprise factor for the week.

I found my room easily, the same one I used last year. The door opened to reveal a twin bed, a desk with a lamp, an armoire with double doors, and a small chest of drawers. The modular furniture was reminiscent of a freshman dorm, valuing functionality over frivolity.

Everything was brown fiberboard. Most of it bore the initials of generations of campers from the last fifty years drawn, in permanent marker, on the underside of every shelf and drawer. It was stark, but it held sweet memories for me—and apparently many others. The unmistakable warmth of camp was as comforting as it was unique and special.

I unpacked, stuffing the dresser drawers with my clothes then organizing my snacks on a shelf in the armoire above my now-empty suitcase.

I brought my own sheets and blanket, so I quickly made the bed. In no time, I was moved in for the week, ready to get started.

I hefted the box of meds to my hip and walked out the door, headed to the Hub, where I could set up shop for the lunchtime medication crew. The box wasn't heavy, but it was a little awkward. It lacked handles, so I just held it as best I could, balanced on one hip.

I headed down the hallway and outside. My heart lifted immediately, inhaling the clean, cool, mountain air. I walked along a path laid with loose gravel. As I walked, I spied a hawk circling. It was beautiful.

I was enjoying myself so much that I didn't see the large rock jutting out into the path, and I tripped. The box would have gone flying, and so would I, but two hands reached out. One steadied me, and the other caught the box and kept it upright. A deep, smooth voice said, "Whoa!" I knew without even looking.

Ryan.

I hadn't seen him there. This was the third time in less than twelve hours this man had caught or helped me in some way. I straightened out of his grip, frustrated with myself. His blue eyes were there, waiting.

"Thank you. Again," I mumbled, my face reddening. "Sorry I keep challenging your reflexes."

He stood, tall and at ease, looking down at me, squinting in the sun. "It's no problem," he replied. "Are you headed over there?" He gestured to the Hub.

I nodded. Without asking, he took the box from me then turned to walk with me. I didn't want to argue or make it any weirder, so I just let him.

"It's beautiful here," he said conversationally. But I couldn't focus. Something was bothering me. I might not get another chance to ask him without other people around.

"Ryan, what did you mean, on the bus earlier, when you said I'm a heartbreaker?" I asked.

"Oh, that. I'm sorry," he apologized, shaking his head. "I was mostly joking. Though, you did break my heart a little bit, disappearing on me like you did."

I rolled my eyes and sarcastically said, "I'm sure you healed just fine."

He said nothing. I stopped walking and faced him. His face was unreadable. Had I hurt his feelings?

"Sorry," I said. "I wasn't trying to be...harsh. I just mean we didn't know each other very well back then, and I assumed you moved on pretty quickly."

He looked at me intently, still holding the box.

"Fair enough," he conceded. "It's been a long time, but I thought we got to know each other really well."

I blushed, bright red, horrified at the innuendo. I reflexively took a step backward. I couldn't believe he would bring that up *here*. He must have read my face.

"Not that way! Gosh, Mia!" He laughed self-consciously, and his neck got very red. "I just meant we *talked* a lot. I mean, we talked on the phone every couple of days for, what, over a month? That was more than I had with anyone else for a long time. We said we loved each other. It meant a lot to me at the time. I was serious about you, and it hurt when you disappeared on me."

I didn't know what to say. He was completely earnest, fully secure. Did vulnerability just not bother this man? But that was a distraction. Right now, we were talking about the same thing—but from very different perspectives.

At first, I thought he was remembering someone else, or maybe I just misunderstood. But no, I'd forgotten. He was right. We *did* say we loved each other. We said it a lot in those few weeks. In fact, the last time we said goodbye, we said it. I hadn't considered what it was like for *him,* when my mom blocked his number with no explanation.

Right there in the sunshine, my many years of therapy kicked in. I realized what must have happened in my brain. The aftermath had changed the story in my mind. I remembered it was a happy weekend, but I focused on what came afterward. I rewrote the story, told myself it was just puppy love, hormones, and I didn't really matter to him. In an instant, the real memories surfaced. Slowing down, I blushed some more, thinking about those moments with this man right in front of me. But my heart sank.

Remembering this forgotten tenderness felt like pressing on a scar. It was sensitive. I had not been fair to Ryan. I owed him an apology and the truth. But I didn't think it was wise to tell him everything out here in the middle of camp, with people flocking to the Hub for lunch.

We were standing there, me processing so quickly my heart was pounding, and him just waiting, giving me time. I was overwhelmed. But one truth came through as the light shone through my memories. I didn't have a lot of opportunities for repairing wounds. I shouldn't squander this one. I took a breath and did what I could.

"I didn't realize it hurt you. I'm sorry." I looked into his eyes. It was the best I could do, here in the middle of camp, surrounded by people, trees, and rocks.

He shifted the box to his other hand. He looked around for a second before meeting my eyes. He was clearly processing a lot too.

"Thank you for apologizing. I appreciate it," he said.

Now was not a good time to burst into tears. Examining this bit of un-expected closure would have to wait. Instead, I released the breath I hadn't known I was holding. I gestured toward the Hub.

"Shall we?" I asked.

"Lead the way." He tilted his head in that direction. I shuffled around him, headed toward the Hub. As we walked along, other paths turned off, headed toward different parts of camp.

People gradually joined us on the path, because it led to the Hub. Everyone was talking. The kids were huddled in small groups, occasion-ally erupting in laughter. Sarah caught up with us. She took my arm as we walked, leaning her head on my shoulder.

"I miss Maddie," she sighed.

"Me too," I agreed. This year already felt different without Maddie there. With no cell service at camp, we couldn't even talk or text. Ryan being here added a whole other layer of weirdness. I sighed, wishing for Maddie and also Anna and Gage. Camp wasn't the same. I *definitely* wasn't the same. Maybe nothing was.

I tried to shake off the melancholy by looking at the lake, the water glistening in the sun. One of the adult sponsors was already on the shore, fishing rod in hand. I breathed in, feeling the breeze soothe my skin, which was still heated from my conversation with Ryan. We walked to the side door of the Hub and walked in.

We were greeted by a long food line, set up cafeteria-style. The camp kitchen staff members were still setting out lunch. The room smelled of food and sawdust, a strange-but-pleasant combination I only encountered here at camp. Sarah walked over to help, as well as to see if she could find a good option for her vegan ways. It looked like today was burger day. Last year, she brought a stash of vegan protein bars, just in case, so she probably had those if she needed them.

The room was large and sunny with several windows along each wall. Sunlight streamed in through the skylights, flickering through the blades of a row of ceiling fans. The fans were on, lazily circulating the air. Tables were set up end to end with rows of chairs lining both sides. On the opposite side of the room, in the corner, there sat a lone folding table with a handwritten sign reading *Nurse Station.*

"You want this over there on the nurse's table?" Ryan asked. I nodded and thanked him. He headed over there, so I followed him. He set the box on the table. I opened it and started organizing the lunchtime pills in tiny cups. There weren't many, only four. I vaguely noticed Ryan walking away as I was putting pill bottles away. When he returned, he brought a folding chair with him so I could sit down at the table. I was touched by his kindness.

I thanked him, and he smiled at me. A peace offering. A small step forward in this new way of being around each other. I could see we were slowly creating some semblance of friendship. It felt overwhelming but good. I was grateful. This wasn't the time to think about everything he said outside. I would need to process that later, in private.

It never occurred to me that I may have hurt him. I told myself he must have had a girl in every town. I wasn't sure what to do with this new information all these years later.

My thoughts were interrupted by the noise of fifty teenagers bounding into the room to get in line. The kids took up their plates and began to collect the makings of burgers, fries, and chocolate chip cookies for dessert. A freshman dropped his plate with a loud clatter, and everyone clapped enthusiastically. He turned bright red, bending down to clean up the mess.

Ryan got in line with Youth Guy Chris. Even through the noise of kids talking and eating, I could hear Chris' enthusiastic yell of "Hey, bro, where'd you disappear to?"

I couldn't hear Ryan's response. A student walked over to get her medication, so I focused on her. After making sure she took the pill, then recording the dose, date, and time in my nurse notebook, I looked around for the rest of the kids. They each eventually meandered up to the table, and it didn't take long to finish up. I walked over to the food line, absolutely starving.

Some of the kids were in line, getting seconds. I grabbed a plate, received a burger and fries, and poured myself some lemonade. I turned to find a place to eat, looking for Sarah, but Youth Guy Chris yelled, "Hey, Mia! Over here! We saved you a seat." People at the table next to him turned to stare at me. *Great.*

I sighed but walked over toward the table, carefully stepping around a puddle of spilled lemonade on my way. I did not fancy a busted tailbone at camp. Chris gestured to show me the seat he saved for me, right next to him, across from Ryan. I felt exhausted. I needed a break. It had been a long day already.

Talking with Ryan took a lot out of me, with so much to process. But I couldn't just turn my back. It would be rude—again—and Ryan *had* saved me from injury no less than three times that day. I set my plate on the table then collapsed into the chair. The guys were talking about sports. A small mercy! I tuned them out, focused on putting my burger together. I was still starving, and even this camp burger smelled amazing.

Chapter 17

The lunch hour passed quickly. Youth Guy Chris sent everyone to their bunks to finish settling in. Everyone else would meet up in thirty minutes to play games and get group assignments, then they would have the first small group session, followed by free time for the hour before dinner. I had the afternoon to myself.

I headed out the door with the crowd and down the rock path to the volunteer dorm. Walking into my room, I felt tempted to just lie down on my bed for a long nap. But a nap would only make me feel more tired. I decided to go for a walk. I put on sunscreen, refilled my water bottle from the water fountain in the hallway, then headed out.

I walked down the path to the lake. A small pier for fishing jutted out over the water. I could hear tiny waves ripple against the grassy shore. I turned, following the dirt path laid out around the lake.

It was a nice little walk, shaded by the many trees, a mix of pine and oak. The mountain rose up gently to the north, the sun bathing the entire area in friendly, bright light. The dirt path was tightly packed with a few other trails branching off, going deeper into the surrounding woods. The trees were dense here. I stayed on the path. It felt good to move.

I wasn't planning to run, but the cooler mountain air was invigorating, and it felt so good to be outside, so I broke into a jog. I moved at a good clip, reaching the other side of the lake within a few minutes. I made it all the way around and decided to do another lap. I had time, and it felt good to move after being cooped up in the cramped bus.

I didn't have my phone, so there was no way to play music, but it wasn't necessary here. I started praying to God. I kept praying through two more laps around the lake.

Finally, sweaty and panting, I turned off the dirt trail then walked briskly up the rock path toward the dorm. By the time I made it there, I was cooled down enough to be able to stretch. I was bent over, stretching my hamstrings, when Ryan came out the door, wearing running shorts and a t-shirt. He stopped when he saw me.

"Hi," he said, tilting his head to meet my eyes around my leg.

I instantly realized my butt was in the air, right in front of him. I popped up quickly. Moving upright so fast made me a little dizzy, but I turned around, smiling as if he hadn't just caught me looking extremely awkward. I felt my face burn with self-consciousness. *Play it off.*

"Hi," I said too brightly as I walked by him. "Just finished a run!" As I said this, my fingers decided to shoot finger guns at him. *Finger guns?! Lame!* He didn't seem to notice.

"Yeah, I'm actually headed out now. The trail just goes around the lake, right?" he asked.

I nodded.

"How many laps did you get in?" Ryan asked.

"Four," I replied. "I wasn't planning to run. It just kind of happened."

"Cool. Maybe I can do five, on purpose," he joked with a smile.

I laughed at his faux competitive spirit. "Okay, hotshot. Enjoy!"

We both laughed then turned to go our separate ways. Feeling content, I went inside the dorm and walked down the hallway to my room. I took a quick shower and dressed in comfy clothes. On one end of the dorm, a deck with wooden rocking chairs overlooked the lake. I grabbed my journal and Bible then went to spend some time with the Lord.

Breathing in the clean air, I snuggled into the rocking chair, deciding to read the book of Philippians. I had time, so I read and journaled through all four chapters, then I took a moment to rest my eyes and meditate on everything I just read.

A flash of movement caught my eye. Ryan was running on the far side of the lake. Sweating, he moved with confidence. Was there anything the man did not do with confidence? I looked away from him, watching some birds twirl through the air, chasing each other.

I was interested to hear Ryan share his testimony at the campfire tonight. Being around him was different than I anticipated—it was weirdly easy. Knowing the things I knew still made me edgy, but just being around him and getting to talk with him felt…simple. I prayed, *Lord, help me do this. Help me have the courage to become friends with him, if it is what you want for us.*

I hadn't prayed for friendship with a man, ever. I especially wouldn't have dreamed of friendship with Ryan Blackstone. It was precarious. It would be wrong not to tell him about my past if we became friends. Once he knew more of my story, he may not *want* friendship with me.

I reminded myself I had to hold this with an open hand. I just had to. I couldn't control anyone but myself. Even more than ten years later, I still had a lot to learn. The work seemed never-ending, but I kept on. I could tell Ryan had done mental health work in his own life and had grown as well. All I could do now was take it one day at a time, praying for wisdom along the way. *God, help me,* I prayed.

A breeze blew across the deck. A shout rose from the field on the other side of camp where a bunch of the kids were playing touch football. A small group of boys were walking down the path with fishing rods and tackle boxes. They were laughing loud enough to scare all the fish, but they were clearly having a great time. Camp was good for us all.

In my periphery, Ryan turned up the rock path, headed toward the dorm. The path curved, and I lost sight of him. I stayed where I was, absorbing everything for another minute. I didn't want to run into him in the hallway, all sweaty. My skin prickled, feeling warm.

Brooke and I discussed this a bit when Ryan first showed up at church. I needed to be wise, and that meant being totally honest with myself. I had never been as attracted to a man as I was to Ryan all those years ago. It wasn't something to be ashamed of or afraid of. It was normal. Anyone could see he was an attractive man.

I told myself it didn't matter. I could push the awareness and the memories down to the back of my mind, and eventually, I would be immune to his eyes, to his face, his shoulders, and the sound of his voice. I would. *I promise*, I reassured myself. I believed me. *At least he's not a drummer anymore, thank God for that*. I got up from the rocker, went to my room, and grabbed some pretzels to snack on. Then I headed out to the field to find Sarah and her girls. We needed to strategize for Capture the Flag.

In the evening, after a big dinner of chicken parmesan with spaghetti, everyone bundled up in their sweatshirts, grabbed flashlights, and headed across to the fire pit. The fire pit was near the lake. It was surrounded by three rows of log benches. The fire was going by the time I got there.

Ryan was standing in the front row, playing his guitar, leading the students in worship, as the stars peeked out, one by one. The students were singing loudly, and it was beautiful. I found a shadowed spot in the back row by Sarah's group. As the worship wrapped up, everyone sat down, and Youth Guy Chris stood up. He introduced Ryan then prayed for his words to be an encouragement to us and to glorify God. Then Ryan stood up, took a deep breath, and began to share his testimony.

Chapter 18

"Thanks for having me this week, I'm excited to be here with y'all. I'll just jump right in. I'm Ryan. I'm thirty-two. And I've been walking with the Lord for about eight years now.

"I grew up in Houston. I'm an only child, and my dad passed away when I was fourteen. He died suddenly, of a heart issue. He was a good man, and my mom is wonderful, but for most of my childhood they were not church people. My mom sent me to VBS with friends a couple summers, to get me out of her hair, but that was the extent of my exposure to spiritual things until after my dad passed away. My mom attended a widows' support group and became a believer through some of the friends she met there.

"By then, I was going into high school. I was grieving and I wanted nothing to do with the Lord. She started praying for me. I was a good kid, a band nerd. I played drums and made the drumline at my school as a freshmen. All through high school I was part of a crowd of good band kids who got in a little trouble here and there but nothing too terrible. No cops or anything. I went to school at Vanderbilt, in Tennessee, on a music scholarship for drums. I picked up other instruments along the way."

I was mesmerized by his words and his voice. I remembered some of this, but I held on to every word, hungry to learn more about how God had shaped this man. Ryan took a sip of water from a water bottle then continued.

"I partied a little bit in college, and I learned a lot. Like lots of music majors, my goal was to be a famous musician. My senior year, I met a guy named Chad at a party. After graduation, he asked me to join his band. They needed a drummer and I wanted to see what I was made of. So, for the next year and a half, I traveled around the West Coast in a black Suburban that smelled like dude, playing shows at clubs, taking care of my bandmates when they got too high or too drunk. I played the drums and mostly focused on the music. Traveling with the band was fun for the first couple months, but I was starting to get bored. Then, at one of the shows, I met a girl. I fell in love for the first time."

My spine tingled with a *zing!* I straightened in my seat.

Wait. What?

Did he say love*?* Was *I* the girl? I wondered. I couldn't breathe. My heart pounded, hearing him speak of the time in his life when our stories intersected. I couldn't help myself. I wanted to know if he was going to say any more. S*he* was *me*. That seemed incontrovertible. Or was it? I couldn't know for sure. Powerless to change the story or direct his words, I sat at the edge of my seat, listening intently.

"It didn't last long. A few weeks later, I lost the girl. My first broken heart. We were traveling to a different town almost daily, but it was all the same. I was just drifting along through life, no purpose, nothing mattered. I was bored. I went looking for something to fill the void. Booze, women, drugs…I tried it all. A lot of it.

"I thought it would help me feel better. But none of it was satisfying. It didn't do what I wanted it to do. I *didn't* feel better; I felt worse. I slowly gave up that lifestyle. A few months went by, and I grew more and more unhappy in the band life. So, I told my bandmates to start looking for a new drummer. It took another six months, but they found one. Once the new drummer came on, I moved to Nashville and started a job as a studio musician for a recording studio."

He paused, took a drink of water, and a big breath. He started again, his voice thickening with emotion.

"At the studio, I met a sound engineer named Jamie Martin. We worked together and became good friends over the first year. He had this *lightness* about him, this *freedom* I wanted to have in my own life. As we got to know each other, he shared with me often. He loved Jesus.

"At first, I brushed it off, thinking religion wasn't for me. I'd done too much bad stuff. I couldn't be good, couldn't be loved. But I could feel this stirring in my heart. I *wanted* to know God, wanted to be loved by Him. Jamie told me I absolutely could be, because God made me in His image and sent His son to die in my place, to pay the price for my sin. He'd told me before, but that day was different. I believed him. It was a good day.

"I started studying with Jamie and going to church with him. We became roommates. I got to live and work with my best friend. He was a huge encouragement to me. I was excited to be a Christian, but it was a slow process, learning, figuring out what all this meant in my life, how to be a new version of *me*. A few years went by, and life was mostly good. I struggled here and there. I made mistakes. But I was growing closer to the Lord, learning more, serving in church, working hard at the studio. I was living in abundance.

"I was playing drums for the worship band at church when a new girl joined the singers. Her name was Lindsey; she was great. Beautiful, graceful, and talented. She and I started dating, and eventually we became engaged. I couldn't believe how good things were going for me.

"Then one day, my mom called. She told me she had been diagnosed with multiple sclerosis. It's a disease which attacks the nervous system. Hers was pretty bad. It was aggressive. I freaked out and went to Houston.

"We visited lots of specialists, got second and third opinions. They all came back saying the same thing. Multiple sclerosis, primary progressive, which is the bad kind. They could help her, using medication and physical therapy, but they couldn't stop it from progressing.

"We needed a plan. We all agreed to the next steps. I got my mom settled in with her doctor and her routine in Houston, then I went back to Nashville, to my fiancée, my job, and my best friend.

"Four months later, Jamie and I were out rock climbing in the middle of nowhere with a group of friends. He slipped and fell. He hit his head just right, and he passed away. That was the worst day of my life."

His voice trembled. He brushed a tear from his cheek, sniffed, and went on.

"Um. Grief is a weird experience, especially as a Christian. We know the big ending. We know the promise of Eternity is waiting for us. But it didn't do much for me when I couldn't figure out how to keep going. How to get up, to live, to go to work…all without my best friend.

"Grief was strong. Stronger than me. It just…*swallowed* me for a while. It was dark. I grew very depressed. I started having panic attacks. I almost lost my job. Lindsey told me I needed medicine, and I needed to go to therapy. I didn't want to, but she said she would go with me, so I tried both. She was right. It helped.

"Climbing out of that hole was like climbing a very tall ladder, going up a few rungs on a good day, then having a hard day and sliding down a couple. Up and down, up and down, day by day. It was the hardest thing I've ever done, but I made it through, for the most part. Grief isn't linear. I still have bad days sometimes, but they are rare now. After about a year, I turned a corner. I could feel myself starting to come back to life.

"Lindsey helped me a lot. She'd been so good to me, but that season really wore her down. She couldn't be in love with me anymore. The romantic part of our relationship ended, and we canceled the wedding. It was hard, and it hurt, but I understood. I still do. I'm grateful for everything she did for me, but I can see now that we just weren't the best for each other, even before. Sometimes things happen *to* us, but later we can see it actually happened *for* us, and for me, this is one of those times."

Wow. I thought that was pretty gracious, knowing how quickly she moved on after the breakup. I reminded myself everyone is a whole person. I shouldn't judge her. *But what a loss,* I thought. Grief was a treacherous, winding road to navigate. Before I could get lost in analyzing this, Ryan had more to say.

"I got a call about ten months after that. It was John Martin, telling me their church was about to start hunting for a new worship minister. He was wondering if I ever considered ministry as a job? I hadn't, but I thought a change might be good. I got my resume together and threw my hat in the ring. I came down and interviewed.

"Long story short, I got the job. As y'all know, I live in Dallas now. My mom moved up from Houston too. She lives with me, so I can help her out when she needs it. I've had a weird last few years, with challenges and changes, but things seem to be looking up.

"I don't share any of this to say it was easier for me because of God or that I handled any of it well. I didn't. Even now, I don't always. But God has met me, carried me through deep darkness, and He has kept me through it all. Every moment. There is no day I look back on where I can't see Him there, working in my life.

"Romans tells us nothing can separate us from His love, and that is my story. The promise holds, even when the circumstances in my life feel like darkness I can't see through. He is good, He loves me, and I'm glad I know Him. That's all. Thanks for having me."

Everyone clapped as Ryan sat down on the bench behind him, picking up his guitar. Youth Guy Chris thanked him for sharing then said a prayer. I wiped a tear from my cheek, grateful I was in the shadows. Ryan stood up, and we all sang a song together by the light of the fire, the stars twinkling overhead. It was a beautiful moment.

I was processing a mile a minute, all this new information filling in the gaps, shining light on a bigger picture. I was getting a more solid understanding of Ryan as a person. It was refreshing but intimidating. He'd gone through so much, yet he still seemed confident. Whole-hearted. He wasn't arrogant, just sure-footed. This was a man who was solidly comfortable in his identity.

We finished the song, then everyone turned on their flashlights and headed back to the dorms, their feet crunching on the gravel. All the kids seemed to be talking. Raucous laughter erupted as one of the senior boys threw a shrieking Emily over his shoulder and headed down to the lake. Youth Guy Chris watched the commotion and hung back, supervising. I considered saying something, as the nurse, but I was worn out. If they needed me, they knew where to find me.

My mind whirled with the fullness of all I'd just heard. Wow. All the information, from how he came to faith, to being engaged to marry Lindsey, to his mom's diagnosis, tore through my mind, but one part made me feel anxious and panicky. The girl he'd lost. *Was* she actually me? Or was it maybe someone else? I couldn't be sure. I was afraid to ask. But he said earlier he thought we loved each other.

Wow.

If it was me he was talking about, his memory was a lot to consider. I acknowledged in my memories that I had fallen in love with him, but with my mom and everything, Ryan was pushed to the back burner.

I remembered being in survival mode, just trying to get through that time, to keep going. I knew now it was God who sustained me through it. Him, and a miracle named Anna. If He hadn't given me Anna, to make me eat and go to class and therapy, I may not have made it through. Once that darkness pulled me under, it took me a long time to come back into the light.

I made it to my room, shutting the door. I showered then collapsed into bed, overwhelmed and exhausted. I was afraid I wouldn't be able to sleep, but I fell asleep immediately and did not wake until morning.

Chapter 19

T he next day was Sunday, the first full day of camp. I woke up groggy after having weird dreams all night, but I couldn't remember any of them. I stretched then got out of bed. I had time for a run before breakfast.

After breakfast, we had a camp version of church service out by the lake, around the firepit. Ryan led a couple of songs, and Chris gave a short devotional. We took communion, then it was over. In the afternoon after lunch, the kids did activities like fishing, the ropes course, or played soccer in the field. It was a slower day, but it wasn't hard to avoid Ryan. I needed to talk with him, but I needed some space to process first.

That evening at dinner, I administered the final medication for the day. I got a plate then looked for a place to sit. Sarah's group was crowded together at a table with a couple of other groups, so there wasn't room. An open seat sat at the end of the next table by Youth Guy Chris. Ryan was there, but Chris would be a buffer—*probably a loud, obnoxious buffer, which was even better,* I thought to myself.

I set my plate of chicken tenders, fries, and salad down, asking if I could sit there. The guys nodded. Chris was in the middle of a story about being out on a date with a girl.

Thinking of Maddie, I was instantly on edge. Apparently, he took this girl out paddle boarding on White Rock Lake, and she had "the worst balance he'd ever seen." To my knowledge, he went out with Maddie in the winter months, so this was probably not her. He was describing what happened when the girl tried to stand up on her board but ended up falling in.

"And the splash, bro! I kid you not. She hit just right, and that wave took out all the people near her, including me. Just *bam, bam, bam*, on down the line! Ten people!" He was gesturing wildly and held up all his fingers, driving the point home. "The bartender said it actually happens a lot, something about how shallow it is in that part of the lake." He nodded and looked around at his audience.

"I'm telling you, look out for first-timers if you ever try paddle-boarding, especially on a first date," Chris said sagely. We all nodded solemnly, as if we were receiving deeply wise counsel. The students started getting up, taking their trays to drop off the trash, ready to move on to the next activity. Chris stood up, joining them.

I was only half-finished with my meal, so I stayed seated. I was surprised when Ryan stayed seated with me. The awareness I felt being at the same table quadrupled, and a swarm of butterflies invaded my stomach. I wasn't ready to talk about last night. I needed more time. I searched for a way to avoid this conversation.

"Don't you need to get down to the fire pit so you can prep for worship?" I asked.

He shook his head. "Nothing to prep. There's no sound equipment outside, just me and the guitar. Putting the strap over my shoulder takes about half a second, but that's the extent of it. I'm good."

"You don't have to wait for me," I said, giving him another out.

"I don't mind," he replied. "I wanted to talk with you. I just haven't seen you all day."

Imagine that, I thought, feeling on edge. I stayed silent, very focused on chewing.

"Have you had a nice day?" he asked conversationally. I nodded, stuffing my mouth full of chicken. He wasn't deterred.

"Me too. I went for a run this afternoon during free time. The trail around the lake is really nice. I explored a few of the trails leading off from it, nothing too crazy, but it felt good to be outside and move."

I was finished eating, thank God. I took a big drink of lemonade and popped up out of my seat. I gathered my trash then took it to the big trash can. I wiped my hands on a napkin before I dropped it in as well.

"Oops, you missed some," he pointed out in his low voice, standing across the trash can from me. He gestured with his hand. "Just there, by your mouth."

I sighed, brushing at my skin, trying to get rid of all the crumbs. "Thanks," I said.

I turned to walk out of the building, headed back to the dorm to get my flashlight. Ryan fell into step with me. "Everything going okay with you so far?" he asked kindly.

"Yes, I'm good," I replied. "Sorry, I'm not trying to be rude. It's just been a full day. I'm kinda tired."

"I get it," he said. "I've been wanting a quick moment with you though, if you don't mind. I felt a little self-conscious, talking about my testimony with you there."

I groaned inwardly. This was happening. I couldn't avoid it. I tried to swallow down my anxious thoughts and breathe.

"I thought you did great," I assured him. "Sharing your testimony is vulnerable, especially with a bunch of teenagers."

"It wasn't the teenagers I was worried about," he said.

I searched for words. We were almost to the dorm. "I'm sorry about your mom. MS is tough."

He nodded. "Thank you. She's doing pretty well right now. Mia, I wanted to—"

I just couldn't. I stopped walking and interrupted him. "Ryan."

He stopped talking, stopped moving, turned, and looked at me. I gathered my courage to speak.

"I am still processing your testimony. I realize now our time together made an impact on you. I was impacted as well. I agree it's important for us to talk soon, but I don't think camp is the best place to do that. Would it be okay if we just take this week and get through camp? Then we can talk after we get home? Maybe we could meet for coffee or something when we have more privacy."

I wasn't sure what he was going to say for a moment. He looked confused at first, then understanding took over. He nodded.

"Of course. I'm sorry for coming on so strong," he said sincerely.

"It's okay. I understand," I answered him. "I appreciate you giving me some time to process."

"Okay," he replied, opening the door to the dorm, holding it for me. "I'm going to run over to the fire pit. I'll see you there."

"Sounds good. Thanks!" I walked in and jogged down the hallway to my room.

I thought my heart might pound out of my chest. Whew! I prayed that when the time for the conversation came, God would give me the right words, because right now, I absolutely did not have them.

The evening's worship passed, filled with beautiful songs and prayers. For the first time since I saw Ryan on the bus, I was able to relax. There was a set time for when we would talk, and it wasn't now. This week could pass, and I could just be here. I'd worry about the imminent conversation when it grew closer.

The next couple of days passed without event. The students were all having a great time, and so was I. I passed out meds, went for runs, and chatted with Sarah in the off moments. Ryan and I were around each other a lot, but the weight of the moments changed. The air wasn't heavy with anticipation anymore. It was just air. My tension settled.

I learned he preferred his cereal crunchy with no milk. He loved coffee as much as I did. He drank it black and hot, regardless of the weather. He had a sweet tooth. It turned out the scar on his eyebrow was from hitting his head on the corner of the bathroom counter when he was three.

The story set Youth Guy Chris off to tell everyone he could, with the colorful punchline, *Who knew potty training could be dangerous?* Poor Ryan. He bore it well, with good humor. He didn't even seem to mind. I learned a little more about him every day, and being around him got easier.

Chapter 20

Wednesday arrived—the day of the big hike. I rose bright and early to pack my nurse backpack with first aid gear. Afterward, I got dressed, put up my hair, smeared on sunscreen, and stepped into my hiking boots. The hike wasn't necessarily difficult, but it would be long. We were planning to be gone all day.

My favorite part of the hike was the meadow where we would eat lunch and rest. I was looking forward to being out in nature, hearing the stream roar over the rapids and small waterfalls. I put on my hat on my way out the door to breakfast.

Bleary-eyed teens were headed the same way. I walked up the path, the rocks crunching under my heavier boots. Everyone loved the hike, but it was always a slow start. I piled my plate with eggs, fruit, and yogurt, filled a mug with hot coffee, then turned to find a seat. I would eat quickly then move around the room, making sure everyone was wearing sunscreen. No skin cancer on my watch!

I was eating breakfast when a sleepy, disheveled Ryan grumpily plopped his plate down in front of me, sat down, and began to eat. He was clearly exhausted and disgruntled. His hair was sticking up at odd angles, and his shirt was on backward.

"Holy cow," I said, "what happened to you?"

Ryan grimaced. I winced, guessing right before he said the answer.

"Youth Guy Chris," he growled.

I groaned in sympathy. Youth Guy Chris was notorious for needing less sleep than the average adult and for using his extra wakefulness to prank friends early in the morning at camp. Ryan began to share his painful story.

The night before, we had mashed potatoes and gravy with dinner. Apparently, the kitchen ended up with lots of gravy leftover, so Chris kept some in a bowl and brought it to Ryan's room around 4:00 am. Ryan's door was unlocked (*rookie mistake*, I thought to myself), which is how Chris got in. He planned to simply place Ryan's hands in the gravy bowl, then tickle his face with a feather, and get him to wipe it all over his face. But Ryan was startled enough that he woke up fighting. The gravy spilled, splattering everywhere.

"It's on my pillow, my sheets, the floor. Heck. It's probably still in my hair, Mia," he complained. "The smell of gravy is going to haunt me forever."

I bit my lip, holding in laughter. A tiny snort escaped, but I held it together. Poor Ryan. I did feel terrible for him. Chris' pranks were typically a little overboard but not this bad. It was a new low, for sure. I gathered myself to try to speak without laughing.

"Did Chris help you clean it up?" I asked.

"He tried," said Ryan, "but I was so mad I threw him out of my room."

"Entirely understandable," I assured him, still valiantly holding it in.

"I don't regret it," he said decisively. "But I do regret cleaning it up with my only towel, in the dark, then going back to sleep. I did a bad job. Now it's dried and crusted everywhere," Ryan deadpanned, rubbing his hands across his forehead as if a headache was brewing.

I stopped laughing. I was astonished. Was he joking?

"Ryan! Gross!" I exclaimed. He hung his head, still rubbing at his eyes.

"I know! It's disgusting. I was just so tired! It was four in the morning! Anyway, I woke up and showered, but of course my towel had gravy on it. I should have just used a shirt, but I was in a hurry. I was in a community bathroom. There's no privacy! I thought I could just dodge the gravy spots. But I was drying off and got gravy in my hair—again. I finally just gave up. I rinsed off as best I could, dried off with the shirt I *wanted* to wear today, and here I am."

Frustrated, he shook his head.

I shook mine too, bewildered. *Boys*, I thought. The interactions be-tween men were fascinating and unfathomable to me. This wasn't the first time I was grossed out and confused by boy pranks at camp. It may not be the last, even this week. We still had a couple days to go. I pursed my lips, searching for less foreboding words to say to Ryan, but they wouldn't come.

"I'm sorry he did that," I said, for lack of anything better.

Ryan met my eyes. Somehow, it was the right thing to say. He smiled a small smile.

"Thanks for listening."

I considered letting Ryan know about my plan for the tuna fish in Chris' *youth-minister-mobile*, but I needed to get moving. I began to gather my stuff.

"Maybe the caretaker has a washing machine," I suggested.

He perked up. "That's a good idea. Thanks, Mia."

I needed to make the rounds with the sunscreen. I'd packed an indus-trial-sized bottle of SPF 75, knowing the kids (and some adults) may have forgotten theirs at home. I stood up and headed over to the nearest table. I focused on the task at hand, and by the time I was halfway through the group, Ryan was gone.

He must have gone back to handle the gravy. In my head, I wished him luck. Even if he was able to wash everything, it still sounded awful. I wondered if Ryan was a vengeful man. Some might say Youth Guy Chris had a pretty punchable face in broad daylight, on a good day. A 4:00 am wakeup call was beyond the pale. I hoped Ryan found a hilarious way to pay Chris back. Shaking my head, I refilled my water bottle at the drink station then walked out to the Hub's porch, ready to help distribute the sack lunches.

We got started a few minutes later, heading down toward the lake, then turning left to walk up the side of the mountain on a wide, beautiful trail. The birds were singing, the sun was shining, and it was only sixty-five degrees. I breathed in the clean air, and smiled at the sky. This was going to be a fantastic day!

Six hours later, we were slogging down the mountain trail, every one of us soaked to the skin and muddy. The hiking songs had dried up, and the camaraderie was dead. Even Youth Guy Chris had lost his patience with the singing and attempts at being happy. He'd skipped the devotional we were supposed to have had at the top of the mountain, due to the thunder making it impossible to hear.

Going up went great. I mingled with different groups along the way, chatted with parent sponsors and students, then we ate lunch and played games with Sarah's group in the meadow. We were all enjoying the day until the rain began coming down in buckets about halfway back. The trail was slick with mud, and we were all walking slowly. Lightning struck farther up the mountain, making everyone feel a little on edge. I was bringing up the rear, having stopped to give a kid his inhaler. It took me a minute to stuff everything back in my bag and get going again.

Lightning lit the sky, and right above us, a crack of thunder split the air. Someone shrieked, and a commotion stirred a little ways in front of me. Everyone started yelling. I hurried up to the gathered crowd to see what was what. I wrestled my way through the teens until I reached the center of the commotion.

Ryan was seated in the mud beside a teen girl, Emily. She was crumpled by his feet, holding her ankle. A couple of senior boys were knocked down too, but their biggest problem seemed to be the mud caking their clothes and hands. They were standing to the side of the trail, attempting to rub the mud from their hands onto the large rocks.

I could see what had happened as the boys explained it to me. The trail was a little steeper here, and a big boulder jutted out, almost blocking the way. Emily was playing around, hoping to lighten the mood. She jumped off the boulder but twisted her ankle, and lost her balance in the mud upon landing. She slid down, knocking Ryan and the boys down like dominoes before coming to a stop.

Ryan appeared to have grazed his head on the boulder as he fell. He was bleeding from the point of impact, but it didn't look deep or swollen. I immediately went into *nurse mode*.

"Everybody back up!" I yelled. The crowd all shuffled backward as I squished through the mud, making my way to Emily and Ryan. I crouched down beside her, using Ryan's shoulder for balance in the sticky mud. I opened an outside pocket on my backpack, removing a wad of gauze. I handed it to Ryan and told him to press it on the head wound, hard. Then I turned toward Emily.

Emily was clearly trying not to cry from the pain. I could see her ankle had already begun to swell, but everything was still pointed in the right direction. I figured it was probably just sprained, but I couldn't find out for sure all the way out here. I reached into my bag for a splint and wrap. I worked quickly, getting her shoe off, splinting her ankle, then wrapping it in just a few minutes. I gave her two Tylenol for the pain and watched carefully as she swallowed water to wash them down.

One of the taller senior boys offered to carry Emily to camp on his back, piggyback style. That was not a good option on the slick trail. Instead, I assigned two girls around her same height and asked them to walk on either side of her. That way, they could support her as she hopped with her arms over their shoulders. I told Youth Guy Chris we needed to get her back to camp as quickly as possible. He got everyone organized, and the group set off down the mountain.

I was planning to walk close to Emily so I could observe her injury, but first I needed to assess Ryan's head wound, to be on the safe side. The bleeding had slowed down considerably. He was all muddy, but he sat very still while I assessed him, looking into his blue eyes, shining my light to check his pupil reflex. The last of the group disappeared around a curve in the trail, but I knew we would catch up quickly.

"Does anything hurt besides your head?" I asked, looking closely at the scrape along his hairline.

"No," he grunted, a dullness in his voice. It caught my attention. He was breathing awfully fast. I checked his pulse. It was flying.

"Ryan? You okay?" I asked. He didn't answer. His eyes were squeezed shut. He curled up in a ball and lay down on his side in the mud. For a moment, I was confused. Then it occurred to me: in his testimony, Ryan shared that he'd experienced panic attacks after losing Jamie. Getting injured, especially in this environment, could certainly trigger a reaction like this.

People had panic attacks in the ER a lot, and of course, I had my own experiences in college. I knew how to help. I sighed. This was going to be squishy and cold.

I lay down in the mud on my side, facing him. He was breathing fast with his eyes still closed. I took his hands in my own and spoke clearly and calmly.

"Ryan. You're having a panic attack. I'm right here. You're okay, Ryan. Breathe with me. Breathe in…one, two, three, four, five. Good. Now breathe out…one, two, three, four, five."

I breathed in exaggeratedly through my nose then out through my mouth slowly. Nothing changed. I pressed one of his hands to his abdomen, the other to mine.

"Feel me breathe, Ryan. Breathe with me." I counted through the next breath. We breathed, again and again. After what seemed like a very long time, I felt his hand press more firmly on my stomach. He was coming out of it. His breath began to slow. His eyes opened, that flash of blue sadder and more tender than I had ever seen it. His eyes were filled with tears. When he spoke, his voice was a trembling whisper.

"Thank you. I'm so sorry."

Empathy and compassion filled my heart, seeing him like this. We kept breathing.

"It's okay," I assured him. "You're not alone."

His hand moved on my stomach. He reached around my waist and clumsily slid closer, hugging me tightly. Cold mud oozed through my hair and soaked through my clothes, but I didn't care.

All I could think about was his body pressed to mine. His strong arms held onto me for dear life as he grounded himself, slowly getting his breathing controlled. His torso expanded against me. His breath warmed my hair. He was shaking.

I realized I was holding onto him too. I told myself it was just a reflex from all the adrenaline. My heart was pounding from all the breathing. He smelled nice. He must have gotten the last of the gravy off. I don't know how long we stayed there. We were quiet for a bit while his breathing normalized. Finally, I allowed myself one more breath then patted his shoulder.

I watched his eyes open, inches from my face. They widened when he registered how close we were. His breath hitched. He released me and rolled away onto his back.

"I'm sorry. I didn't mean to—" he said.

"It's okay," I told him. I repeated it, for myself. "It's okay."

I sat up slowly. He did the same. I looked down at myself and breathed out a laugh.

He looked at me and realized immediately what I was laughing at. The entire right side of my body was caked with mud from head to toe, but the left was clean, except for my muddy left hand. He smiled, but before he could laugh, I said, "Oh no, Mr. Mud Pie, check yourself."

I waved my hand, gesturing to his entire...well, everything. His left side and back were completely smeared with the stuff.

We both erupted. Positively howling, I could hardly catch my breath. Laughing with Ryan in this weird, intimate moment, I felt something heavy in my heart warm, loosen, and float away. Deep healing brought a lightness to my chest, as simple as a breath of clean air.

This whole situation was so strange and heavy. A week ago—gosh, a *day* ago—touching Ryan was unthinkable. Now we'd held each other in the mud through a panic attack. And it didn't hurt. It was right to help him. It felt good to laugh, to release some of the tension. It felt even better to recognize more healing in myself. This was good.

Progress and thankfulness were great, but they didn't make me any warmer. I was starting to shiver. We were both soggy from the rain, and now we were all muddy. We needed to get moving. Ryan seemed to realize it at the same time. He carefully got to his feet.

"Man, taken out by a teenager. I'm getting old." He shook his head and held out a hand to help me up.

I put my hand in his. He hauled me up, surefooted, even in the slippery mud.

I looked at his bandage once we were standing. It looked good. There was no fresh bleeding. He assured me he wasn't hurt, just tired from the panic attack and cold from the mud.

"Let's catch up with the others," I suggested. I needed to check on Emily. Surely we were getting close to camp after all this hiking.

Walking down the muddy trail, side by side with Ryan, was not something I planned on, but I was glad to have him. He seemed to know, instinctively, the best places to put his feet. I, on the other hand, slipped, slid, and even fell a couple of times.

Every time I slid, Ryan's hand was there to steady me or help me up. I was grateful, though touching him set off something in me every time. I tried to be gentle with myself, but I felt like all of me was in overdrive.

My mind and heart acknowledged the breakthrough, and I was glad for it. But my body had just been held close by Ryan for the first time in over ten years. *The body remembers.* After our little breathing session a few minutes ago, my skin felt like it was covered in fireworks. I had to re-focus every other step. *Keep moving, Mia.*

We caught up with the group pretty quickly and walked in companionable silence for a bit. The kids were singing a marching song to pass the time. The singing reminded me that I had a question for Ryan.

"I've noticed you lead a lot of hymns, which I enjoy. Hymns are my favorite. But they're not the usual, are they? How did you get started leading hymns instead of only newer songs?"

Ryan took a few moments and thought about it.

"I try for balance, but I have always preferred older music traditions in any genre. I'm not into pop music, even though I played a lot of it in the studio. I can play pop; it's just not my favorite. But the hymns have stood the test of time, and they're still true. They're still beautiful, with words I have to really concentrate on to sing correctly. The hymns feel meaningful. They're full of truth and doctrine. It's a simple answer, but there it is: I like them."

I nodded. "Your answer is sufficient."

"Glad to hear it," he said and smiled distractedly.

His attention was on something ahead. I turned to look. I could see the lake through the trees. We were finally back. The kids started whooping and yelling. They took off running toward camp. Emily and her support girls looked tired but glad to be there.

"Why don't we get cleaned up, then I can re-wrap it, get some ice on it, and use the caretaker's car to drive you into town for an x-ray?" I suggested.

Emily nodded. Held up by her friends, she continued hobbling down the trail.

When we got back to camp, I took a super-fast shower and changed clothes in my room. From there, I ran to help Emily in the girls' dorm. Luckily, her room was on the bottom floor, and her friends helped her, but she was exhausted.

Sarah was with us since she was Emily's group leader. I examined her ankle, checking the swelling. With an injury like this, the best thing I could do was elevate it, compress it with a wrap, and ice it. Emily told me she didn't hear any pop or snap, just felt the ankle twist on impact. This seemed like more of a sprain, but I didn't want to take a chance.

It was dinner time, so I asked her friends to run to get Emily, Sarah, and me each a plate of food. Then Sarah and I would take her into town in the caretaker's car. I went to my room to grab my purse and the binder of medical forms, then we were off.

Chapter 21

I was dead asleep the next morning, when a sound pierced my ear drums and attacked my brain. I sat up so fast I almost fell out of the bed. For a moment, I was completely disoriented and tangled up in the blanket. I was on the verge of panic when Youth Guy Chris' raucous laughter drifted through the open window.

Oh. Was he literally pranking the entire camp now? I groaned and waited for my heart to stop pounding. This was the last straw. I couldn't wait to put that can of tuna in his car. I wasn't the only one who was furious about this rude awakening. A couple of teens shouted at him from the dorms. I recognized the voice of another adult sponsor doing the same from somewhere on the floor above me.

The air horn went off again, and I gave up the idea of going back to sleep. I wanted nothing more than to stay in bed a while, but I had a job to do. I needed to go check on Emily, and get the morning meds ready. Slowly extricating myself from the wreckage of the blankets, I realized I was still wearing my clothes from the night before.

The ER two towns over had been packed and had taken forever. It was after midnight when we got back with crutches and pain meds for Emily's badly sprained ankle. I'd fallen into bed, exhausted. Her parents were driving up to get her today.

Still in a sleepy daze, I stood and shuffled over to look out the window. Chris was standing on the porch of the Hub, in the middle of camp. I grumbled at him one more time for good measure. Before I turned away, a movement caught my eye and my grumble turned into a smile. Two teen boys were on either side of the porch, sneaking up on Chris, presumably to avenge the rest of us. They attacked from both sides and tackled him to the ground. He went down with a yelp. I couldn't help but laugh. It was a beautiful morning for the last day of camp.

One of the other adult sponsors took possession of Chris' air horn at breakfast and everything went much more smoothly after that. The kids were all a little rumpled and tired but everyone wanted to make the most of the last day, and we did. While the groups met for their sharing time, I went for a mid-morning run around the lake and it was wonderful. The birds were out, and the fish were jumping. I even saw a deer from a short distance. No matter how much I missed my own bed, I would miss this when I ran back home in the oppressive heat of Dallas.

After lunch, Emily's parents arrived to pick her up. I helped them get all her stuff to the car and wished her well. She was inconsolable, in pain, and frustrated with the crutches on the gravel path. I felt bad for her having to leave early, but it was the right call.

After Emily's group all waved tearfully until the car disappeared down the lane, Sarah invited me to join them for some games to cheer everyone up. In the way of kids, the girls bounced back quickly and we all laughed until our ribs ached. During one of the games, I caught a glimpse of Ryan fishing down at the lake with a group of boys, but I didn't get to talk with him.

Later in the afternoon during free time, I reflected back over the week as I packed my suitcase. So much had happened. I needed to process through this week with everything that occurred.

Obviously, the biggest factor of the week was Ryan. With so much history there, he was a loaded subject. On one hand, he turned out to be fun and enjoyable to be around. I was glad to have a fledgling friendship with him. On the other hand, it wouldn't be honest to grow any closer without him knowing the rest of the story. This simple truth felt complicated and terrifying.

Hopefully, Brooke could help me figure out the best way to share it with him. I was eager to discuss my healing epiphany with her. Maybe I should book a double session next week—an hour may not be enough time.

The sun was starting to sink in the sky, and the bell rang for dinner just as I was folding the last pair of dirty socks. I picked myself up off the floor, glad to have a distraction from all the thoughts swirling in my head. Still lost in thought, I left my room and walked down the hall. Reaching the main door of the dorm, I pushed it open. With a guttural *oof*, the door bounced right back at me.

Oh no! I wasn't looking and accidentally slammed the door right into a very sweaty Ryan. Through the window, I watched in what seemed like slow motion as the impact sent a jolt through his whole body, knocking him back a couple of feet.

"Ryan!" I yelped in surprise. "I'm sorry! Are you okay?"

Opening the door much more carefully, I moved outside and began to check him for injuries. He stayed standing and brushed me off.

"I'm fine, Mia. I promise. Just a little surprised. You ladies are keeping me on my toes this week," he joked.

If he could joke around, he must be okay. I calmed down about hurting him but avoided eye contact. I wasn't ready for sweaty Ryan, no matter how much had changed. He stretched his quads one at a time.

"I wanted to get in one last run around the lake," he said conversationally. "It's so nice here. I'm going to miss it."

I nodded in agreement. The weather here was perfect. It was going to be tough going back to the Texas heat. "Yeah, running outside at home is torture already. I run inside on the treadmill if it's already hot in the morning, which has already happened a couple times."

Ryan nodded. He seemed to want to say something else. I risked looking into his eyes and waited.

"Well, better get to dinner," he said. "I'm going to shower real quick, then I'll be over there."

"Okay," I agreed. I turned and walked toward the Hub.

Hmm, that felt like an odd interaction, but I couldn't put my finger on why. I hadn't seen Ryan all day. Maybe I misread him. I was also tired from being up late the night before. *Focus*, I thought. I didn't have time to worry about a conversation. I needed to get in the zone for the big game of Capture the Flag.

I reached the hub in plenty of time and got the dinnertime meds distributed. I grabbed a plate of tacos and sat down. Youth Guy Chris plopped his plate down across from me, immediately starting in with the trash talk. When Ryan sat down, he told him all about the decoy flag from last year, laughing uproariously.

My teeth were grinding together, and my eyes were growing tired from being rolled by the end. The story wasn't any funnier, even a year later. It was still infuriating. I was taking a breath to let Chris know what he could expect if he pulled a prank like that again when Ryan quietly asked, "Isn't that cheating?"

The gentle warmth of victory swept through me. With a simple sentence, Ryan put Chris in his place. I basked in the glory for a moment. It was nice to know Ryan stood for truth, as opposed to winning at any cost.

Chris took a second to pause and possibly to evaluate whether calling a spade a spade was, in fact, within the bounds of Bro Code or not. He seemed speechless, so I couldn't tell one hundred percent. Then he shrugged. "It's all in good fun, bro." From there, he launched into more strategy talk.

I didn't want to listen to any more. I stood, cleared my area, and walked over to where Sarah was sitting with a bunch of the girls, talking intently about our strategy. We had already planned it weeks ago. One big change was necessary. Emily was the fastest one of all of us. With her gone, we had to move some girls around. A junior named Kelsey was going to be our flag runner now.

Once dinner was finished, everyone had twenty minutes to get ready. I had an all-black outfit to change into, so I headed to my room. I braided my hair to keep it out of my eyes. I was just finishing up tying my shoes when there was a knock at my door.

I looked over, wondering if maybe this was a trap. I wouldn't put it past Chris to lock me in my room or something to keep me out of the game. The timing was certainly suspicious.

"Who is it?" I asked cautiously.

"It's Ryan."

Oh. That, I was not expecting. I opened the door. Ryan was standing there in his jeans and t-shirt. My first thought was he didn't seem to grasp the importance of this game of Capture the Flag at all. He stood in the doorway, looking sincere. "Can we talk privately for a second?"

I thought about saying no, but I could tell he really needed to talk. I remembered he acted a little weird after I body slammed him with the door earlier.

"Sure. But we don't have long," I reminded him. I stepped out into the hall, and we walked to the deck with the rocking chairs. The lake was there in the darkness, but I couldn't see it. The rhythmic song of frogs and crickets pulsed through the air, punctuated by the buzz of moths hitting the dim porch light. The rocking chairs were empty, but I stayed standing.

"What's up?" I asked, turning to him.

"I wanted to apologize about yesterday. Grabbing you like that on the ground. That wasn't appropriate. I'm sorry, Mia. I haven't had a panic attack in months. I forgot how powerful they can be. You were kind about it, and I appreciate your grace, but I'm afraid I made things weird between us or made you feel uncomfortable in some way. I'm so sorry."

Wow, the word vomit was back. But he was being really sweet, and I appreciated that. I nearly channeled my mother and Pam Martin with a *Bless your heart,* but I caught myself.

"Thank you, Ryan, I appreciate your apology. But it's okay. I don't feel weird about it. People do all kinds of things when they're having panic attacks. Sometimes we just need a hug. I'm glad I could help you. That's why I'm a nurse. We're good, I promise."

Ryan let out a breath.

"Thank you, Mia. I'm grateful."

The air seemed to grow thicker around me. I felt a heightened awareness of everything going on: the animal sounds, the breeze rustling the tree leaves, the students yelling and laughing in the distance. Fireflies blinked on and off in the shadows nearby.

Most of all, I was aware of the man standing in front of me. I looked at him in the dim porch light, taking in his face, his height, the slope of his strong, broad shoulders. The light touched the stubble on his chin, making it more of a contrast than usual. For a second, I was taken back in time.

I could see him in the flashing light of that club. His hair was longer back then, and he was all sweaty in a tight black t-shirt. I remembered the thrill of him smiling at me across the room as Anna and I danced.

I shook my head, unsure what to say, so I just blurted out my thoughts.

"It feels weird to be around you and have *this* Ryan overlay the Ryan I met ten years ago."

Ryan nodded, pushed a hand across the back of his neck, and looked out at the blackness before meeting my eyes.

"I know what you mean. It's weird for me sometimes too. The old me, who I was, feels like a stranger in a lot of ways now. Sometimes when I wake up, I remember it all and realize again that I really am new. It's confusing, being so different now. To want different things. It was a slow transformation. I've surprised myself a few times. But I'm grateful for Jesus." He took a breath. "It's heavy for me too, being around you."

I nodded, looking down at the ground. "That's fair."

He said nothing, and the silence wrapped around us for a moment.

I looked out at the darkness, and said, "I wonder if it's like this for everyone who comes to faith, or just some."

Ryan considered this. "I don't know. Maybe. They say everyone has a past."

I was tempted to jokingly ask if everyone runs into their past *at church*. But this wasn't the time for chit chat.

I gestured in the general direction of the field. "Well, I'd better get out there. I have a youth minister and a bunch of teen boys to dominate by stealing a flag."

"Oh yeah." Ryan seemed to have forgotten all about Capture the Flag. "They told me their plan. You've got your work cut out for you. I'm going to go get packed and maybe read a while before bed."

"You're missing out," I teased. "But that's your choice."

"You can tell me all about it on the bus tomorrow. I look forward to a harrowing tale of victory!" He smiled.

I laughed. "Here's hoping!"

We walked down the hallway of the dorm, parting ways at the main door.

"Have a good night," I waved on my way out.

"You too," Ryan replied then turned to go up the stairs.

I walked out to the field, seeing lots of shadows already running across, tagging each other and laughing. I breathed in deeply. That went well. *I think I'm officially friends with Ryan*, I told myself. *Anna's going to wet her pants*. I jogged into the field, heading straight to my post, ready to guard the girls' flag.

As soon as I arrived, I checked in with Sarah, who was already there by the fallen log, flat on her stomach in the grass. She was holding a pair of binoculars in one hand.

"Wow, where did you get those?" I asked, lying down and leaning over to take a look. Sarah handed them to me so I could check them out.

"They're my dad's. He uses them to hunt." She made a face that clearly said, "Blech."

I nodded with understanding. Sarah didn't expect anyone else to be a vegan, but she held her conviction firmly. She'd had a sad animal experience in college and couldn't stand to consume animal products since. For her to borrow her dad's hunting gear meant she was all in on the girls' team, willing to do just about anything to win this year. I was about to thank her for her sacrificial service, but a movement in my periphery caught my attention. I hunkered down, stealing a look at Sarah. "Shh."

Two teen boys came running across the field, staying low. They were scouting the perimeter just as we anticipated they would. Our flag was well-protected on the other side of the field in a copse of trees. We stationed guards all along the field in small, deceptive clumps. Usually, the strategy was to place lots of guards around the flag, but this way, the boys wouldn't be able to tell which clump of girls was guarding the actual flag and which ones weren't.

We just needed to slow the boys down so our scouts had time to search the boys' side. Our scouts were instructed to explore carefully, moving strategically from the perimeter to the center of the boys' side. There were a couple of places they could have hidden their flag. Our best guess was a different spot than last year, closer to the water. It was a dark area, full of good hiding spots. The risk in that situation was all the hiding places—the boys could conceal themselves too well. We could too; we'd just have to be sneaky.

A cry rose from behind us—one of the boys. It was a false alarm, nowhere close to our flag. We'd known to expect that. We learned the hard way last year; these guys favored decoys. No one revealed themselves. Our girls were too smart to fall for an old trick.

I tapped Sarah's shoulder, pointing in the direction I was going to attack. She nodded enthusiastically. I stood silently and ran around the other side of the log, following behind the two boys. They went deeper into the trees, but the tricky ground slowed them down. I stayed on the side, knowing we'd added bigger rocks and branches to the middle of the path to do just that.

I snuck up silently, tagging each of them with ease. They looked dejected as I escorted them to our jail, which was in the far back of our part of the field. I noted with satisfaction that our jail held a good number of boys. I'd just turned the boys over to our jailers when, suddenly, a lanky figure came running toward us, moving fast, straight down the middle of the field.

It was Chris! This was a daring jailbreak, but it might work. He was excellent at evasive maneuvers. He'd be tough to catch. But we *had* to catch him, or he'd break all these guys out of jail, and they'd swarm toward the flag.

I ran toward Chris. He was headed right for me. We were about ten yards from each other when he started taunting me obnoxiously. His focus was entirely on me, which was helpful. He didn't see Faith before she came barreling out of the trees to Chris' left and tackled him at the knees.

Down he went. YES! I ran to Faith and gave her a high five. Chris was still catching his breath on the ground. I stopped near his shoulder, bending down, face to face.

"You've been captured, bro!" I yelled. The girls around us clapped and cheered. Everyone loved to take down the youth minister. It was part of the job. Chris stood, our reluctant prisoner, good-naturedly shaking his head. Faith took hold of his elbow in case he tried to escape.

"You girls and your strategy. It's not gonna work! There are too many of us," he gloated. I was about to answer him sarcastically, but a sound caught my attention.

A disturbance rose across the field. We all turned to look. A girl was running fast, followed by three boys. From this distance, it was hard to tell, but a long dark braid flew behind her. It must be Emma, our flag runner. This could only mean one thing: She'd done it! She must have the flag!

The boys were running out of gas, but Emma didn't slow down at all. The boys yelled with frustration, urging one another on as she increased the distance between herself and them, but they couldn't catch her. From our viewpoint, we watched, cheering as Emma ran all the way through the girls' side and held up the boys' flag right before she got to our home base, where our flag still hung in the trees. It was over. Victory!

Cheers filled the night air. I held up both my hands, looking down at Chris. "YES!" I yelled with all my might. I jumped in the air, spinning around, celebrating and laughing. It felt so good to win fair and square! Sarah ran up to me, cheering. We attempted to do the thing guys do. We jumped up and bumped our chests together. *Oof*! We hit a little too hard. We both fell back, laughing. I looked over, expecting Chris to say something about cheating or checking the flag. Instead, his shoulders slumped in defeat. Then he did something I never thought I'd see. He smiled and held out his hand. "Congratulations, Mia. Well played."

Chapter 22

The next morning dawned, bright and beautiful. A light fog rested over the water of the lake as I jogged around it. I was up extra early with time to get in one last peaceful run before heading home.

A hawk swooped over the middle of the lake then dove down. It surfaced and flew back to its tree, a fish wiggling in its claws. *Nature is rough*, I thought, cringing a little. I kept running and concentrated on regulating my breathing. I had just turned a curve when I heard the pounding rhythm of footsteps behind me. I turned to look just as Ryan came around the curve. He caught sight of me, slowed, and smiled.

"Mornin'! I hear congratulations are in order!" He beamed, matching my pace to run next to me. He held up his hand for a congratulatory high five.

I smacked his hand and smiled.

"It was a good night!" I admitted, taking the high road. On the inside, of course, I was jumping for joy.

"Glad to hear it," said Ryan. "Some of the guys were up early, and they told me about it on my way out to run."

"It was a team effort, for sure," I told him. I remembered why I was surprised to see him. "Don't you typically run in the afternoon?"

"Yes," he answered. "I have been this week. But I woke up early today, and it's going to be miserable when we get home, so I took the opportunity now."

We chatted easily about the weather, running, and travel through three more laps around the lake. We finished the run in good time then broke off the trail to follow the rock path. Crunching on the rocks, I walked with my hands on my hips, cooling down, and waiting for my breath to slow.

Somehow, I didn't see a tree root jutting out on the path. My foot caught it, and I tripped. Ryan reflexively turned and caught me, one arm wrapped around my waist. Once again, Ryan saved me from falling on the rough rocks.

He stood me upright and asked, "Are you okay?"

Embarrassed and frustrated, I rolled my eyes.

"Yes, I'm fine," I sulked, barely resisting the urge to stomp my foot, and wave my hands like a child. I settled for using my words. "Why do I keep falling this week?"

"Maybe your equilibrium is off from the altitude or something," Ryan suggested.

"Well, I'm not usually this clumsy," I said crabbily. I sighed, looking at him in my periphery. "You have caught me a lot this week. Thank you. You have excellent reflexes. I guess it's a good thing you're here."

Ryan smirked. "Was it hard for you to say that?" He barked out a laugh.

I blushed, tempted to cover my face for a second. "I'm sorry. I know I wasn't exactly happy to see you earlier in the week. I just…" I held up my hands in defeat. I didn't know what to say or where to begin without bringing up everything.

Ryan took pity on me and acknowledged what I couldn't say. "It's a lot."

"Yeah," I agreed, for lack of a better response. "But it's been good. I'm glad you're here, even if it's only to repeatedly save me from injury," I joked sassily. He smiled with me.

"I feel the same way. It's nice to be here doing something useful," he said sarcastically, and we both laughed.

We reached the dorm. We said a quick, 'See you at breakfast,' and headed to our respective rooms. My chest felt full with warmth. I felt…different. These weren't butterflies. It was peace. The unimaginable had happened. We really were friends.

The more I got to know Ryan, the more grateful I was. He was a kind, sweet man, who was trying to serve the Lord the best he could. I admired those qualities.

To think, if I'd had my way and avoided him forever, I would have missed out on a very special person. I understood I might always have to put in that little bit of extra effort to move beyond the past about him. He still had those eyes after all. But I was okay. This felt healthy and good, like a gift of redemption.

The reminder of why I needed redemption surfaced in my mind, and the cold, heavy reality that this friendship may very well be short-lived cooled the edges of that warmth. I could hear Brooke's voice in my head. *Live in the moment, Mia. You don't know the future.* I sighed. I may not know the future, but I knew my past, and if all that rejection was any indication, it wasn't looking good. But I couldn't worry about that now. I needed to hand out the morning meds.

The moment I walked into the Hub, I froze in my tracks. The smell of syrup permeated the air. Waffles. My heart skipped a beat. So much for moving beyond the past. I sighed.

Of course they would serve waffles for breakfast on the last day of camp with Ryan. The night I met him, we went out for waffles with the band after staring at each other all night at the club. Thinking about waffles led to thinking about…everything else. *Get a grip, Mia.* I took a deep breath, gave myself a moment, and kept moving.

I took my time. I got the meds ready for distribution then packed everything carefully in the nurse box as the kids came by. By the time I was finished, I was one of the last people in line for a waffle. At least there was bacon too. I took a couple pieces for emotional support.

It would be weird to sit somewhere else after eating with the guys all week. I steeled myself for the awkwardness and walked over to the table. The guys were already eating. Chris saw me first and immediately began to pout, his shoulders hunching down.

"Don't even say it," he grumped.

"Don't say what?" I asked, eyebrows raised, the picture of innocence. "I didn't say anything."

"You were thinking it," mumbled Chris, shaking his head.

Actually, I was thinking I was glad to have him as a buffer. But he was thinking about the game. Chris had impressed me last night. He shook hands with all the girls after we won, in a pleasant moment of unexpected sportsmanship. I didn't want to ruin it. The jury was still out on him being tuna-ed, and that sportsmanship was a big factor.

"We don't have to talk about it, Chris. Let's just eat. I'm starving," I told him.

I sat down next to Chris, across from Ryan. Chris mumbled something about checking on the bus then stood to go. Once he was gone, it was just Ryan and me. He took a big bite and chewed casually.

Butterflies slammed into my stomach. My mind went into overdrive. Was Ryan thinking about that night? How we'd laughed together? The way my heart pounded as he grabbed the corner of my chair and dragged me closer to him? The moment he leaned in...*no*. Of course he wasn't, and neither should I.

Ryan and I were friends now. He was probably just thinking about how delicious waffles were. I searched my mind for something to talk about. But nothing else surfaced. I sighed, feeling agitated and wrapped up in my thoughts.

Whose idea was it to serve waffles anyway? Some terrible, friendship-destroying villain? Just when we were finally getting more comfortable around each other, now this?

Right as the anxiety had me ready to jump out of my skin, Ryan swallowed and made eye contact with me. He pointed at the waffles on our plates and asked, "Is it too soon to laugh about this?"

Relief coursed through my body, neutralizing the anxiety along the way. I released the breath I hadn't known I was holding. I wasn't crazy or alone in being reminded of the past. It was normal, part of the process. I didn't need to overthink it.

I couldn't help but laugh, even as I tried very hard not to blush beet red and keel over from the onslaught of memories and awkwardness. But now was the present. It was important to stay present. I shook my head.

"Nope, it's definitely ironic." I took a breath and rolled my eyes. "But please, can we move on?"

He took mercy on me and grinned. "Sure. Tell me about your epic win. I want to hear all about it."

It felt so good to think about winning the game, my heart slowed and warmed up all over again. I gave him a play-by-play of the game while we both cleaned our plates. He even stole some of my bacon, and it was just fine.

Chapter 23

The bus air conditioner gave out the last (and warmest) hour of the trip. Naturally, it was expected for the adults to set a good example, to keep a positive attitude. Sarah was the only one who succeeded. She tried to help the rest of us, but we eventually sunk into grumpy silence and read our books. The other adult sponsors had their hands full in the back, with the boys wanting to take off their shirts in the sticky heat. Fifty teenagers. Do I even need to mention the smell?

In the end, Youth Guy Chris resorted to using an extremely serious tone to get everyone under control. The students obeyed like meek little lambs after that. We'd finally seen his adult side, and it was…effective. I was glad I hadn't tuna-ed his car before we left. All this growth might have been wasted.

We got back late in the afternoon. I pushed through the door of my apartment, covered in sweat, with what felt like an inch-thick layer of bus grime on my whole body. I was so ready for a shower I could have cried.

I absolutely enjoyed the very-strange-but-good week, but I was thrilled to be home. My little apartment had become a haven of warmth and peace, and it felt wonderful to be back after such a long time.

I showered, savoring the water pressure and spoiling my skin with my favorite products. Then I unpacked, throwing all my clothes directly in the washer. I played music while I put on makeup and scrunched mousse through my hair. It was too hot to even consider straightening it.

I set out for Anna and Gage's in a cute yellow sundress that sort of billowed away from my skin. It was hot here in Dallas, and I was still cooling down from the super-stuffy bus. The bright color contrasted nicely with my brown hair. It looked good, but best and most importantly, it had pockets.

I was worn out from camp. I didn't plan to stay long. Anna and Gage were hosting a game night at their house with a fun mix of single friends and some couples they knew. I was excited for this meshing of their worlds.

When I arrived, the party was in full swing. I took a moment to drop my purse in the guest room then headed to the kitchen to see if I could help. I passed Gage in the living room, looking serious, with a PlayStation controller in his hand. He was playing Madden with a guy I recognized from church but didn't know. I waved and walked toward the kitchen. Anna stopped her conversation with Maddie as soon as I entered the room, immediately wrapping me in a huge hug.

"Oh man, I missed you! I can't wait to hear all about camp! We have a LOT to catch up on!" Anna smiled, giving me a look of significance I could only describe as *crazy eyes*.

I smiled, not sure what was up. I reached over to hug Maddie as well. She told me Kevin was out on the deck with the guys, having some *bro time*. I rolled my eyes at her.

"I just spent a week with Youth Guy Chris. No more bros, please," I joked.

Maddie and Anna both chuckled a little awkwardly. Maddie cleared her throat.

"Actually, Youth Guy Chris is out there with Kevin right now."

I couldn't hide my surprise.

"Wow. Okay, I have questions…" I raised my eyebrows.

Maddie shrugged her shoulders. "I don't know. We started hanging out the week before camp. He grew up with dogs. He's been helping me with Kevin, giving me advice and stuff. It's not serious or anything. He called this afternoon, wanting to see us, so I invited him to join in over here."

Anna said nothing, though I could tell she was full of opinions. She looked like she was about to burst. She obviously already knew this was going on, since they'd been here for a while. I wasn't sure what to say. I decided to be supportive.

"That sounds cool, Maddie. I'm glad he could help with Kevin. It's a big adjustment, right?"

She nodded, looking relieved. Then she looked fierce.

"I'm not playing around with him, Mia. I promise. He said he wants us to talk tonight. I am going to tell him I'm not up for being anyone's distraction."

I high-fived her. "Good for you, girlie!"

"Okay, enough about that," said Maddie. "I want to hear about camp!"

There was so much to tell. Where to begin?

"Well—" I was cut off by a yell splitting the air.

"Mia!" Youth Guy Chris was standing in the doorway, holding Kevin under one arm. He raised his other arm, pointing right at me. The people in the room all turned to stare.

"I have a surprise for you outside! Come on out here!" He turned, walking back outside.

Embarrassed at being called out in front of everyone, I quickly followed him. The sooner I put whatever he was up to to rest, the sooner I could enjoy my evening with my friends. Anna and Maddie followed me through the back door and onto the deck. Several guys were out there. My eyes almost immediately landed on Ryan Lyles. Chris was right, I was surprised. Ryan was standing there, playing cornhole like one of the bros. What in the world?

Chris leaned in, an excited smile lighting his face. "I invited Ryan to come too. You're welcome."

I looked at him, aghast. "I'm sorry. I don't think I understand what's happening."

"You have a thing for him, right?" Chris asked, smiling like he'd just solved world hunger. He put his hand next to his mouth like he was going to whisper then said, "You're welcome!" in a high, breathy voice. He walked away toward the cornhole setup.

I looked at Anna. She looked horrified. "I was trying to find the right moment to tell you Chris brought him. I can ask him to leave."

I held up a hand. "No, it's fine. I have a lot to tell you. I just need a minute."

Maddie was baffled. "What's up, Mia? What happened?"

I looked at Anna. "Can we talk in your room?"

She nodded, gesturing toward the hallway. We walked through the house, passing small groups of people here and there, all of them talking and laughing. I walked into the dark coolness of Anna's bedroom then spun to talk to her and Maddie.

"I'm just going to tell you, then we can discuss, if that's okay?"

They both nodded, looking very concerned.

"I'm totally fine," I assured them. I looked at Maddie. "Maddie, I haven't told you this yet, because there hasn't been a good time, and it took me a while to process it. You know I had an abortion in college, remember?"

She nodded.

"Ryan, the new worship minister, is The Guy."

Maddie's eyes grew huge. Her jaw dropped. I held out my hands.

"I'm okay. I'm good. I was really freaked out at first, but I'm good now," I assured her.

Maddie looked relieved, but she was clearly bursting with questions. I paused to take a breath, grateful to have friends who loved me so much.

"I didn't expect it, but Ryan was at camp the whole time. We were around each other all week. I am doing a lot better about him. It's still a little weird sometimes, but it's good. He's actually great."

It was Anna's turn to look surprised. I nodded at her. "I know. It's a lot."

They both started talking at once.

"How did this come about?" Maddie asked.

"What's he like?" Anna wanted to know.

I felt overwhelmed, having just dropped this little bomb on them, but I did my best to answer.

"I'm still learning what he's like. He's really nice and funny. You already know, he and Jamie Martin were best friends, so he is close with Pam and John. He's a lot more humble than I remember him being, and he has been through a lot. That's everything I know, in a nutshell." *Whew*! I blew out a breath.

Both girls looked stunned. Anna spoke first.

"Wow."

Maddie and I just nodded. Yup.

"Why did Chris say he brought him for you?" Maddie asked. "That seems odd, even for him."

"I'm not sure," I told her. "Chris said I have a thing for Ryan, but that is not what is happening there." I wanted to reassure all three of us.

"We became friends over the course of the week, kind of slowly," I said. "It's weird for both of us. I haven't told him about the abortion yet. So the friendship may be over soon, but for now, that's what I know."

Saying that aloud felt mortifyingly tender. I could feel my eyes getting teary at the idea of losing his friendship, but I blinked them back.

Both Maddie and Anna took hold of me then. They hugged me, assuring me it was going to be okay. Maddie asked if she could pray, and I was grateful. I wasn't prepared to see Ryan again this soon, and I needed God's wisdom. After the prayer, we were all a little teary-eyed. Anna got us tissues, then we left the room together. Once again, I was reminded I was not alone.

Anna went to get us drinks, and Maddie and I walked outside. There were more people out there now. Some girls were huddled up chatting, and the guys were still playing cornhole.

I didn't see Ryan immediately, but when I found him in the crowd, he was looking right at me. His blue eyes smiled, and I smiled back, giving a little wave. It had only been a few hours since the bus, but his eyes hit me all over again. I took a calming breath.

Youth Guy Chris brought Kevin over, handing him to Maddie. "Here you go, milady," he gave a little bow then jogged back to finish his game.

Maddie cuddled Kevin then set him down in a fluffy pile on the ground. I looked at Kevin and smiled.

"He's adorable, Maddie."

"Thanks," she said. "I'm sorry Chris was obnoxious earlier. I don't think he always understands how he comes across."

I needed to tread carefully here, but I didn't want to waste my shot. "Do you think that might be difficult in a relationship?"

Maddie paused. "I'm honestly not sure. I don't want to write him off for something he can grow past. Like I said, it's super new, and I don't even know what IT is. But I'm not going to waste a bunch of time on a man-child with potential."

I nodded, satisfied. "Sounds like you're being wise about it."

She let out a breath, shaking her head. "I'm trying, girl."

Just then, cheers rose up from the other side of the cornhole game. Some of the guys were clapping while Chris held Ryan's hand up in the air. Apparently, they'd won.

Anna came out with our drinks. We all clinked our clear plastic cups together. I sipped my wine. It was cool and refreshing. I felt extra aware of everything around me. The sun set and the patio lights, bright against the dark sky, lent a festivity to the moment.

Maddie asked Anna about the changes they'd made to the house. While Anna answered, the slow thump of the cornhole bean bags hitting wooden boards gave the night a beat. I could feel my skirt dancing in the breeze, sending goosebumps across my skin. I felt at peace here. It was good to be home with my people.

My little moment came to an end when Ryan crossed into my line of sight. He was ambling toward me with his long, confident stride, a beer bottle in his hand. His eyes seemed darker blue in the shadowy light. Something in me awakened—a slow, fluttering butterfly. My heart threatened to warm, maybe even burst into flames. Chris' words echoed in my head.
Nope, I told myself abruptly. *That's not it. It can't be.*

Friendship with Ryan was a miracle I didn't deserve. I wouldn't dare ask for anything more. It would be too weird. He must feel the same way.

I had to remind myself that even friendship wasn't guaranteed. He didn't know everything yet. The knowledge pressed like a lead weight in the pit of my stomach, even as those eyes drew me in like a magnet. It wasn't fair. My mind felt like a string on a guitar, pulled taut by the tension. I braced for the sound of his voice.

"Hi," he said and smiled.

Anna and Maddie stopped talking and straightened, standing in solidarity by my side. I wasn't alone. I drew on their strength. I stepped forward before my courage dissipated. No time like the present.

"Hey. Can I talk to you for a minute?" I asked.

He looked surprised. He looked down at his beer bottle then back at me.

"Sure. I was gonna get another beer. Want to walk inside with me?"

I nodded. He smiled at Anna and Maddie then walked to the door, pulling it open for me. I walked through, into the blessedly deserted kitchen. I could hear noisy people in the other room, but we had enough privacy in here for this. Before I could lose my nerve, I took hold of the moment and turned to face him.

"I was wondering if we could get together on Tuesday?" I asked casually.

Ryan looked surprised. He took a second to digest what I said. He smiled at me gently then replied, "Mia, it's nice of you to ask. I would love to, but I just…I'm not sure this is the best timing."

I listened to him say all that, shocked he seemed to be saying no, until I realized what was happening.

"Oh!" I exclaimed. "No! No, Ryan. That's not it." I blew out a breath, huffing a little laugh. It relieved the heaviness in my chest, at least for a few seconds.

He seemed totally baffled. Trying again may mean brutally destroying his ego, but I didn't feel bad, considering he'd just essentially rejected me.

"I'm not asking you out. Do you remember at camp, after you shared your testimony, you asked if we could talk? I'd like us to talk this Tuesday, if you are free."

He blinked, taking it all in. He seemed perturbed. But he nodded, running a hand through his hair.

"Yes, I can do Tuesday."

I took out my phone and asked for his number so I could text him details. He recited the numbers obediently then reached over for a plastic cup, filling it with water from the sink.

I said, "I thought you came in to get another beer."

"I did," he replied, "But then I was just a total imbecile with you, so I'm switching to water. I'm sorry, Mia, that was…I was an idiot."

His words were more satisfying than they should have been. Ryan was a good apologizer.

"You're forgiven," I said magnanimously and changed the subject. "So, are you and Youth Guy Chris besties now or what?"

He chuckled. He raised his eyebrows then sassed right back, "Don't be jealous."

I scoffed, but Ryan's laughter was contagious. I couldn't help but giggle.

"He's not that bad," I admitted. I figured if Maddie could give him another chance, I probably should too.

We walked back outside together, stopping by Maddie and Anna. I had just introduced them both to Ryan when an unmistakable voice hollered from across the yard, "Ryan and Mia sitting in a tree! K-I-S-S-I-N-G!"

I take it back, I thought. *No number of chances could absolve this level of obnoxious behavior.*

Frozen to the spot, I happened to look at Maddie. She looked like she could have beaten Chris to a pulp for embarrassing me while simultaneously begging the ground to open up and swallow her. Poor thing.

To my right, Ryan cleared his throat. In a strained voice, he murmured, "I'll talk to him."

I nodded, incapable of making eye contact with him in this moment. "That would be helpful. Thanks."

Ryan excused himself then walked across the yard like a man on a mission. I was grateful dealing with Chris wasn't my burden to bear but his. This way, I was able to focus and help Maddie through what was sure to turn into a moment of self-loathing, since she was the one to invite Chris.

Deciding humor might help most in this terrible moment, I looked at her poor, humiliated face and simply said, "Bro." We all burst out laughing. Maddie put both hands over her face, laughing quietly. Anna snorted with laughter. When she got her breath back, she gently took hold of Maddie's forearm.

"I'm serious, Maddie. I'll set you up with someone great, I promise," Anna insisted.

Maddie always refused to let Anna set her up, but she nodded. "That would be good. Thanks." She turned to me. "Mia, truly. I'm so sorry. I was foolish to bring him here. It's no excuse, but he is a different person when it's just the two of us."

I waved her off. "Don't even worry about it. It was embarrassing, but this will be a funny story by tomorrow. We're good."

The game of cornhole resumed. I could hear cheering coming from the living room too. I yawned. It had been a long week. I was ready for a good night's sleep in my own bed. I hugged the girls good night, thanked Anna for having us all and walked out to my car and headed home.

Chapter 24

Saturday morning, I laced up my shoes to go for a run then got coffee at the little coffee shop in my neighborhood on the walk home. Time was ticking. I was planning to tell Ryan on Tuesday, and the dread sat heavy on my stomach. I needed to stay busy, so I was very productive that day, running errands and cleaning my apartment.

That night, I had a movie night with Maddie, Sarah, and some other girls at Sarah's house. Sarah was not at Anna's the night before because she was with Ben. Maddie and I couldn't wait to hear how things were going. Sarah blushed, saying it was going really well. Being away from him for camp helped her see how much they meant to each other.

I was glad to hear this and was super excited for my friend. After the other girls left, I told Sarah about my past connection with Ryan. She was simultaneously horrified on my behalf and amazed.

"I *knew* there was history there!" she muttered triumphantly. She encouraged me, saying she would absolutely be praying for Tuesday, which I appreciated. Over and over, I was reminded that I wasn't alone, and that was a bigger relief than I expected. It helped.

Sunday dawned, cloudy and brutally humid. Sarah and I were supposed to serve that morning, so I set my alarm a little earlier. I got dressed in a loose, flowy dress to combat the heat and humidity then drove over to church. I was excited to see my friends and worship. Camp was great, but I missed church last Sunday. Sarah and I arrived at the same time, and we walked in together.

Taking up our posts, we stood at the doors, welcoming the people and keeping traffic flowing. Miss Alma watched closely for dalliers, but the dalliers seemed to have slept in. We gathered our things to walk inside as they began the second verse:

My sin, oh the bliss of this glorious thought,
My sin, not in part, but the whole
Is nailed to the cross, and I bear it no more!

Praise the Lord! Praise the Lord, oh my soul!

I probably would have been fighting tears during that song anyway, but I couldn't stop them from rolling down my cheeks today. My heart was torn between the dread I felt at the idea of telling Ryan on Tuesday and the hope I clung to. Once again, I was glad I knew the Lord.

I knew it was Jesus who had paid for all my sins, but now it was real in a new way. My sin from years ago was catching up with me. It was going to hurt my friend. Ryan was going to hate me. I felt so nauseated during church I almost went home, but Maddie begged me to come to lunch. She knew going home alone would only give me more time to focus on the dread.

"Come on," she urged. "No point in going home to stew on something you can't control. And we can go for a walk afterward with Kevin." She was right. It was better to be distracted. I agreed to go.

As usual, ten of us were squished into a huge round booth more suited for eight. I happened to be on the end when Ryan showed up, having just finished cleaning up with the band. Everyone shuffled around, and he ended up shoehorned into the table, right next to me. Another wave of anxiety hit, and my armpits turned into showers. He didn't seem to notice. He greeted me with a smile then turned to answer a question one of the guys asked him about one of the songs from that morning.

When the food came, he elbowed me playfully. He needed more room for his barbacoa tacos. When I reflexively elbowed him back, he slid right off the edge of the booth. Everyone laughed while he picked himself up. I sheepishly apologized then squished myself against Maddie to make more room. We chatted easily the rest of the meal.

After we paid, we all walked out in a big, chaotic group. Ryan walked next to me so we could work out a time and place for our meeting on Tuesday. My stomach turned, thinking about it, and I was glad I hadn't eaten much lunch. I was going to miss the ease of this friendship. Ryan was really fun, and wise—a good man. I enjoyed being around him more and more.

Looking back, I was amazed. In just a week, God had done all this. I wondered if there could be any hope that Ryan wouldn't hate me once he knew. Anything could happen, and I was powerless to know. So I just kept praying.

I tossed and turned Sunday night, then working on Monday was exhausting. I almost regretted scheduling a session with Brooke, but I really wanted to talk to her before my meeting with Ryan. We talked through the best way for me to tell him. After imagining all the scenarios, I was still weighed down with dread. If the roles were reversed, I wasn't sure what I would do or how I would receive that information. It almost seemed there was no way a conversation like this could go well.

My session with Brooke was helpful in an unexpected way. I'd assumed it was best to expect nothing, but Brooke asked me to consider something else. She felt it was important to honor myself and all the work I'd done around this situation. Brooke reminded me that while there could be fallout, I could not lose the gift of God's love and grace. That truth seemed elementary, but I never tired of coming back to it. The way Brooke reminded me of what God had done for me, I found myself rejoicing in the gift of grace.

When I left Brooke's office, I was still dreading the next day, but I was walking in freedom. If Ryan didn't want to be friends, or couldn't, I would survive. I would keep going. It was his choice, but I was worthy of consideration too. It took a lot of work to heal from that time in my life, and it wasn't for nothing. I felt the nerves, but I felt the peace more.

Tuesday morning, I woke up refreshed, having finally slept. I prepared to face the day. I went for a run then tried to eat breakfast, but I couldn't eat more than a couple of bites. I spent some time with the Lord, reading my Bible and praying. I focused on the facts: God had been completely faithful to me. He wasn't going to let me go on this day or any other. I belonged to Him. I could trust Him. *Your Kingdom come, Your will be done*, I prayed.

I kept a list of God's attributes in the cover of my journal, and I read over it. The sovereignty of God and His omnipresence were a comfort to me, as always. He already knew what was going to happen and He was in charge of all of it.

I dressed in jeans and a t-shirt then left my apartment, feeling the heaviness of what I was about to do. I focused on my breathing the whole way to the coffee shop near the church building. My body was as relaxed as I could get it.

I arrived a few minutes early. It wasn't crowded. Ambient music played while the sound of the steamer split the air periodically. I sat down. Within a minute or two, Ryan appeared, looking gorgeous and relaxed in a soft blue t-shirt and jeans. I stood to hug him briefly, thanking him for meeting with me.

We ordered our coffees and sat down across from each other at the small table. No one sat near us, so I felt a little less self-conscious. Ryan took a careful sip from his steaming cup then smiled at me. It warmed my heart. I let myself enjoy the feeling, knowing he may not smile at me ever again after this conversation.

"Thanks for taking the time to see me like this," he said kindly. "Especially on your day off."

"That's no problem. I appreciate you being here. I was a little abrupt about it at camp, and you were really gracious. I loved hearing your testimony and about how God has worked in your life. Seeing you now, it's a huge encouragement to me. I really enjoyed getting to know you a little bit at camp," I babbled. *Now who had the word vomits?*

"Thanks," he said, oblivious to the sheen of nervous sweat breaking out on my back. "I'd love to hear more about your life, how you came to faith, and what you've been up to the last decade."

He was so enthusiastic. I smiled, nervous and a little sad too. *Here goes nothing*, I thought.

"Ryan, a lot changed for me after I met you. Um, there's a lot…" I drifted off, my courage leaving me. I didn't know what to say next. My mouth was dry. I had no words. Ryan shifted and cocked his head, ready to listen. I could tell he was growing concerned. *God, help me do this*, I prayed.

I took a sip of coffee and pushed through, staring hard at his coffee cup. Brooke told me to choose a focal point. It was right there, as good as anything else. I took a deep breath and spoke to the C in the word *coffee*.

"A few weeks after I met you, I found out I was pregnant." I stared at the C and blew out a breath.

His thumb had been toying with the corner of the cardboard sleeve around his cup, but it stilled. He said nothing. Nausea rolled through my stomach like it always did when I told anyone this part of my story. I kept going.

"I didn't know what to do. I was totally in shock. My mother came. She told me if I kept it, they would cut me off. They wouldn't support me. I would be alone. She made an appointment under a fake name, and I had an abortion."

My voice broke on the last word. I breathed through the nausea, in and out, in and out. My hands shook. I held them together tightly, pressing them between my knees.

Ryan was quiet. I wanted to look at him, but I was terrified. What was he thinking? A tear slid down my cheek. I thought about how much I had come to value Ryan in a short time. Losing this friendship was going to be even harder for me than I imagined. But it was too late now.

"I'm so sorry, Ryan." It was all I could think to say. Of course there was more. The nightmares, the horrible guilt, the fear, my parents' awkwardness and distance, the fact that I lost all my self-worth and looked for love in the stupidest places before I found Christ. But the main thing was finally said.

Ryan's reaction to this information would decide how things would be moving forward. Finally, I couldn't take it anymore. I needed to look. I braced myself for whatever was in those blue eyes, then I lifted my gaze to his face.

He was pale and very still. His eyes searched my face. He opened his mouth to speak then closed it. This was it.

Ryan sniffed and cleared his throat. "Um. Thank you for sharing this with me. I…" He looked at me, drew a breath, and tried again, his voice soft with shock. "A baby?"

I nodded. "I'm so sorry." I couldn't think of anything else to say. It was a lot to process. He would need some time to wrap his mind around all of it.

"It was mine. You're sure?"

I was surprised to suddenly feel even more awkward. But it was a fair question. "Yes, I'm sure. You were the only person I'd ever...been with at that point." I looked at the table.

He closed his eyes, rubbing his hands over his face. "Mia, I'm sorry. That came out terrible. I–" His voice cut off. He sighed then tried again. "I have so many questions. A baby. The baby is...the baby is gone?"

I nodded. *Here it comes*, I thought. The next words from his mouth would be, *How could you do that, Mia? Why didn't you tell me?*

Ryan shook his head slowly, looking at me. "You must have been so scared. Are you—are you okay? Is, like, your body okay?"

My eyes filled in response. I marveled. I knew the hard part wasn't over. This conversation could go anywhere. But this was already different. For him to even think of me when I had done this. Who could be so kind?

My heart knew the answer: *Jesus*. I'd heard the phrase *to love as Jesus loved*. I had experienced it before, but I had not expected it today. Something cold in me warmed and lifted. How could it be, that even in this moment, God was healing me?

"I'm okay now," I assured him. "Physically, I healed well. I was young and healthy. The emotional part took a long time, but I'm much better. I've done a lot of therapy over the years."

He nodded and sipped his coffee. He rubbed his face with his hand and sat back in his chair. "Ten years. Okay. Um, can I ask you more questions?"

I nodded, bracing. "Of course."

Ryan took a breath. I could see his mind working, trying to process, trying to figure out what to ask. His voice trembled a little bit when he asked, "Do you have any information about the baby? Was it a boy or a girl?"

My eyes overflowed with tears. I assumed he would have questions. I thought I was ready for anything. I was wrong. Shame came roaring back, its teeth sharp and piercing. I had imagined a few scenarios, mostly with yelling accusations or crying. But I wasn't prepared for Ryan to be gentle, much less tender.

It was clear: This man already loved a baby he never knew existed until sixty seconds ago. He wanted to *know* about it. A baby I had let go of out of fear. The baby was gone, and it was my fault. My breath sped up. This was even harder than I'd anticipated. I looked away, unable to meet his eyes.

I felt hideously ashamed. I wanted to panic. To run away and hide. All the counseling in the world couldn't help this. *I can't do this.* I shook my head and covered my face. I needed to do this, but it was so overwhelming. I talked to myself, the way Brooke had told me to. *No. Stay here, Mia. Be present. Do this. Answer the question.* I took a couple of deep breaths and answered him.

"No, it was early, too early to tell. They didn't do testing. So no, I don't know for sure. But in my mind, when I picture the baby, she's a girl."

He stood and walked over to the counter. He returned with a stack of napkins. I took one and blew my nose.

"And your mother? She just *left* you in that?" he asked, as if that part was even more shocking. His eyebrows drew together in a frown as the story continued to sink in.

I shook my head. How could I help him understand them? "It's complicated. My parents are politicians. The job is their whole identity. It's been that way for a long time now. Back then, my dad was running for the Georgia State Senate for the first time. It was a tight race, and the local press was watching him closely, scrutinizing every little thing. I think they just *reacted*. They were terrified it would cost him the election, and all that work would have been for nothing.

"I'm not excusing it. It's still difficult. It changed my relationship with them, maybe forever. But at the time, they were working really hard. They built that campaign for a couple of years. It took all they had. They were totally focused on winning. A pregnant teenage daughter was their worst nightmare."

Ryan looked at me, taking it all in. I kept going.

"I was on the phone with my mom when it occurred to me that I could be pregnant. I'd been throwing up in the mornings that week, and she was worried it was an ulcer or something. She was reading off WebMD. She made a joke. She said *thank goodness I wasn't pregnant.* And it hit me. I hung up with her and went to buy a test. I was terrified. She read between the lines and flew out the next morning."

I started to cry again, just remembering that feeling of seeing my mom in the doorway that morning. I'd been so relieved, until I saw the look on her face. She looked like a stranger, pale and resolved. She told me she'd made an appointment at a clinic in the next town over. I was shocked.

That was the biggest argument we ever had. The image of my mother standing in my room, so calm and cold, was burned into my brain forever. I couldn't believe she'd even suggested something like that, and I'd told her so.

"Well how could you be so stupid?" she'd spat, shaking her head. Then when I wouldn't comply, the threat: "If you don't do this, you can't be our daughter anymore. You will be alone. Good luck paying for college and daycare."

The pain of that moment never faded, even all these years later. It took a long time to forgive her. I took a breath. The coldness crept through my veins, as it had that morning long ago. Coming back to the present moment, I sniffed and looked at Ryan.

"I was completely overwhelmed," I admitted. "I was relieved to see her at first, until I realized what was happening. We argued—this huge fight. It was terrible. I didn't want to do that. I thought there must have been another way. But she told me it was our only option. If I didn't do it, I couldn't be their daughter anymore. They would cut me off. I would be alone. And I believed her. I've never been that scared—ever."

I held onto the napkin in my hands, wringing out the strength to explain the rest.

"It was done that afternoon. She dropped me off at home afterward and left for the airport as if she'd never come at all. She blocked your number on my phone plan, and that was it. The trail was covered, like nothing happened. But we were never the same after that."

Ryan nodded. "I can imagine. Do you still see them?" he asked.

I nodded and took a deep breath.

"Honestly, in some ways, we never recovered from it. I think they feel ashamed. They're my parents. I know they don't want this to be my story. They paid for all my therapy in college. We still check in on the phone pretty regularly, and I go visit a couple of times a year.

"We all try, but neither one of them can really look me in the eye anymore. They don't know how to handle it. They just keep going. They both work all the time. They won't discuss it. I have forgiven them. I love them, and they love me, but we're not very close, you know, emotionally."

He digested everything for a few seconds.

"So you've carried this alone? All these years?"

I shook my head. "Not alone. Anna and I stayed roommates until she got married a couple of years ago. She stayed with me through all of it. She made me eat, made me go to class and to therapy, helped me heal. We've stayed close.

"She and Gage are basically my family here in Texas. I do a lot of holidays and stuff with them at Anna's parents' house in Fort Worth. Or with the Martins. Pam and John know I had an abortion when I was nineteen."

He repeated the word. "Nineteen. A teenager. A kid. Mia, I'm so sorry—" He broke off. His eyes were glassy, and now they overflowed. At a loss, I put my hand on his shoulder as he cried. When he seemed calmer, I straightened in my chair, pulling my hand back.

"Ryan, I don't expect anything from you. This is a lot. If you're angry, or if you hate me, or if you—" I would have kept going through all the things I feared he would say, but he raised his head and met my gaze.

The look in his eyes silenced me. Full of tears, they looked like blue fire.

"No, Mia. That's not how I feel. I could never hate you, and I don't hate you for *this*. I'm sad. I'm—I'm *devastated*. I wish I had known. I wish I could have been there. I wish…I wish a lot of things. I'm angry at your parents for putting you through that. But if I hate anyone, I hate myself.

"I lived for my own appetites back then, Mia. I was so selfish. I told myself I loved you, but I made *all* of that about *me*. Even now, seeing you again, I let myself get distracted, and I focused on you ghosting me instead of asking better questions. I'm sorry." He paused, took a breath. "I don't know if I could have been a better man then, but I wish I had been around to try. I'm so sorry."

I hadn't been sure what to expect. Judgment? Anger? Maybe piety or begrudging forgiveness? Definitely not this.

"Thank you, Ryan. You're being very gracious. I appreciate you saying all that. Truly, I don't expect anything from you, and I hope you can forgive me someday," I said, tears still falling.

Ryan stood up from his chair then knelt next to mine. He looked at me, his eyes a blue storm. He wiped a tear off my cheekbone with his thumb and wrapped his arms around me. I melted into him, wrapping my arms around him too.

He murmured quietly, "Mia, of course I forgive you. You were so young. And you didn't get pregnant by yourself. I was stupid and selfish and thoughtless. I should have been there. I should have tried harder. Can *you* forgive *me*?" He was so sincere.

I nodded. "Yes, definitely."

Forgiving Ryan was part of my healing process early on. But I didn't blame him for something he hadn't known about. At this point, I only blamed myself. Forgiving Mia Browning was much more difficult and much more of a cyclical reality. Brooke told me once in therapy that, one day, I would forgive myself for the last time. I was grateful to think that day would come, but it probably wasn't coming anytime soon.

We held onto each other, both of us softly crying. When Ryan released me and returned to his seat, he wiped his eyes. Then he looked at me like he could read my thoughts.

"Mia, I know this is very personal. I don't have the right to ask, but have you forgiven yourself?" he asked kindly. He was ministerial, even in this.

I nodded. "Yes, hundreds of times. And I will again. I've put in a lot of work, emotionally and spiritually. I've healed a lot. Even telling you today has helped me. But it's a process. Kind of a cycle. November is always a little rough."

He nodded with understanding. "I can understand that."

We stayed quiet for a minute. Tears running down his face, Ryan looked at me. "Mia, this is hard. I don't know what to—" He broke off.

I nodded. "It is. We can talk about it more, if you like, after you've had more time to process."

"Thank you," he said. I was amazed at his humility and kindness. *This man is a miracle*, I thought to myself.

"You said you did counseling. Would you be willing to come to counseling with me? Help me process this?" he asked.

I nodded, grateful he was handling this so kindly. "Of course."

Ryan blew his nose on a napkin. "This is heavy for a Tuesday. I'm not sure what to do from here."

I nodded. "I'm honestly not sure either. I thought you might never speak to me again. I didn't make plans after this immediate moment."

He nodded. "I get that." He paused. "Mia, I have a lot to process. I need to take this seriously, and I do. But still, I would love for us to be friends. Maybe we could spend some time together, get to know each other? Is that too weird?"

I shook my head and smiled. "I'd like that. But you have to plan the next activity. This one has too much crying."

He gave a watery chuckle. "Deal."

We finished our coffee. I was sure to be all red and blotchy. I wiped my face carefully, trying to get as much mascara off my cheeks as possible. When we left the coffee shop, Ryan hugged me for a long time. I let myself enjoy holding onto him. I breathed in his cologne; it was light and fresh. Like a new day.

He told me he'd let me know when his counselor was available. I walked away, feeling lighter than I had felt in ten years. A huge part of my story was finally at rest, and I could be too. I never could have imagined my conversation with Ryan going so well.

The sun was shining, and the morning breeze rustled through the trees dotting the sidewalk. I got in my car to leave. The release of all that anxiety left me emotionally and physically drained. I was tempted to go home and go back to bed, but I had errands to run.

I prayed, thanking God the whole way to the grocery store. I needed to get groceries and prep my lunches for the rest of the week. I was working the next three days in a row. I knew from experience that it would wipe me out. Taking care of future needs today would be very helpful for Future Mia.

Anna, Maddie, and Sarah were all praying for me that morning. I texted to tell them it could not have gone better. They all responded with supportive words and encouragement. My heart was full.

I knew I would never fully let go of that terrible decision or the precious baby I missed out on. But God never left me alone in the darkness, and I believed He never would. He brought light after light. The promise of restoration and goodness for eternity was real. Every sad thing would be untrue, and one day, that would be all we knew anymore. My heart longed for the day. I was grateful to know it was coming.

Chapter 25

W orking three days in a row made the week pass quickly. On Saturday, I rested and caught up on laundry. That evening, I went to the Martins' house for dinner. I was excited to see them both. They still hosted the Fourth of July gathering every summer, and it was coming up. I drove over early to help Pam get ahead on the cooking.

Pam put me to work as soon as I arrived. I donned a frilly black apron with *Southern + Sassy* embroidered across the front, and started making six batches of brownies. Pam would freeze them then have them ready for the upcoming party. She worked on making sangria to freeze in ice cubes so the fresh sangria wouldn't get watered down as the ice melted in the heat. We worked companionably, side by side, chatting the whole time. It was refreshing to my soul.

John was outside in the heat, bravely manning the grill. The meal was simple: Caesar salad with grilled chicken. I was excited. It was too hot for anything warmer than salad, now that the relentless heat of summer held Dallas in a death grip. It was brutal outside. Everyone was sweaty all the time, and the drivers had all gone crazy. I made sure to look extra long at every light because you never knew when someone would run a red light.

Pam's kitchen featured a double oven, which was great for baking six batches of brownies in a hurry, but the kitchen was positively stifling. John had just brought in the chicken from the grill and set the plate down on the stove. He took off his grilling mitt and set it down, wiping his sweaty forehead. He sliced the chicken, cutting it into bite-sized pieces.

"How else can I help, darlin'?" he asked Pam.

She told him he could set the table in the dining room. I widened my eyes at that.

"Fancy!" I wiggled my eyebrows.

Pam rolled her eyes. "Oh, don't be silly, hon. It's just too hot in here 'cause of the oven. We'll be much more comfortable in the dining room.

There!" she exclaimed, pouring the last of the sangria into the ice cube tray. She expertly carried the trays two at a time to the freezer, setting them inside without spilling a drop. I was reminded of my clumsiness at camp. I was glad that had gone away. Maybe it really was the altitude. Whatever it was, I'd been walking successfully all week.

Pam pulled a large salad bowl full of lettuce out of the fridge, along with a bottle of dressing. She dressed the salad, added homemade, freshly browned croutons, the cheese from the grater bowl, and the chicken. She then tossed it with two big spoons and turned to me with a smile.

"I put the good stuff in here, Mia, the par-mi-jahno!" She shimmied her shoulders. I shimmied along with her enthusiastically.

"Yum!" I said as we shimmied. I wasn't faking it. Parmigiano Reggiano was the best! Pam taught me the difference between it and the other, pre-shredded parmesan cheese, which was basically wax in comparison, and I couldn't go back. *Buy the good cheese, honey,* she always said. It was just one of her many tips on life and living but maybe my favorite of all. I obeyed it to the best of my ability. I was dusting off the counter when the doorbell rang.

"I'll get it!" John called from the front of the house. I heard the sound of the door opening, and John's usual enthusiastic greeting. A couple seconds later, John came into the kitchen followed by Ryan.

This was a surprise. Out of habit, my heart picked up speed for a second, but I reminded myself to breathe. He'd texted me during the week to thank me again for talking with him and to let me know he was glad we could be friends. We texted back and forth a few times about attending a joint counseling session with his counselor. We planned to go the following week.

Ryan walked across the kitchen to hug Pam. He handed her a bottle of white wine. She exclaimed, "Ooh, it's nice and cold! We should open this now, Johnny!" John got to work, taking the bottle from his wife and walking to the bar cabinet for a corkscrew.

Ryan saw me and paused for a second. I held my breath. He might need time or space away from me. Should I offer to leave? But then, he smiled. He stepped closer to give me a hug.

"Hey, I didn't know you'd be here," he greeted me. He looked down at my flour-dusted apron. "Southern and sassy, huh? I'll consider myself warned."

I laughed at his joke, feeling relieved. "I didn't know you'd be here either."

Pam hadn't mentioned Ryan was coming. It wasn't a terrible jolt, like it would have been a month ago. I was getting used to him being part of my life.

"You've got a little flour on your nose," Ryan pointed out helpfully.

I groaned. Of course I did. "Thanks," I replied, rubbing my nose.

"You got it," he assured me. I untied my apron and walked over to hang it on a hook.

At that moment, John returned with the opened wine then poured us each a glass. We all clinked glasses and sipped. The wine was cool and refreshing. Pam picked up the bowl of salad and asked John to get the crusty bread out of the oven where it was warming. I picked up her wine glass, carrying it into the dining room, where the table was set beautifully, complete with candles.

"Wow, Pam, this is impressive," Ryan observed in his smooth, deep voice.

I nodded in agreement. "It's beautiful."

We sat down, and John said grace. Then we ate the delicious, refreshing meal. Ryan told us the salad reminded him of a time he and Jamie took two girls out to a fancy French restaurant. They'd all eaten Caesar salad as an appetizer, then one of them accidentally ordered snails. We all laughed, and Pam cried a little bit, wishing for Jamie. It was a sweet time. For dessert, John served one of the pans of brownies I'd baked, with vanilla ice cream and hot fudge sauce.

"Sorry to waste your efforts, Mia, but I think it's best if we find out now if they're poisonous," John teased. We all laughed and dug in.

For a moment, I let myself reflect. I loved the joy Pam and John shared in inviting others into their lives. When I looked ahead in my own life, I wanted to be like them. For the first time in a long time, I let myself consider the possibility that something like this could happen for me.

Over the last decade, dating was a minefield for me. I was starting to think being alone was inevitable. But now I wondered. I could tell I was healing more and more. Sharing with Ryan had brought a lightness to my soul I never could have anticipated. Hope was springing up like a tiny sprout. Could I let myself dream? Could I consider the possibility of opening up a home I shared with someone? Could I love and be loved?

Those thoughts didn't make my stomach churn with anxiety as they once had. God must be healing me in ways I hadn't even known to look for. Telling Ryan was the right choice, and I was glad he was here now. It was good.

Pam released me from the thoughts in my own head by asking a question. "Ryan, how's the softball team going?"

Ryan was leaning back on his chair, obviously very full. He smiled and laughed to himself. "It's going okay so far. Our first game was last week. We lost to the Methodists from across town."

"It's the Baptists who cheat, Ryan, remember that," John warned him, waving his finger ominously in Ryan's direction. Ryan's eyebrows raised. He looked as surprised as I felt. Who knew softball would strike such a nerve for John?

Pam rolled her eyes. "Johnny. It's been fifteen years, honey. Maybe it's time to let it go."

This unlocked a hidden vault of emotions in John Martin. I watched in amused wonder as he crossed his arms over his broad chest. "I'll do no such thing. They cheated! That ball was IN! Fool me once, shame on you; fool me twice, shame on *me*, woman!"

Pam held up her hands, agreeing. Ryan looked at me, clearly trying not to laugh. I was in the same predicament. I looked away until I could trust myself to hold it together. When we were both calm again, Ryan's eyes lit up with an idea.

"You should come to our game next week if you want, Mia. It's on Wednesday at 8:00 pm. Are you working then?"

I thought ahead. "I'm off Wednesday. Anna told me about the team. I promised her I'd go with her to watch some games."

"I don't know who we're playing, but it may not matter. We're not great, to be honest." He looked at John. "We could really use the expertise of Big John Martin!"

John shook his head humbly. "Eh, y'all will be fine. A couple of those guys played ball in college, didn't they?"

"I think so." Ryan nodded. "Maybe Preston?"

Pam perked up at that. "Preston, as in *your* Preston, Mia?"

I smirked. "He's definitely not MY Preston. We broke up. I thought I told you." I looked at Ryan. "And yes, he did play baseball in college. Apparently, Youth Guy Chris was a star sportsman in high school too. If he hasn't told you yet, I'm sure he will."

Ryan looked amused.

Pam continued the conversation from earlier. "Oh! I forgot. Yes, you did mention that. Well, I hope Preston is better at softball than he is at dating."

I smiled at Pam. "Thank you for your loyalty, but I'm sure he's fine at both, with the right person."

"You and Preston?" Ryan tilted his head.

I waved it off, shrugging. "Briefly."

"Is that why you said you were freshly dumped, on the bus?"

"Got it in one," I answered, tapping my nose. I changed the subject. "So, are you a strong athlete?"

Ryan shrugged, looking a little pained. "I can hold my own, but I'm very much a musician."

I nodded. "Good to know."

He turned the tables. "What about you? I know you run. Are you packing The Heater in that arm?" He reached out to give my bicep a friendly squeeze.

I shrugged. "I can athlete. But I'd rather just eat. Are there snacks at the ballfield?"

He shook his head, looking pained. "Sadly, no."

Pam started clearing the dishes. The clatter of the plates caught my attention. I shook myself then jumped up to help. I gathered myself as best I could, feeling a little embarrassed. In just a few seconds, I'd totally forgotten John and Pam were even in the room. What was wrong with me?

I took the stack of dishes I'd gathered into the kitchen and put them next to the sink. Pam started the water and looked at me.

"I've got this, Mia. Why don't you go out back and take a look at my new flower bed? John built me an arbor, and the jasmine vine is creeping along beautifully. And take Ryan with you. He loves gardening. I don't want him to miss it."

Giving me no chance to excuse myself, she turned her head and yelled, "Ryan! I want you to see my new arbor John built for me! You'll love the jasmine! Go on now!"

Ryan ambled into the room. "Yes, ma'am."

He turned toward the door, and Pam called, "Mia, you go too. Show her, Ryan!"

Okay, I thought. That seemed odd. Ryan looked at Pam for a second then nodded obediently. He walked over and held the door for me. I went outside into the beautiful Martin backyard.

The sun was just about set. I thought the patio lights would be bright overhead, but they weren't lit. John had woven tiny twinkle lights all through the shrubs, which bordered the entire perimeter of the yard. A stone path cut through a break in the shrubs. The walkway was dotted with small lights, softly illuminating the way out to the rest of the yard.

We walked through the gap in the shrubs and stopped. The next part of the yard held a gorgeous pool with a lavish garden of plants and flowers. I could see the arbor in the bluish glow of the pool lights. A second later, more twinkle lights snapped on, and we were looking at a twinkling fairy land in the shrubs. I stared in wonder at the beauty, noticing the scent of jasmine in the air.

"This is really nice," I observed. I walked along the flagstone path to get a closer look at the arbor and the plants around it.

"Careful," Ryan said quietly, walking beside me.

I smiled good-naturedly. "Ha ha. I have actually been walking like a pro all week."

"I don't believe you," he said humorously. I gave him a playful shove. He dodged it, laughing mischievously.

"So, you're a gardener?" I asked.

"Well, my mom is a gardener, but she has a hard time doing the gardening now. Plus, the heat is really dangerous for her. So I am her hands and back and legs, but she is the gardening mastermind. I just obey her orders."

"That's so kind of you to do that for her," I said. "I'm glad she has you."

"I'm glad I have *her*. My mom is great. You should meet her sometime. She would love you."

"Does she go to church?" I asked.

"She does, if it's not too hot or cold. When she comes, she sits with Pam and John."

We stopped to admire some flowers. I decided now was as good a time as any to check in. He'd had a lot to consider the last few days. In the dim light, I looked him in the eye.

"How are you doing with everything?" I asked.

He nodded, quieting. He took a deep breath. "I think I'm doing okay. I mean, it's on my mind, but it doesn't take over. I've been pretty emotional privately. You know grief and I are well-acquainted. I know it's necessary, but this feels different than losing Jamie. I don't know if it's because I never knew the baby?"

His eyes shone with unshed tears. His voice scraped along his vocal cords as he continued. "I feel even more guilty about that than how sad I feel about the whole situation. It's just hard. I'm glad to know, though. I'm grateful you told me, Mia. Thank you. And thank you for checking on me. It's good of you."

My eyes filled at his kindness again. I'd learned at the pregnancy center that many, many people were not kind at all. I'd heard women's horrifying stories of surgical abortions done while they were awake, women who'd been beaten or kicked out by their boyfriends or parents, and the list went on.

Trauma is a very real and terrible thing to experience. Many things can make it worse. Yet, here I was, having the sweetest man offer me grace and kindness. I couldn't make sense of it. *Lord, this is heavy and confusing. You bear our burdens. Help me keep the right perspective.*

Ryan sniffed, wiping his eyes. The light was dim. He said, "I think counseling will be helpful."

I nodded. "It has been for me," I told him, wiping a tear off my cheek. We sunk into a comfortable silence. We walked over to the arbor, looking over all the fragrant flowers and vines.

I reached over to smell a rose, pulling it closer to my nose, and pricked my finger on one of the thorns. "Ouch!" I muttered, startled.

"Let me see?" Ryan asked. He took out his phone, turning on the flashlight. He took my hand in his, angling my pointer finger so he could look. A tiny drop of blood was seeping out, but the thorn wasn't stuck in there or anything.

I looked up. Ryan's face was bent low over my finger, close to mine. He lifted his head a bit, and we were eye to eye before I even realized what had happened. I hung there for a second, drowning in those eyes. Was I moving closer to him? That would be a bad idea. I took a breath then looked down. I searched for something to say.

"I'll go see if Pam has a Band-Aid."

Ryan nodded, releasing me. We turned wordlessly to walk through the yard and in the door. Pam was finished with the dishes. She and John were talking quietly in the kitchen. She went to get a Band-Aid while I washed my hands with soap. When she returned, I dried it thoroughly and wrapped the bandage around my finger.

"Expert-level Band-Aid placement, I have to say," Ryan observed from the other side of the kitchen island.

I shrugged, smiling. "That's why they pay me the big bucks." I turned to Pam. "Thank you for having me tonight. I had the best time. I'd better go so I can get up for church tomorrow." I gathered my purse and keys then hugged both Pam and John. I said good night to Ryan and gave him a little hug too. I smiled toward him but didn't make eye contact. We had enough of *that* in the backyard.

I was grateful to be growing closer in friendship with Ryan. But I needed to be careful. I didn't like this feeling of confusion. I certainly didn't think it wise to encourage any more of it. *We just need some space*, I told myself. *There is a lot of emotion to feel right now. It will pass.*

As I walked to my car, I thought back over the evening. If I didn't know better, I'd think Pam had been trying to create a *moment* of some kind with Ryan and me. That would have made things even more complicated. But Pam wasn't manipulative. She didn't meddle. I shook my head as I got in and started the car.

I was halfway home when I remembered I was out of coffee. I stopped in at a grocery store on the way and bought some. When I was back in the car, I drove towards my neighborhood and stopped at a red light. The light turned green. I looked both ways and started going.

I was halfway through the intersection when, out of nowhere, head- lights approached quickly from my left. I barely had time to respond before the impact of the other car knocked me sideways. Lights spun around me as the car whipped around and around. I felt myself fly upward, and then the loud squeal of something being dragged filled my ears. The car came to a stop, and everything went black.

Chapter 26

Something was pressing on me really hard. It was hurting my right hip. *What is that?* I wondered. I tried to move, to roll over, but something was off. I opened my eyes. It was dark, so it took me a second to understand where I was. I was inside my car, but the car was on its side.

The air bags were deflating. I was dangling in the air, hanging from my seat belt, the buckle digging into my hip. *What in the world?* My breathing sped up. Fear flashed through my mind and body. I could see lights flashing outside. A voice pressed through the darkness.

"Miss? We're gonna get you out. Hold on."

Everything felt foggy. *I'm a nurse,* I thought muddily. *I can help.* But it was me who needed help. The fear built again until I remembered, *I'm a nurse. Focus, Mia! Assess! Bleeding?* Giving myself a task calmed me down. With a clinical eye, I looked down at myself.

In the dim light, I could see my left hand was a little scraped up, and my arm was in extreme pain. I couldn't move it. I did not see any blood on my torso or legs. That was good. Something tickled the left side of my face. I brought up my right hand and gingerly wiped at it. I looked and gasped. Blood. *Stay calm. Breathe. Blood is a normal part of a car accident. I'm okay.*

So I was bleeding from the head. And my arm was almost certainly broken. The hip pain was probably just from the seat belt. *Now, neuro. Check for concussion.* I was not vomiting. I could see pretty clearly, but my head hurt a lot, and I was feeling nauseated. It was a strong maybe on the concussion. *I'm not great, but I'm okay. Lord, help me.*

The voice came back. "Miss? We're gonna lower your car back to the ground now. Hold on."

The car shifted and slowly lowered. I tried to stay calm. The movement hurt. I focused on my breathing. As I came down, I realized I wasn't being lowered by a crane, but by a group of very large, very muscular men.

Who are these people, the Dallas Cowboys? I asked myself. I would find out later they turned out to be witnesses. They were ten insanely muscular CrossFit friends, out at a bachelor party, who stopped to help when they saw the accident happen. I was grateful for their kindness.

A firefighter came to my window, which was shattered but still holding together. I couldn't see his face, only the silhouette of his helmet. He said they were going to open my door, but it was going to be loud. They needed to use the jaws of life. I gave him the thumbs-up sign with my right hand. The nausea was getting worse. I was afraid I would vomit if I tried to speak.

A bunch of creaking and screeching later, the door was open. The firefighter turned out to be a guy I knew from work named Cade.

"Hey, Mia," he said kindly. "Fancy meeting you here." He held a flashlight up to take a look at my head then asked, "Are you nauseous?" I gave him another thumbs-up. It hurt too much to nod.

The next thing I knew, I was vomiting into a bucket while Cade gently held my hair back and told me I was going to be okay. When I finished, he wiped my mouth with a napkin. He wrapped a stabilizing brace around my neck then cut my seatbelt. Then he carefully pulled me out, and carried me to a gurney.

He laid me down as easily as if I were a little kid. *Superhero strength*, I thought muddily. The rest of the EMTs leapt into action, assessing me some more. I tried speaking.

"I'm Mia Browning, female, age 29. I'm a nurse at Methodist Hospital." I rattled off my date of birth, blood type, no known allergies. I told them my information was in my purse inside the car.

My purse was already in my lap. Cade had grabbed it when he lifted me out of the car. *Wow*, maybe the man really was a superhero. A tow truck arrived, and my car was up on the truck bed in no time. The operator gave me his card, then one of the EMTs put it in my purse.

I felt extremely sleepy, and my head hurt worse. I thought I might vomit again, but I wasn't sure. They loaded me onto the ambulance and got to work. Someone started an IV in my right hand before we got going. It was organized chaos. I closed my eyes just for a moment.

When I opened them again, I was in the ER at the hospital. My friend Cindy was there, the lights too bright above her. They hurt my eyes. She noticed I was awake and spoke quietly.

"You're okay, Mia. A broken arm, probably a concussion too. You got lucky. The drunk teens who ran the red and hit you also got lucky. They're alive. They've already gone home with their parents. We started a police report. How's your pain?"

I answered her as best I could. Then I threw up a little more. I asked her to call Anna, which she had already done. Right then, Anna and Gage appeared by my bedside. *Wow, that was fast.* Anna was crying. I could tell Gage was freaked out but trying to stay calm. He put a hand on the bed. "You gave us a scare, champ."

"Sorry," I mumbled, starting to cry. Anna looked at Gage murderously. Gage looked panicked.

"No, no, no! Please don't cry! I'm sorry, Mia!"

"I can't help it. I'm concussed," I sobbed. "It's not you; it's me."

Cindy interrupted us. "She'll be fine, y'all. We'll take good care of her. First thing's first, we've got to x-ray that arm. Have a seat in the waiting room, and I'll let you know once we see what's going on."

Anna and Gage agreed and stepped back, waving goodbye to me. I was already rolling away.

The X-ray took longer than it should have because of where the break happened in my wrist. I would need surgery to pin the bones into place. *Are you kidding me?* I just wanted to go to sleep. I felt so out of it. Cindy got me admitted as quickly as she could, and the orderlies moved me to a room on the floor. Anna and Gage met me in the room.

"How do you feel, *amiga*?" Anna asked, calmer now. "I can stay with you tonight. I don't want you to be alone."

It hurt too much to shake my head, and the pain meds were making me fuzzier by the second.

"No, go home and sleep. I'm okay. Can you bring me some clothes tomorrow? I think they'll send me home tomorrow."

Anna nodded. "Okay, I can do that. But you have to promise to call the second you need anything."

A nurse was getting my IV tower and blankets situated. She gave Anna a reassuring smile. "We'll take good care of her, ma'am, I promise."

Anna did not seem convinced. Afraid she was going to put up more of a fight, I held up my good hand.

"Anna, I love you. Go get some sleep. I'll be fine," I insisted. I could feel myself drifting off.

When I woke up later, Anna and Gage were gone. I spent a restless night being awakened by kind nurses every hour or so. Before the sun came up the next morning, I was rolled down to the OR and introduced to Dr. Bertram, an orthopedic surgeon, who was going to set and pin my wrist. He asked what color cast I wanted. I must have told him pink because that's what I woke up with, a neon-pink cast. I woke up briefly in recovery. My headache was better, but my arm hurt a lot. They gave me more IV pain meds.

I woke up in a hospital room filled with cheerful sunlight. *Ouch. My head.* I squinted against the painful light, looking around the room. Anna was dozing in the chair by the bed. A backpack sat on the windowsill, hopefully full of clothes for me. My clothes from last night were probably in the trash somewhere. I hoped she'd remembered underwear.

A knock at the door announced someone. A nurse swept in and began looking me over. Her name was Courtney, according to the whiteboard. The IV machine beeped and whirred as she looked at the settings. She recorded my answers to her questions and told me I would be discharged sometime later in the afternoon. She gave me a cup of ice water with a pain pill and told me to buzz her if I needed to get up. The clock read 1:12. Wow, I'd slept a long time.

Anna stirred then jolted upright. I expected this, but still braced for it. Anna was a violent awakener. She couldn't help it, but waking her up was—and always had been—terrifying. As I knew she would, from experience, Anna remembered immediately where she was, and she was back to normal. I smiled at her. "Hi, roomie."

Anna leapt out of the chair and started checking me over frantically, as if anything could have changed since she had fallen asleep. I held up my IV hand and said, "Anna, I'm fine. Can you help me get up? I need to pee."

Anna helped me navigate the IV tower to the bathroom and back. Once I was settled back in bed, she fluffed my pillows.

"My phone is blowing up," she told me, glancing down at it before putting it back in her pocket. "I took the liberty of telling everyone to stay away. I hope that's alright."

It was more than alright with me. I had seen myself in the mirror, and it was ugly. The nurses had done their best, but my hair was still matted with blood on the left side, and the cut on my temple was swollen. Bruises spread across the left side of my face, an angry purple and dark blue. My whole body ached. I was horribly sore.

"That's a relief. Thank you," I told her, speaking softly. "My head is still pretty painful, even with the meds. I don't want to see anyone else."

Anna smiled down at me. "I'm so glad you're okay," she whispered. Her eyes filled with tears again. My eyes filled with tears too, but that made my head hurt more. I groaned.

"Enough," I begged. "Crying hurts my head."

"Sorry." Anna sniffed and obediently tried to staunch the flow of tears.

"Do you want anything?" she asked.

"I want to go home," I grumped. "Did you bring me some clothes? I want to be ready to go as soon as they come to discharge me."

Anna helped me into the clothes she'd brought. I was glad she remembered about the cast. She'd chosen a racerback tank top with larger arm holes.

"Thank you," I told her. Just being out of the hospital gown and wearing my own clothes, I felt like a new person. I said yet another little prayer of thanks for my friend. Where would I be without her? My purse was also there. I got out my phone. I had about fifty text messages of people checking on me. All the letters ran together, and the light of the screen hurt my eyes. I put my phone down.

I'd just sat back down on the bed, exhausted from getting dressed, when a knock sounded at the door. Anna and I looked over. The ER charge nurse walked in, an older woman named Linda. She was no-nonsense, formidable, but also fair. I liked working with Linda because I always knew where I stood with her.

"Just here to check on the patient," Linda said cheerfully. "How are you, Mia?"

"I've been better," I told her, "but I'm okay."

She tsk-ed and raised an eyebrow. She started straightening the blankets. Linda wasn't a sitter; she liked to stay busy.

"Well," she said conversationally, "I just got finished with the doctor and the scheduler. We've cleared your schedule for this week, and we want you to rest up and heal. That's doctor's orders, you hear? I don't want to see you before next Monday morning." She raised an eyebrow, letting me know she was serious.

I wasn't going to argue. I gave her a thumbs-up. "Yes, ma'am."

"Sounds good. I'll see you next Monday." Then she gently patted my shoulder. "I sure am glad you're okay, Mia. You're a blessing to this old battle ax." She winked at me and walked out of the room.

Shortly after Linda left, the nurse came in with the floor doctor. I was discharged with a prescription for pain medication and a long list of orders regarding my care. Obviously, a concussion was a big deal. I was loopy from the pain meds, but I assured the doctor I wouldn't take it lightly.

An orderly brought a wheelchair while Anna went ahead to get the car. I asked the orderly to take me outside via the ER so I could see my friends and give them proof of life. I didn't feel much like visiting, but it was the least I could do.

It was busy in the ER, as usual. But we swung by the nurse station to let them know I was okay. Anna texted to say she was parked at the door, so we headed in that direction. We were almost to the lobby when an exhausted-looking EMT turned the corner ahead of us. It was Cade. I waved at him. He stopped and waited for us to catch up with him.

"Hey, superhero man," I greeted him quietly, trying not to hurt my head.

He smiled and spoke softly. "Hey, Mia! You breaking out of here already?" He held out his hand for mine. When I acquiesced and placed my good hand in his, he squeezed it. "How ya feeling, champ?"

I nodded carefully. "I'm okay. Thank you for helping me last night."

"I'm glad you're okay. I'm sorry you're hurt, though. Concussions are no fun," he said. The memory of him holding a vomit bucket under my chin chose that moment to resurface. *Oh, man.* That was super embarrassing. I felt myself begin to blush under my bruises. I needed to get out of here. But Cade was still talking.

"I was planning to come up and check on you once my shift was over, but I'm glad you get to go home instead."

"That's sweet. Thanks, Cade. My ride is waiting. I'll be back at work next week. I'll see you then." I pulled my hand back from his and motioned to the orderly to get going.

"See ya." Cade waved, smiling at me. We started moving, then he was gone from sight. Up ahead, the big glass doors opened to let us through. Anna was waiting. She and the orderly got me settled in the car. I thanked the orderly, and we were off.

When we got to my apartment, Gage was there waiting. He offered to carry me, but I didn't trust Gage to have Cade-level strength, so I declined. Going up the stairs was slow, but eventually, I was settled on the couch with a pillow and blanket. Anna fussed over me, making me eat, offering me drinks, snacks, and more pillows.

I rested a few minutes, but I desperately needed a shower to wash off the blood and just not feel so gross. Anna helped me cover my cast with a plastic bag, then she insisted on staying in the bathroom while I showered, just in case. I was thankful for her help with washing my hair, but I was exhausted by the end of it. I needed to rest, and everything was starting to hurt again. It was time for another pain pill.

Anna and Gage took great care of me, making sure I was comfortable and everything I needed was within reach. But I was beginning to feel a little smothered. I finally told them both I was going to lie down and sleep, so they could go. Anna worried and fussed until I reminded her she could come back anytime. She hugged me carefully.

"Please be careful, Mia. You're my family too," she murmured.

I rested the unhurt side of my head on her shoulder. "I know. I will, I promise. You be careful too," I said.

Gage hugged me gently, then they left. I sighed, worn out. Being hurt was frustrating. Yesterday, I ran three miles and did all kinds of things and still had energy. Today, I showered and felt like I had been run over by a truck. Well, technically, it was a Honda Civic. But still. I sat down on the couch, thanking God for my blessings.

My phone began to ring. I checked the display. It was my mom. *Oh.* I hadn't let them know about the accident yet. I took a breath and answered the call.

"Hi, Mom."

"Hi, honey, how are you?" Hearing my mom's voice brought tears to my eyes. Stupid concussion. I cleared my throat.

"I'm okay. I had a little fender bender last night, but I'm okay," I answered.

Mom freaked out. "*What?* Oh my gosh, Mia! Are you sure you're okay? Were you injured?"

I switched over to nurse mode. "Honestly, Mom, I'm fine. I'm a little banged up, but nothing to worry about."

"Oh, honey. Well, I'm glad you're okay. Please don't scare me like that!"

I smiled in spite of myself. "Sorry, Mom."

"Can I do anything to help? Do you need money? Should I fly out there?" she asked. "I have a fundraising lunch, two ribbon-cuttings, and a dinner this week, but I can move them if you really need me."

"Oh no, Mom. I'm fine. Please don't do that," I begged.

It was time to get off the phone before she asked more questions. "I'm going to let you go so I can rest. I'll talk to you later?"

"Of course, honey," she replied. "Please keep me updated, and let me know if you need anything. I love you."

"Thanks, Mom. I love you too. Bye," I said, and we hung up.

I set the phone down, and it began to ring again almost immediately. It was Sarah. She and Maddie were at Target. They wanted to check on me. Anna kept them updated, but they wanted to know from me that I was ok and ask if I needed anything from Target.

I told her I was fine, just tired. I promised I would call her back to-morrow. We hung up. I checked the time—5:00 pm. It was late enough to acceptably go to bed after such an exhausting twenty-four hours. Feeling loopy from the pain pill, I went into my bedroom and got into bed.

Chapter 27

I woke up early the next morning, feeling fuzzy and sore with a headache. I took my time getting up and around. I was out of coffee. I thought longingly of the ground coffee from the other night. It was at the tow yard now. I ate a little cereal then took a pain pill. I turned on the TV, hoping the light wouldn't hurt. I ended up turning it off.

The pain pill kicked in quickly. I was feeling loopy but trying to read my Bible in the morning light when a soft knock at the door startled me. I shuffled to the door then looked through the peep hole.

Was I hallucinating? Ryan was standing there, holding a coffee cup in each hand. *Coffee.* Desire for coffee overrode my self-consciousness about how atrocious I must look. I opened the door. He was real. He was sweaty from running, but his eyes were the same blue. *Good Lord, those eyes.* I wondered if it was the concussion or the morning light making his eyes even bluer than usual.

"Sorry?" Ryan asked, looking confused.

Oh no, I must have said that out loud. No!

"Nothing," I replied. "Um, what are you doing here? It's early."

He held up the coffee with a grin. "I guess you didn't get my text? Sorry. I'm on a mission. I have orders from Pam to check on you since I live a few blocks away. I hope that's okay. I tried to tell her you might think it was creepy, but she insisted."

It hurt my head to laugh, but I couldn't help it. I couldn't say I was surprised. Pam loved big.

"She would have come herself, but she and John are leaving for Alabama first thing this morning," Ryan reminded me. "They're going to see her folks. She strongly suggested I bring this by and check on you, see if you need anything. Then I am supposed to report back."

I took the coffee he offered. "Thank you. Please tell her I'm good."

He didn't move, just kept standing there, beautifully sweaty. He was studying me. Conscious of the fact that I looked terrible, all swollen and bruised, I fought the impulse to touch my hair. Focusing was a challenge. My mind began to wander. I looked at Ryan. *How is he even more hand-some all sweaty?* I wondered. *It's not fair.*

"Thank you?" he said, sounding amused. He tilted his head to the side. I'd thought out loud again. *Where was a convenient sink hole when you needed one? Lord, make me immune to sweaty Ryan.*

Ryan cocked his head to the other side and squinted. "I think your concussion is working on you. Let's get you back inside. I don't want you wandering off on my watch."

He herded me inside carefully. I felt tired, and my brain was fuzzy, so I obeyed. *But*, I told myself, *only this once.*

"Just this once, I promise," he agreed.

Mia, seriously, stop it!

Ryan tucked me in on the couch, under the soft gray blanket, checking to make sure I could reach the coffee on the coffee table. He perched on the arm of the couch by my feet.

"How are you feeling? Any pain?" he asked, concerned. Goodness, he was sweet. My heart warmed and expanded.

Aloud, I told him, "I'm sore, but I'm okay. My head is already better than yesterday. So is my arm."

"I'm really glad you're okay," he said quietly. He checked his watch and said, "I've gotta go, but I'm signed up to bring dinner tomorrow night. Text me if you need anything before then, okay?"

"You don't have to do that," I argued weakly.

Ryan looked at me, his eyes on *full-blast blue.* "I'd love to do that. Be-sides, what would Pam say?" I laughed at that. He smirked.

"I'll see you tomorrow. If you're good, I'll bring you coffee after my run in the morning."

I sighed. This man. *Gosh, he's so great. He's so kind, and funny, and unreasonably attractive. Oh no. I know I said that out loud just now.*

He laughed aloud as he stood up. "No, you didn't."

Ugh. I groaned and covered my face with my good hand, humiliated. When I looked up, he was crouched down near my head. His smile was kind.

"It's okay, Mia. Remember how I had an embarrassing panic attack in the mud on a mountain, and you were kind to me? Now, we're even," he said gently. Peeking out from behind my hand, I nearly got hung up on those eyes again. *Sigh.* I could feel myself zoning out a little bit. These stupid meds were so strong.

To keep from embarrassing myself any further, I shifted my gaze. From this angle, the scar on his eyebrow seemed more prominent than usual. Loopily fascinated, I lifted my hand and pressed my finger to it. Ryan held still, letting me. We stayed quiet for a second. He lightly skimmed his hand up my forearm and squeezed my hand, warming it. His thumb brushed across my skin.

His tone was gentle when he murmured, "I'm really glad you're okay." He swallowed then took a deep breath and carefully placed my hand back by my side. He checked his watch, then looked back at me and said, "Now I've got to go. I have to get ready for work, but I'll see you tomorrow."

He patted my hand twice as he stood then let himself out. I sipped my coffee, resting my head on the pillow. The coffee helped clear my head. I reflected on that sweet moment. After everything he'd been through, it would make sense that a friend being hurt might be tender for Ryan. I was glad to be okay too. And I couldn't help but notice how comfortable it felt to have him here. We really were friends.

Anna came at lunchtime, bearing salads. I was surprisingly hungry. She set the bag down next to my empty coffee cup.

"Where did that come from?" she asked, eyeing it curiously.

"Oh, Ryan brought it by this morning," I replied. Anna arched an eyebrow at me, clearly wanting more information. I shrugged. "He came to check on me. He didn't make a special trip or anything; he was out running. It was on his way. He got a coffee for himself too. He's just kind like that."

Why was I over-explaining? *Shut up, Mia!*

Anna nodded sagely. "Yeah. Nothing like a hot coffee after a run in June. Sounds perfectly reasonable to me."

My mouth was full. I just kept chewing through her sarcasm. I was feeling better but still too tired to formulate a dignified response. Then I got distracted by the memory and started to worry about everything I said.

"I think the pain meds made me weird," I confided in Anna. "The pain is already better. I think I'm going to switch to ibuprofen."

Anna nodded. "That's probably smart, especially if you're going to have sweaty, beautiful man-visitors coming to check on you."

I stopped chewing and looked directly into Anna's dark-brown eyes. "Anna Elizabeth Salcedo Jones, are you making fun of me when I am injured?"

Now, Anna's mouth was conveniently full. She shook her head, her eyes full of innocence. "Mm-mm."

Rolling my eyes made my head hurt. I decided to change the subject instead. "Are y'all coming to the Martins' Fourth of July party in a couple weeks?"

Anna took a sip of her tea through a bright-green straw and nodded. "We wouldn't miss it!"

I was excited too. The party was lots of fun every year. I was certain I'd be better by then, but I'd still have the cast. I felt tired just thinking about it. I had eaten about half my lunch. I put the salad bowl on the coffee table and rested my head on the couch. Anna finished her meal and threw away all our trash. When she came back, she fussed with the blanket, tucking me in for a nap.

"Don't worry about being weird with Ryan. I bet he loves every minute with you, medicated or not," Anna encouraged me. She kissed me on the head and left.

I woke hours later to a knock at the door. It was Sarah and Maddie with dinner. I couldn't believe I slept so long. They sat with me, and we all ate together. It was great, but I was still pretty loopy. *No more pain meds*, I decided. I didn't like that feeling.

Before they left, they helped me change my pajamas. I thanked them for the meal and apologized for being no fun. They sweetly insisted I was always fun, concussed or not. After they left, I thought I might try to read, but the lamp light still bothered my eyes a little bit. I was surprisingly tired and fell asleep easily.

The next day, I woke up early with a dull, aching pain in my arm, but I could tell my head was a lot better. I took some ibuprofen and ate a cereal bar for breakfast. A little bit later, sweaty Ryan knocked softly on the door and wordlessly handed me a coffee. He looked as handsome as ever, but I was able to keep my thoughts to myself this time, thank goodness.

"Thank you for being my coffee fairy during this trying time." I smiled.

He grinned, taking in my epic bed head. "It's a joy. You seem more like yourself today."

I nodded. "Definitely. No more pain meds for me."

"That's too bad. You were pretty funny on pain meds," he teased, his eyes twinkling.

Incredulous, I glared at him, trying to stop myself from blushing insanely red. He took mercy on me and changed the subject, though a cocky grin stayed on his face.

"I have a surprise for you this evening," he said.

"What?" I was intrigued. "Like, a fun surprise? I love surprises."

"Well, then, I will tell you the surprise will *certainly* like *you*. But that's your only hint!" he said playfully. "I have to go get ready for work. See you later."

And with that parting shot and a wink, he sauntered down the stairs without another word. What a punk. I wiped the smile off my face and turned to go back inside.

I waited excitedly all day, wondering what the surprise would be. With such a cryptic hint, it could be anything. Maybe he'd gotten a puppy. I liked puppies. Who didn't? I picked up my apartment, making sure it was tidy.

I'd never had a reason for friends to bring me a meal, but since every effort made me so much more tired than I expected, it was nice to have the food. I loved getting to see a friend for a little bit when they dropped it off too. It made me resolve to take more meals to friends in need. Bible Study didn't meet during the summer, and I was missing seeing everyone each week.

At lunchtime, Anna helped cover my cast for a quick shower. She even helped me wash my hair, so I was as fresh and clean as possible, wearing athletic shorts with a clean tank top.

Around six that evening, a knock came at the door, and I was ready. I opened the door to Ryan and a smiling older woman who was about my height. She was slender and wearing a medical cooling vest over her clothes to offset the heat. Her salt-and-pepper hair was styled in an attractive bob. Her sparkling blue eyes were the color of an October sky. She was unmistakably Ryan's mom.

He was right; I was thrilled to meet her. I welcomed her with a hug as she walked in, smiling.

"I'm excited I'm finally meeting you, Mia! I'm Stella. Ryan has talked about you so much. It's wonderful to put a face with the name."

I blinked. I hadn't expected Ryan to talk about me, ever, to anyone. *What would he say?* I was curious, but before I could ask, Ryan butted in, asking his mom where the sauce was. She walked into the kitchen to help him serve the food on plates.

When they came back to the living room, Stella was carrying two plates piled with spaghetti and meatballs, and salad. Ryan set his plate on the coffee table then went back for glasses of ice water for each of us. Stella and I sat on the couch, balancing our plates in our laps. Ryan sat on the floor, his plate on the coffee table.

The food was wonderful. We ate and visited, laughing together throughout the meal. Stella told me about Ryan taking to different instruments over the course of his childhood. Apparently, the trumpet was her least favorite of all the instruments Ryan brought home to try over the years. It hadn't gone well. Trumpet aside, she was clearly incredibly proud of her son.

While Ryan did the dishes, Stella talked to me about the ways Ryan was like his dad, David. He sounded like a wonderful man. He'd loved music and reading. I could tell they loved each other a lot. Stella asked me questions about my job, church, and my community.

She was familiar with the hospital I worked for, having spent plenty of time there, she mentioned with a grimace. Her MS was progressing, slowly but surely, but she was thankful for great doctors. She did what she could every day to keep her body healthy. I didn't know much about MS, except it was a terrible disease.

Ryan spoke up then, pointing out it was getting late, and I was still recovering. They should probably let me get ready for bed. Stella mock-pouted, but she nodded and stood up to leave.

"Thank you for having us, Mia!" She hugged me. "I'm so happy I got to spend this evening with you!"

I hugged her back and thanked her for coming. "I'd love to see you again, anytime," I said. Ryan hugged me gently and told me he'd see me tomorrow. Then he got Stella wrapped in her cooling vest, and they were off.

My apartment felt large and quiet afterward. I was grateful for the wonderful evening. I could tell it was good for me. I wasn't used to being holed up in my apartment, and I appreciated how Ryan broke up the day for me, bringing me coffee and then dinner.

I smiled, thinking of Stella. She was great. Ryan was lucky. I tried not to be jealous of others when they had wonderful parents and were close with them. I had everything to be grateful for, but Stella hit a nerve. I was glad I could call her my friend.

The rest of the week passed slowly. I improved a little bit every day. Anna came to check on me daily during her lunch break. Different friends brought me dinner each evening. Ryan brought me coffee in the mornings after he ran. I told him I was getting spoiled, but he just smiled and passed it to me. Switching to ibuprofen for the pain proved to be a good decision—no more embarrassing myself, thank goodness.

By Thursday, I was walking in the cooler morning air when Ryan came walking up the sidewalk, holding a cup of coffee for me. He joined me, and we walked around the block, then he brought me back home. We chatted about all kinds of things—hobbies, embarrassing moments, what our respective work days looked like, etc.

He shared with me about the counseling appointment we were supposed to attend together. He'd gone alone and found it helpful. The counselor suggested a post-abortion support group for men and women. He was planning to go the next day. I told him I'd be glad to go with him if he wanted company. He thanked me, saying he'd think about it.

We walked again Friday morning. He asked if I felt up to going with him to the support group that evening. I said yes. I wanted to be supportive to Ryan in this, and I was honored he would allow me to be part of his processing. I could tell Ryan wanted to work through this as well and as quickly as possible. I didn't tell him grief doesn't work like that. I figured he knew. I understood wanting to simply check off a list and be free. Everyone wants that.

I had seen and been a part of a few support groups through the pregnancy center when I volunteered there. It was helpful to work through the emotions and to have a safe place to do it. The pregnancy center used a six-week curriculum. At the end, they held a memorial service for the babies. Going through that experience helped me a lot, for the most part. We'd been encouraged to give our baby a name. I hadn't been ready to do that, but maybe someday I would be.

Chapter 28

T hat evening, I was ready on time. Ryan picked me up and drove toward a church several miles away, in Richardson. "Thanks for giving
me a ride," I told him.

He nodded. "Of course. I'm glad to."

We were quiet on the way to the support group. I didn't feel nervous,
necessarily, just very aware—anything could happen. I wasn't sure how
prepared Ryan was to do this. The meeting took place in a classroom in
a local church building. When we arrived, I unbuckled and started to get
out of the car. But Ryan didn't move. I shut my car door to keep out the
heat and turned toward him.

"Ryan?" I asked. "You okay?"

He gripped the steering wheel and nodded. He took a breath then unbuckled his seatbelt. He looked at me and admitted, "I'm just nervous.
New environment. Big emotions."

I nodded, understanding. It was not easy to do something like this. I
felt nervous too. I took a breath and looked at him. I said the only thing I
could think to say.

"You're not alone."

Ryan looked at me, his eyes drawing me in, even here, even in this.
He took my hand in his and squeezed.

"Thank you for being here," he told me. I squeezed back, nodding.

"Anytime," I replied.

We got out of the car and walked into the church building. When we
found the brightly lit classroom, men and women were finding seats, getting settled into rows of metal folding chairs. I guessed there were about
twenty people in all. A table against the wall held an arrangement of silk

flowers. It was the only other thing in the room. Ryan and I found two seats next to each other in the back row.

The leader stood at the front, welcoming everyone. She spoke briefly, sharing her story of abortion years ago, and how she'd found healing from the trauma and grief. She informed us the purpose of this group was to encourage and help us move through the grieving process into healing. Then she asked if anyone wanted to share.

A man stood and shared, expressing his shame and self-hatred over paying for an abortion years ago. After that, a woman stood and shared how this day was the anniversary of hers. She was feeling crushed by guilt and shame. Many people pulled out tissues as they cried. A couple more people shared. The leader hugged each of them after they spoke.

At one point, I saw Ryan discreetly wipe his eyes. I knew he could be feeling anything. I didn't want to intrude. Thinking back, I remembered feeling like I was floating, like I needed to anchor myself to something, somehow, when the grief got overwhelming. I laid my hand on his arm. He took it, squeezing gently. He didn't let go but clung to my hand. I squeezed back, hoping to comfort him.

The leader spoke and told us all of these feelings were normal. She encouraged us to let ourselves feel all of it, to move through the grief. Then she shared the hope of the gospel.

"Jesus died on the cross for the forgiveness of ALL sins. His grace and freedom from shame is available for you. I hope you will let yourself grieve this terrible thing, then I hope you will embrace the forgiveness Jesus offers and rejoice in the promise of Heaven. He didn't save us so we could stay in bondage. It is for *freedom* that Christ set us free," she said in closing.

We all stood to leave, people wiping their eyes, giving each other hugs, gathering their purses and things. Ryan stayed quiet. He kept hold of my hand until we got to the car. He opened my door, and I got in. When he got in, he started the engine and stared straight ahead instead of driving away immediately. I fidgeted with my cast and waited for him to speak.

"Mia, what was this like for you? How did you move through it?" he asked, sounding tired.

He turned his head and looked at me. I could tell he felt a little lost. I decided to just be honest.

"It was dark. I was filled with shame for a long time. I got really depressed. Anna made me go to counseling, and I was surprised how much it helped. But healing took a long time, lots of twists and turns. Bad decisions. Toxic relationships. I hated myself, Ryan. I felt so worthless. I was just desperate for love of any kind. And there were a lot of times when I just wanted to feel better.

"But Anna wouldn't let me go down that path for very long. She said if I kept doing all those things, she'd find a new roommate. I didn't want to lose her on top of everything else, so I stopped. God protected me from so much, Ryan. If He hadn't given me Anna, I would have gone down a much darker road for much longer, I think."

He nodded, understanding. "I get that. I did the 'comforts of the world' thing—before. I'm not going back to that. I know it's important to feel all of this, but I get the impression it's more of a journey than a momentary-pain-and-healed thing."

I nodded. "I'm so sorry, Ryan."

He looked at me and nodded. He leaned his head on the headrest. "I know. I forgive you. Again."

We smiled at each other, but he grew serious. "I've made a lot of mistakes over the years too, Mia. I know forgiveness is a cycle. I hope you can forgive me as many times as it takes. I forgive you, and I am so sorry. Thank you for not leaving me alone in this. Truly."

I nodded. "It's hard, seeing what we do to each other and ourselves. It took me a while to start counseling, then it was a long journey. I found some healing, but the deeper healing happened when I met the Lord. That freedom. Jesus changed everything for me."

I shrugged, unable to find better words. Ryan nodded. He understood. I don't know why, but I kept going.

"Every story is unique and different, of course. I did a support group like this at a local pregnancy center. It was just for women. At the end of the semester, we had this memorial service for our babies. We were supposed to name them. I didn't name mine. I didn't feel ready."

Tears welled up in my eyes. "Even after all this time, I haven't been able to name her. I felt like such a failure; I couldn't even get that part right. Then the guilt and shame were always there, waiting, telling me I'm worthless, the worst person in the world. It's a little too easy to believe sometimes, even now."

Ryan looked stricken. "Mia, you said it yourself. Jesus changes everything. He redeems it. Nothing is wasted! All this pain has brought you to Him! You shine so brightly with His love. I see it all the time, and it's such a beautiful thing about you. You are new! You are His, and the hope we have in Christ is indestructible! That little girl is waiting for us in Heaven. We'll see her there."

Oh gosh, now I was *really* crying. "Thank you, Ryan."

He paused. "Mia, if you'd like to name her with me, I'd be honored, if you ever do feel ready."

I sniffed, wiping my eyes. "That's kind, Ryan. Thank you. I may take you up on it someday."

I took a deep breath. I wanted to give Ryan as much space as he needed to process. But I was starting to feel a little overwhelmed. I could use some levity. It was impossible to stay down in the mess of it, without things getting dark, fast. I could tell we were both ready to go back to lighter subjects for now.

"Ready to take me home?" I asked. "Maybe we could stop for ice cream on the way."

Ryan blew out a breath and nodded, "I'm always up for ice cream. Let's go."

When I got home that night, I sat down to read Psalm 121. *The Lord is my Help*, I reminded myself. I thanked Him for helping both Ryan and me through the evening. Grief, shame, and pain were such strange things to navigate. Throw in my past with Ryan, and the deep attraction that was always sort of a low hum, and it all got confusing.

I prayed for wisdom. I thanked God for the friendship He was giving me with Ryan, despite the very real weirdness of this situation. *God, thank you for this dear friend and all the ways you are healing me*, I prayed. *Help me to be a good friend to him.*

Chapter 29

S aturday was a day of rest for me. I slept in, then went for a walk to get coffee before the heat set in. The sun was shining, and small gusts of wind rustled in the trees, flapping through the awnings on the businesses I passed. Something was missing. I was surprised to realize I was looking for Ryan on the sidewalk.

I looked around, but there were no unreasonably handsome men out running. I was mildly disappointed. I had become spoiled with our walks. I got a text message, so I looked down at my phone, and I felt my face bloom into a smile. *Ah.* He may not be out here on this sidewalk, but he'd just become part of the moment.

Ryan: Hi Mia, would you be open to coming to a counseling session with me this coming week? She has an opening Monday night at 7:30. I know that's late. No pressure.
Me: That is late, but I'm available. I'll meet you right after work. I'm happy to go, if you think it will be helpful.
Ryan: I think it will be. Thank you for being there for me. I appreciate you.
Me: You're not alone, friend. Send me the address? I can Uber over from work.
Ryan: Sounds good. Then I can take you home, if you're okay with that.
Me: Yes, thanks!

I put my phone away, and kept walking. I knew I would be tired from working on Monday, but if I could be helpful to Ryan, it would be worth it. Many of the men and women I'd met at the pregnancy center were traumatized, tortured by the choices that had been made. It was a hard road. I wouldn't wish that on my worst enemy.

I got home and did a few things around the apartment. Then I took a nap. That evening, I went out for Italian food with Maddie and some other girls. It felt so good to go out and do something normal after a week of sitting around the house. By the time I got home I was exhausted, but it was a wonderful evening.

When I awoke Sunday morning, my bruises were a neon patchwork of yellow and green, much improved. I decided I didn't care if they were bright purple; nothing was going to stop me from going to church. I rode with Anna and Gage, since my car was totaled, and I hadn't received the insurance money yet.

When we got there, different friends came up and gently hugged me. Ryan shot me a smile and waved a friendly hello from the stage. I enjoyed every minute of the service. It felt wonderful to be there. The band played every song acoustically, just the instruments and the voices, no speakers. When I realized Ryan must have done that for me, knowing the concussion made me sensitive to sound, it brought me to tears.

My heart overflowed with gratitude, to get to be there and have all these people to love and be loved by. There was lots of time to think, to consider things over the last week. I'd seen countless victims from car accidents very similar to mine, and not everyone got to walk away at all, much less have this gift of community. I had a lot to be thankful for that morning. I couldn't help but cry a little bit, singing the words to the hymn.

Amazing grace,
How sweet the sound,
That saved a wretch like me.
I once was lost, but now I'm found.
Was blind, but now I see.

That grace was precious to me. I embraced it and thanked God yet again.

Afterward, I was walking out of the sanctuary with Maddie when I heard my name. "Mia?" I turned to look. A tall, muscular man with short, dark hair and blue eyes was smiling at me. It took me a moment to place him out of context. It was Cade from work.

"Oh, hi!" I greeted him.

I introduced him to Maddie. Maddie looked like she was very interested to hear more. I turned to Cade and said, "It's good to see you. Do you usually come here for church?"

"This is actually my first time here," he said. "One of my buddies from work goes here, and he invited me." He gestured to a muscular, bald man standing with a pretty woman who was holding a baby. "How are you doing? You look like you're feeling better."

"Much better, thanks. I'll be back at work tomorrow, then the cast should come off in about a month," I said. "I hope you enjoyed the service. Do you have lunch plans? There's a group of us going out for Mexican food. You're welcome to join us."

He smiled, "I'd like that."

I told him where to meet us, then Maddie and I headed to her car. It felt fantastic to be out doing something normal. I was excited to return to work the following day too. The week of rest had been necessary and good, but I was not used to sitting around the house.

Maddie and I chatted about the sermon on the short drive to the restaurant, then we went inside to join the group. Cade came in a minute or two later, sitting down by me. I introduced him around the table, and everyone greeted him enthusiastically. The server was taking our orders when Ryan walked in and took the seat we'd saved for him at the table. He was seated on the far side of Maddie. He introduced himself to Cade and shook his hand.

The meal passed quickly, all of us talking at once, joking around, complaining about the heat, and thinking about the week to come. Everyone was excited for the Fourth of July party happening later that week. I told Cade about it. He said he didn't have plans, and maybe he'd join us. I was glad we could give a new person a place to feel belonging.

After everyone finished up and paid the checks, Maddie and I walked out with Cade. He asked if he could text me about the Fourth of July party later in the week. I gave him my number, then he told us goodbye and went to his car. Maddie and I were almost to her car when Ryan jogged up to us, asking if I was going to work the next day. I told him I was, and he said he'd be praying for me and to let him know if I wanted to go for a walk or try a run sometime this week. I thanked him and told him I would.

We got in the car. Maddie turned to me, a sly smile lighting up her face. "Oooh, girl, you're in demand this week."

I rolled my eyes. "Ha ha, yeah right."

Maddie shook her head. "You didn't see how they both looked at you. *Veeerry* interested, if you ask me. Cade is really cute too."

Out of habit, I shook my head. This was an immediate no. I looked at my friend, unsmiling. "Maddie. You know I am a disaster at dating. I don't date. I may never date again."

She turned serious and insisted bossily, "Correction: you DO date, and you will again. You've just been through some heavy stuff. Don't roll your eyes at me, young lady! Hear me out. You've found some important healing in the last couple months. Maybe it's time, Mia. You could try and see how it goes. That's all I'm saying. It's just a suggestion."

I shook my head. I hadn't thought about it since that night at the Martins. "I don't know, Maddie. Maybe."

"That's all I want! A maybe! Will you consider it? If he asks you out, will you go?"

I covered my face with my good hand. "Fine. But he's not going to ask out a co-worker he just ran into at church. That's too many overlaps."

Maddie pumped her fist in victory then smiled smugly and said, "Never say never."

I was out of energy. I rolled my eyes some more then changed the subject. "How's Kevin?"

Mercifully, as I knew she would, Maddie talked about the dog the rest of the way to my apartment. I was grateful for that little furball.

At home I laid down for an afternoon nap. Church and lunch had worn me out. I slept too long. When I awoke, I felt out of sorts, groggy, and a little lonely. That didn't happen often, but I didn't want to sit in that feeling. I needed to move.

I got out the vacuum. I would move with purpose. I only needed one hand to vacuum effectively. Then I unloaded the dishwasher. I started a load of laundry. I got my scrubs and lunch ready for the following day. I preheated the oven for a frozen pizza for dinner. Finally, I sat down and found the movie *Jaws* on TV. It was the perfect way to relax before returning to work the next day.

Poor Alex Kidner had just been eaten when my phone buzzed. I checked the display, expecting a text from Anna. We hadn't talked yet that day. I was surprised to see the name on display: Cade.

Cade: Hey, Mia! I was thinking about going to that party for the Fourth. Is it too late to join?
Me: Of course not! You are welcome!
Cade: Great! Any chance you'd like to have dinner together beforehand?

I put my phone down, staring at it as if it was about to attack me. *That was unexpected.* I took a breath. Why was I reacting like this? I got asked out from time to time. Sometimes I went; sometimes I said no.

Over the last couple of years, I said no more often than not, with the exception of Preston. But I'd come a long way, especially recently. Maybe I should try. I tried to think about this sensibly. I had no reason to say no, but I still felt unsure. I made a list in my head.

Pro: Cade was really nice and attractive.
Pro: He was a Christian.
Pro: He was employed.
Pro: He had all his hair. (Not a sure thing when one is pushing thirty.)
Pro: He carried me across the scene of the accident. That was swoony.
Con: He'd seen me throw up. *So* embarrassing.
Pro: He still wanted to go out after witnessing that.
Con: We were co-workers. That could be awkward.
Pro: I promised Maddie I would try.

I reminded myself that going out on one date to see if I liked him and wanted more dates was a normal thing to do in my twenties. Dinner was low commitment. I didn't have to marry him unless I wanted to, which I would never know if I didn't get to know him a little bit.

The pros won. I held my breath and typed: Sure.

I sent him the address of a restaurant I could walk to from here, then we settled on a time.

Cade: Looking forward to it.
Me: Me too.

I made a mental note to book a session with Brooke soon and put down my phone. *I don't have to think about this right now,* I told myself. *I am taking a break from thinking.*

I hit play and finished the movie.

Chapter 30

I took an Uber back to work the next day. It was great to be back but exhausting. *Being down one arm shouldn't be this big a deal*, I thought a few times. I adjusted quickly, but I was glad I didn't have to have the cast for much longer.

I made it through the day then called an Uber to go meet Ryan for counseling. He'd sent me the address. It was the same building I went to for my sessions with Brooke. *Maybe we're seeing someone from the same practice*, I mused.

When I walked in, Ryan was waiting for me in the atrium. He greeted me with a hug and thanked me for being there. He led me down the hall. We checked in and sat down in Brooke's waiting room. I was just about to tell Ryan that I thought we might be seeing the same counselor when Brooke came out of her office. She smiled at Ryan then noticed me and looked surprised.

"Oh my goodness!" she exclaimed, a smile filling her face. "Is this seriously happening?"

Ryan looked between us, not understanding. I gestured to Brooke and said, "Brooke is also my counselor."

Brooke clasped her hands together. "This is a therapist's dream come true!"

Luckily, Ryan laughed and seemed okay instead of freaked out.

We walked into Brooke's cozy office. The rug had a pleasant geometric pattern on it. A black leather wingback chair sat near one end of a gray sofa full of throw pillows. The wall behind the couch held an abstract painting with soothing grays, greens, and blacks, with one big splash of magenta.

The setting sun shone through the blinds, giving the room a pleasant coziness. I loved this room. It was your typical therapist's office, but it had become a safe haven for me. Brooke always sat in the chair during our sessions. I took my usual spot on the sofa. Ryan sat down next to me. Brooke got settled in her chair then looked at me.

"This is wild," she declared. I couldn't help but smile. I shook my head slowly and held up my hands in a helpless gesture.

I turned to Ryan. "Are you sure you're okay with this?"

He nodded, looking hesitant. "It could be helpful." He looked at Brooke. "I assume you are putting together some puzzle pieces right now?" He turned to me. "Have you told Brooke about me?"

"That's confidential," I told him in a prim voice. That set Brooke off, and she snorted a laugh. Ryan laughed too, so I was glad I could lighten the mood a little bit. I reassured him, "Yes, Ryan, I've told Brooke about you. She knows my story, and she's helped me a ton."

Brooke tilted her head at me and smiled. "Aw." Then she looked at Ryan and cracked a joke of all things. "Nothing too juicy, I promise."

I choked out a shocked laugh at that and looked at the floor. I could feel myself blushing. Ryan cracked up and didn't even look bothered. He was so confident. *How did we get here?* I asked myself.

But I was grateful. Laughing helped loosen us all up. Ready to get down to business, I looked at Brooke. "Do you do the breathing with him too?"

Brooke nodded, all professional again. We did the usual deep-breathing exercise together. Then Brooke jumped right in, asking Ryan to tell his side of the story, to catch her up to speed. He told her a quick summary, then as a starting point, Brooke asked him if he was struggling to understand the reason I had the abortion. At this point, I'd stayed pretty calm, but at that question, my skin prickled with sweat. *What would he say?*

"No, I'm not struggling with that. She was young. She had no choice, no support. Who could stand against their parents pressuring them like that?" He turned to me. "I don't blame you, Mia. But I do blame your parents. That was a terrible thing to do to anyone, and you are their daughter. It's not okay. I am very angry toward them."

I nodded, agreeing. "I have felt the same way. *And* I still miss them—how things were before."

He nodded. "That's understandable."

I smiled. "Thank you."

He looked between Brooke and me. He took a breath and said, "Speaking of parents, I keep thinking about my dad. What would he think of all this? I think of my best friend. He always knew what to say. They're both dead. And I'm just left here. Needing them. Grieving. I wish I could talk to them about this. It makes me miss them both even more."

Brooke nodded, understanding. They had clearly talked about his dad and Jamie a lot. Ryan shifted and changed the subject.

"But I think my biggest problem is that I am just really sad. I would like to have children one day. To think that I have one I never knew about is hard to wrap my mind around. I feel really...cheated. I wish I could have been there. But I feel guilty because I don't know what I would have said, if I had known. I feel ashamed of that."

He turned to look at me. "I feel ashamed that I didn't try harder with you, Mia. Like I could have prevented this or saved the baby. I should have come to your apartment or something. I should have done better. But I didn't. I'm sorry."

Brooke talked with Ryan about the importance of accepting what is, rather than dwelling on what-ifs. It was familiar advice. I sat quietly. Then she looked at me. "Mia, how does all this make you feel?"

I sighed. "Is it bad if I say grateful? I'm grateful you have been so kind instead of hating me, Ryan. I've felt a lot of fear about that since you came back into my life. I feel terrible for cheating you out of a child you clearly love, even now. I feel horrible about that decision. I am still so sorry. I always will be. I will always wish this was different. If it wasn't for the Lord being such a safe place for me to lay my sins down, I don't know what I would have done."

Ryan nodded. "I know what you mean. But like I said, you've been gracious with me too. Mia, I failed in a lot of ways, and you've been kind and forgiven me. And now years later, you didn't have to be my friend, but you are. It means a lot."

I didn't know what to say. I hadn't thought about it like that. Ryan looked at Brooke and asked, "Is hugging allowed in therapy?"

Brooke nodded. "Definitely, if everyone is okay with it."

I scooted across the sofa toward Ryan. His strong arms came around me, and I fit there against him perfectly. He held tightly to me for a few seconds. I was grateful to be here with him, working through these things. I could see how much Ryan valued our friendship, and I was grateful.

We talked more with Brooke about grief and boundaries. Ryan asked her about what to expect in this specific grief journey. Brooke was supportive of both of us but also reminded us that being honest with each other was important work, even when it was hard. She reminded us that this was a trauma. Triggers would happen, and that was normal. Ryan seemed very open and appreciative the whole time.

When we left, Ryan held the door for me and walked beside me out to his car. He opened the passenger door for me then went around to the other side.

"Thanks for doing this, Mia. I appreciate it," he told me.

I looked at him. "Of course! I'm glad to. Ryan, you've been really brave about the healing part of this. I just want to acknowledge that. It's important work, but it's not easy."

"Thank you for that. I could say the same about you," he said. "Now let's get you home. I can tell you're exhausted."

He was right. I fell asleep in the car on the way to my apartment. I woke up to Ryan gently rubbing my shoulder and quietly saying my name. I stirred, quickly realizing what was happening. It was a little embarrassing, but Ryan was a safe person to be embarrassed in front of. At least no drool was involved. I thanked him for the ride and said good night. Then I trudged up the stairs, ready to sleep.

The next day, I was tired all day, but in a good way. The ER hit a couple of rare slow moments, so I had a minute here and there to process what happened the night before. I felt more settled and at peace than I had in a long time. I was grateful.

Chapter 31

I was off on Wednesday. As much as I wanted to try running, my body was exhausted. I also didn't want my arm to sweat and turn stinky in my itchy pink cast. So I walked in the cool morning air, before it heated up too much. I walked over to my neighborhood coffee spot and went in for an iced coffee. I got in line and heard my name.

"Mia!" Ryan's pleasant, low voice washed over me unexpectedly. I looked over. There he was, sitting at a table with a cup of coffee and a book in front of him. He smiled and invited me to join him. I got my coffee then sat in the chair he offered.

"I didn't expect to see you here. Is this close by for you?" I asked.

"Yeah, I live a few blocks from here," he said. "I like to come here sometimes to read a little bit. It's a change of scenery from the office or the house, and it's air conditioned."

I hadn't known he lived so close, but it made sense. I sipped my drink and asked, "How's your mom?"

He told me about Stella and some changes they were making to his house to make things easier for her in the long run.

"It's a slow process," he admitted, "but I think it'll be worth it. They should be finished by the end of the week."

"I'm glad she has you," I told him, appreciating how well he loved his mother.

"Well, she really loves you," he pointed out. Then he asked me about going back to work. I told him it was great but exhausting. We chatted about the weather and the softball team's losing streak. I checked my watch. Wow, I thought we'd been talking for a few minutes, not an hour! I started gathering my trash. I needed to get going. I had errands to run.

"Where are you headed?" Ryan asked. "Did you get a car since I saw you last?"

I told him no. I was planning to Uber to the grocery store. He perked up.

"Could I take you? I don't mind at all."

I refused, shaking my head. "Oh, no! I don't want to take more of your time!"

"I was actually planning to go to the store today. I'm going anyway," he reasoned.

I sighed. It *would* be helpful.

"Fine." It was hard, needing help. I missed my independence. Ryan read my thoughts.

"I know it's hard to need help, but it's not for long. I wouldn't offer if I didn't want to. I've done too much therapy," he joked.

That made me laugh. "Boundaries are good for everyone!"

He smiled, nodding. "Exactly."

"Thank you," I said quietly.

He smiled at me. "I like hanging out with you."

My heart swelled with warmth—more than it should. I squashed it. *No, Mia.*

To him, I said lightly, "Well, that works out well for me."

We left the coffee shop and drove to the store in Ryan's car. I felt a little self-conscious, struggling to navigate the cart with one fully working hand. Ryan took over the handle, gently hip-checking me out of the way.

"How about you let me drive?"

I chuckled and said, "Just this once."

We walked companionably, side by side, through the aisles. We each picked up some different things to cook, lunch and breakfast items, and fresh fruit. Then we headed to the snack aisle—my favorite. In an unprecedented twist of events, I was completely out of snacks at home. This could not be. I loved snack foods, and I enjoyed trying new things. I wondered about Ryan.

"What kinds of snacks do you like?" I asked him. I kept thinking of things I wanted to learn about him.

"I'm an ice cream guy. We can hit the frozen section next. How about you? Where do we start? Salty? Sweet?"

I looked at the shelf nearest me. I was face to face with the Teddy Grahams. Ryan paused. I could tell he'd seen them too. My eyes went to his, of their own accord. He smiled softly. His low voice sounded a little scraped up when he quietly asked, "Want to start with salty?"

I nodded. I hadn't had a flashback in a while, and for a moment, it took over. I could see him standing in my college kitchen in nothing but a pair of boxers, tossing Teddy Grahams in the air and catching them in his mouth, laughing. I could see him offering them to me only to pull the box back at the last second, wrapping his hand around my waist and drawing me in—*No.*

I shook myself, wrenching my mind back to the present. This was terrible timing. Breathless, I turned and hurried down the aisle, hoping my cheeks were not as red as they felt. Ryan stayed at my side, saying nothing. I didn't let myself wonder what he might be thinking about. I chose pretzels and Oreos, the items at the opposite end of the aisle, then we headed to the frozen foods.

My heart rate calmed by the time we got to the ice cream. Ryan stood there, debating on ice creams longer than I expected. "Sorry I'm taking too long," he mumbled. "I don't want to miss out on something amazing, you know?"

This was new. Even shivering in the freezer aisle, I couldn't help but grin. Who'd have thought Ryan was picky about ice cream? It was endearing to learn about his quirks.

But I couldn't relate. I scoffed. "Every ice cream is special. It's a no-lose situation, every time. It's ice cream!"

Ryan raised his eyebrows, and held his ground, grinning at me.

"I beg to differ, ma'am," he drawled, his voice getting deeper. A different kind of chill ran down my neck and arms. Ryan continued, his voice tingling along my spine. "In no iteration of ice cream is mint invited to the party. It could be lurking anywhere. Looking at the individual pints is as much about choosing greatness as it is about protecting myself from an accidental mint invasion."

I giggled, shivering. I couldn't help it. When he used an exaggerated Texas accent like that, he sounded ridiculous. Yet, I couldn't object. I secretly enjoyed it. I shook myself, coming to my senses. Time to move on. I rolled my eyes and stepped over to the next freezer. I reached in and grabbed a pint of Blue Bell strawberry ice cream.

"Here you go," I said tartly. "Consider yourself marked safe from mint in any form."

He wrapped his hand around the ice cream, his callused fingers brushing against mine. He smiled, his eyes sparkling. "Don't mind if I do. Thank you."

He put the ice cream in the cart, then we walked to the checkout. Ryan helped me scan and bag my groceries since the bulky cast slowed me down so much. We carried our bags out to the car, then he drove me to my apartment.

Ryan insisted on carrying my groceries up the stairs. Once inside, he set the bags down on the counter in my tiny kitchen. I opened the fridge to put the cold foods in. Ryan opened the pantry, placing the pretzels and Oreos in the snack spot. I closed the fridge right as he shut the pantry, and suddenly, we were face to face.

We both froze. The kitchen mysteriously shrunk, smaller than ever, his broad shoulders filling the space. We stood close, just inches apart. *Holy moly.*

"Thanks for your help, I appreciate it," I breathed. I knew better than to look at his face, but my eyes couldn't go anywhere else. Before I knew it, I was trapped in a sea of blue. He looked down at me, nodding.

"Anytime," he murmured huskily.

We stood there, breathing, for just a couple of seconds. Ryan broke the silence.

"Mia…" He swallowed, his Adam's apple bobbing up and down. His eyes traveled around my face. My skin felt like it was shimmering. He was so close. Leaning in would be the easiest thing in the world. In fact, the distance between us seemed to be shrinking.

What am I doing? I thought.

I quickly looked down at a magnet on the fridge. "You should probably hurry," I said quietly. "I don't want your mint-free ice cream to melt."

He exhaled slowly, nodded once, and looked down, smiling. He licked his lips then looked at me again. He spoke softly. "Thanks for going to the store with me. I had fun."

I nodded. "Me too. Thank you for taking me. You helped me out a lot."

He turned and walked to the door. His hand was on the doorknob when he turned to me. "Can I give you a ride to the Fourth of July party on Friday?"

It took me a second to process his words. I was still focusing on getting my breath regulated. "Hm? Oh, no thanks. Cade's going to bring me."

Ryan paused for a second, absorbing that information. He looked at me then down at his hand on the doorknob. He took a breath.

"Sounds good. I'll see you there, then. Bye!" Then he was gone.

I collapsed onto the couch, my whole body limp. I may never go into the kitchen again. *What was that?* I reminded myself, one more time, that just because everything in me came to life when I was around him didn't mean Ryan wasn't off-limits. He absolutely was.

I accessed my nurse brain to remind myself, yes, feelings of attraction to Ryan were scientifically normal. But he was so much more than the most wonderful man I'd ever known. In spite of everything, Ryan was an important *friend* in my life. I didn't want to lose that. I needed to fix this little crush, to move past it, once and for all. I shook my head and squared my shoulders. *I can do this. I WILL do this*, I told myself fiercely. I thought of Cade. *I AM doing this.*

Chapter 32

I worked the following day. It was a long one, with multiple heat stroke victims and two car accidents. Late in the afternoon, I was doing paperwork at the nurses' station when Cade walked in, looking red and very sweaty. One of the accidents was ugly, with multiple cars involved. It would have taken a long time outside. He tapped on the counter at the front of the desk.

"Hey, Mia!"

I looked up. "Hi, Cade! You hanging in there? It's a hot one."

"Yeah." He nodded. "It really is. I'm excited to see you tomorrow, though. It will be nice to relax a little bit."

I smiled. "Definitely. It's going to be fun!"

He tapped on the counter with his knuckles. "See you later." He smiled at me then turned to walk down the hall, getting back to work.

I reminded myself how anxious I was before my last first date, with Preston. This was already easier than that. I wasn't anxious this time. I was…resolved.

A party with all my friends may not be the best first-date spot, but it was too late now. Dating had historically been pretty bleak for me. At this point, I didn't really think having my friends there could make it worse.

I texted Anna, Sarah, and Maddie, telling them I had a date. They cheered me on, excited for this new development. They all knew how hard I tried to enjoy dating Preston. I could see now it was a mistake to force something. If I didn't enjoy tomorrow night with Cade, I would simply step back and say, *let's be friends*. I wouldn't push it.

Friday dawned, clear and hot. It was a perfect day for the Fourth. I walked down to the coffee shop for a cold brew. I wove my way through the crowd of spectators watching the neighborhood parade. Little kids collected candy and beads. A local high school band marched along, playing "The Star-Spangled Banner." I was tempted to stick around and wave at the floats, but I was already getting sweaty. I didn't want my cast to be any itchier. I hurried into the coffee shop and ordered.

As I was leaving, I pulled up short. Ryan was walking toward me on the sidewalk, clearly finishing up his run. The memory of my kitchen slammed into me. *What to do?* He hadn't seen me yet. *I should hide!* I looked around frantically, but the coffee shop was small. There was nowhere to go. I looked up. Ryan was almost to the door.

I froze, just taking him in. Sweat glistened in his dark-blond hair, and his shirt clung to his muscles. Longing sparked in my brain, watching him, but I told myself to shut up and breathe. He smiled broadly when he saw me, drawing me in. I knew he couldn't help it, but he was truly, *relentlessly* beautiful. And that was just on the outside. Look within, at his heart, and the man was totally irresistible. It wasn't fair.

Slow down. Breathe. I sipped my icy cold brew. I took my time swallowing, forcing my eyes to look at the ground. As he got closer to me, my eyes were drawn to his again, like a magnet. Honestly, who could look at this man and keep from melting a little? Not me. *Ugh. Shut up.*

I burst through the door, just before he reached it. I summoned a breezy smile. "Hey, Ryan!" *Yup, totally chill. That's me. No feelings whatsoever.* "Happy Fourth!"

He smiled. "Hi! You too."

"It's a hot one," I said, gesturing to his sweaty hair. He smiled, agreeing. I was still holding onto the door.

"Here you go." I gestured for him to go inside. "See you later," I called as he walked through the doorway. I turned toward home, not looking back. *Move on, Mia!*

Once home, I wanted a distraction. I thought about doing my nails, but I wasn't proficient enough with the cast. Sloppy nails would only add insult to injury. I called Anna.

"Hey! What are you doing?" I asked.

"I'm pickling some vegetables I bought at the farmer's market over the weekend. What's up?"

"I was wondering if you might have time to paint my nails for my date?"

"Ooh, yes, please! I can come over in about an hour. See you then!"

We hung up. I had an hour to kill. I took advantage of the time. I sat down and spent some time with the Lord, reading my Bible and praying. I made a salad for lunch. I called my parents and caught up with them for a little bit. I pulled out a novel. About ten minutes into the story, Anna knocked on my door and swept in, hefting a large bag on her shoulder. It was full of nail stuff, facial masks, even a hair mask.

"Anna. I'm not doing that to my hair," I deadpanned.

She just laughed. "Of course not, Gimpy. I'M going to do it! You will be my masterpiece!"

I shook my head and laughed. "You are so bossy sometimes."

Anna smiled at me. "You love it." I nodded. So true.

We chatted while Anna did my nails. While finishing up the top coat, she looked at me. "So, a firefighter. Are you excited to hang out with him?"

I smiled widely. "Yup, I can't wait!"

Anna smiled but seemed unconvinced. "Uh-huh. Great, glad to hear it."

Since Anna pointed out her ability to take me down, even if I had two working arms (Which was, unfortunately, true. Anna had three older brothers and an older sister. She was remarkably tough.), she gave me the choice: either I could do the masks with a happy heart, or she could pin me down, and I would do the masks anyway. I chose to be beautified with masks all afternoon.

Anna pulled my hair back then began expertly slathering a pleasant-smelling goo all over my face. She told me about the softball game earlier in the week. Another loss. I still hadn't been to a game, but I wanted to go. She told me "Stupid Preston" had a new girlfriend named Presley.

Apparently, Presley was petite and blonde, a physical therapist. Anna observed her voice was a little nasally, especially while cheering, but she was kind and fun to talk with at the games. I told Anna I hoped it was a good match for them both, meaning it. She gave me a sly smile then told me it was looking good so far; they both favored the use of the pet name *babe*.

A bit later, skin admittedly glowing, I was lying on my kitchen counter, having mask residue washed out of my hair in the sink, when Anna spoke.

"This makes me miss *Mondays with Mia*. I hope we can get in our rhythm again soon." I nodded, agreeing. She went on. "So, are you excited about going out with Cade tonight?"

"Yeah. I already told you, I can't wait," I insisted.

Anna nodded, "You sure did. Can I ask one more question? Why are you going out with Cade and not Ryan?"

I gasped. "Anna! How can you ask me that?"

Nonchalant, she turned off the water then wrung out my hair. She wrapped a towel around my hair and helped me sit up.

She looked me in the eye and calmly said, "I'm just curious. And a little worried. I think you might have forgotten the truest thing about my best friend."

I did not want to talk about this. "I don't want to talk about this," I asserted.

"That's okay, you don't have to talk. I will. I know it's weird to even consider it. I'm not romanticizing an experience that was horrible for you, and for me, as your best friend. But..." She looked me right in the eye, hand on her hip, before she went on.

"You hang out with him, for any amount of time, and you come home *glowing*. You came back from a week at camp with him, and there was this *peace* about you. Something is different, Mia. Last week was scary and hard for you. He made it way better. He spent time with you *every single day*! When you told him about your past, he met you there with compassion and kindness. He invited you to counseling with him!

"You tell me everything, and I'm telling you, Mia, when you talk about him, which is all the time, it is with *joy*! Ryan is not who he was. He is a new creation. And you are too! Our whole past is true about all of us, but it's not the truest thing. The truest thing is what Jesus did for us, and I think you may be forgetting it: He made YOU new too! Mia, don't believe a lie. Believe the truth, that you are lovable! You are valuable! You are worthy of joy! You are *worthy* of the love of an amazing man!"

By the end of her little speech, Anna was practically yelling, clapping her hands to emphasize every one of my attributes. I loved her for it, but I wasn't sure what to say in response.

"Wow," I said, catching some water dripping down my temple with the towel. "Thank you, Anna. I appreciate you reminding me of the truth. I do. I need to hear it sometimes."

Then I told Anna the same things I kept saying to myself. "Honestly, I think Ryan is great. Wonderful, even. I admit I'm very attracted to him. But it's not like that between us. He spent time with me last week because he's a minister. It's his job. We hung out at camp because we were volunteering, in the same place at the same time. I'm a nurse, and he experienced a medical issue."

Anna shook her head, and I could tell she was ready to yell some more. I held up a hand to stop her.

"We are building a *wonderful* friendship, and I'm thrilled about that," I admitted. "It's more than I could ever have dreamed. And I am not going to throw it away on some whim of *attraction*!"

But Anna still would not be denied. "What about the way he looks at you? It's there, Mia. I know you see it!"

"That's just how his face looks," I insisted stubbornly.

Anna paused, smiling. "Falling in love takes a lot of courage, friend. I get it. I do. But if he loves you back, which I think he does, what you find together will be worth the risk. You can do this, if you will be brave. Do it afraid, Mia! That is the definition of bravery!"

I'd had enough. "Please don't talk to me like I'm in a Hallmark Christmas movie, Anna. *You* didn't have to be brave. You and Gage were meant for each other from the first date! And you didn't have this gaping wound from the past waiting to be an issue. You've never hated yourself! You never had to wait to see, wondering if *he* would hate you for something you did. This is completely different, and it is not even *happening!*"

I hopped down from the counter.

"Here is reality: I'm going out with Cade tonight. That's all I want right now. A normal date, with a cute firefighter, who can use his big muscles to carry me around if I get tired. It's enough!" By the end, I was waving my arms around like a crazy person. Anna seemed to finally understand.

She shrugged and nodded. "Okay. You have valid points."

"Thank you," I murmured. I was relieved she seemed to be ready to let it go. But the relief was premature.

"Just one more question." Anna held up a finger. " Do you feel even remotely as alive around Cade, or *anyone*, as you do around Ryan?"

"What does that have to do with anything?" I asked, exasperated.

"Everything." She left it at that. I said nothing. Anna held up her hands, accepting defeat.

"Okay. Let's move on." She clapped her hands together once and spun around, marching back to my bedroom, and headed for my closet. I stayed where I was, processing that last exchange.

"Come on," she called from the bedroom, interrupting my thoughts. "Let's get you ready for this studmuffin!"

I sighed. This confrontation was rattling loose a truth I'd locked down for a long time. It burned through my brain like a lit fuse, illuminating all the secrets I'd kept from myself these last few months.

Anna was right, but it was terrifying to me.

I felt unworthy. How could I deserve something *that* good? I knew the "right" answer, but it was still hard to believe sometimes. Of course this was understandable. The fact that it was *Ryan* made it exponentially more complicated. Were these feelings old or new? Or both?

Anything good about what happened ten years ago was tainted by what came after it. But since then, nothing had ever come close to the way I felt with Ryan back then. Mind, heart, body, soul…I knew him. Ten years ago, he felt like home, and he did now. How could that be?

It was messed up. I knew that. What sane person would latch on this tightly to something they experienced as a teenager? Especially with the trauma that followed.

Being around him now, I had to admit, a slow-burning ember was still there, glowing under the surface. But now, it hurt. The stakes were higher. It made me afraid of more pain. More loss. I was terrified of failure, and even considering it felt like jumping off a bridge. I didn't have the courage or the strength to go there and lose him. It was too much.

Considering these things reminded me that a relationship took two people. Ryan never said or did anything to make me think he was entertaining the idea either. He'd certainly had opportunity. I blushed, thinking about our moment in the kitchen the other day. But, by some miracle, we were friends. This was a gift I could not take for granted. It was enough. It would continue to be enough. I needed to move on.

Resolute, I walked into my bedroom. Anna may not have agreed with my thinking, but she didn't hold back. She picked out a casual-but-cute royal-blue sundress with sandals for me. She'd thought of everything—my pink cast added a fun pop of color against the blue.

Anna carefully did my makeup, keeping everything light. It was going to be hot outside; a lot of makeup would just sweat right off. She kept it simple with a swipe of mascara and blush, topped off with a shiny lip gloss. She left my hair curly, and let it air-dry. Between the mask and the products Anna scrunched in while it was still wet, my curls shone, defined and bouncy. Gold stud earrings completed the outfit. I was ready.

Anna kissed me on the cheek. "You look gorgeous! Have fun! I'll see you there!"

I took a deep breath, grabbed my purse, and headed out to dinner.

Chapter 33

C ade was already at the restaurant when I arrived a few minutes later.

"Hi! You look great!" he said as he stood and greeted me with a hug.

He looked good, even in this heat. He wore a soft golf shirt and nice shorts. We sat down and looked over the menu. I ordered ice water, knowing I would probably sweat a lot throughout the evening, as the Martins' party took place in their backyard.

Cade asked me about my hobbies, then the conversation flowed easily. We laughed a lot. Cade loved his job. He had tons of stories, most of which were just plain weird, but laughing about them took the edge off any awkwardness. We discovered we had several friends in common at the hospital.

Our food came, and we continued chatting as we ate. Cade told me he got out of the habit of going to church when he moved here a year ago from Austin. His sister and her family lived in the area. He wanted to live close to them so he could be a good uncle to his nieces and nephews. I thought that was sweet.

"Anyway, I grew up in church, but moving was a big adjustment. I live alone, so I don't have roommates for accountability. But I'm getting back in the swing of things," he said.

I sipped my water, nodding. I could see how church could fall by the wayside, especially with the ever-changing schedule of a firefighter. We were talking about the things he was looking for in a church when the server brought the check. Cade insisted on paying, then we left for the party.

I'd enjoyed our time together so far, but as we got closer to the Martins', I began to feel antsy and nervous. Cade parked the truck on the street, then I hopped down carefully. I could hear the laughter and conversation noise coming from the backyard. Nothing to do now but go in. I took a breath, grounding myself, secure on my feet. Cade was a really nice, fun guy, and this was going to be a great night. He gestured for me to lead the way, so I did. We walked through the fence gate into the Martins' huge backyard.

We weren't late, but we weren't early either. People stood scattered throughout the yard. Some carried big platters of food out to the long tables by the pool. A group of guys played bocce ball. Lots of people hung around, chatting and laughing. It was hot outside, but John was at the grill, fragrant smoke curling into the sky.

I walked in, immediately spotting Maddie, Sarah, and Ben out by the pool. I led Cade across the crowded yard, through the fragrant shrubs, to the second part of the backyard. I could see the arbor John built Pam even better. He had done a good job, and the vines climbing on it were a rich green. It was gorgeous and peaceful out here.

As we approached my friends, they made space for us. I introduced Cade to everyone. He remembered Maddie from Sunday. I hadn't seen Ben in a while. I told him I was glad he was here with us. Sarah beamed at me from across the circle. It was clear all her doubts were gone, and she could just enjoy being with Ben. I couldn't help but notice they were extremely cute together. Some things were just *right*. This was one of them.

Cade asked if I wanted something to drink. I asked him for a cup of Pam's excellent sangria. He walked toward the drinks table. As soon as he was gone, Sarah held up her hand for a high five. I was puzzled but didn't want to leave her hanging, so I slapped it.

"What was that for?" I asked.

"You!" she replied. "That is one good-looking firefighter. Well done!"

I huffed a surprised laugh. "I'm glad you approve. He's also a nice person and a community helper!"

"Yeah!" Ben piped up sarcastically. "That's way more important than being good-looking, Sarah." We all cracked up. Sarah sassily bumped Ben with her hip. He took the opportunity to put his arm around her, hugging her to his side. He looked down at her, and it was clear the world disappeared for both of them. I was happy for them, but I turned to Maddie, giving them a little privacy for their Special Eye Contact.

Maddie jumped right in, asking me how the date was going. When I told her *so far, so good,* she smiled. "He seems genuinely great. I'm glad you decided to give yourself a chance, Mia. Cade's a good one to try with."

I shrugged. "We'll see. He's great so far, super nice, an interesting, fun guy. I'm giving it a shot, and I'm grateful to be here with all of you fine people. I've certainly had worse first dates."

"Glad to hear it!" Cade said, coming up beside me and handing me my drink. I hadn't seen him walking up to the group, but here he was. He didn't seem bothered that we'd been discussing him; he just smiled at me, clinking his beer bottle against my sangria. "Cheers." I liked his confidence.

Sarah looked past me, toward the shrub path, and waved. "Hey, Ryan!" We all looked over, and there he was, walking out toward us, looking relaxed and handsome. Watching him walk past the arbor, I remembered our time out here a few weeks ago. A warm breeze was blowing. I could feel it heating my neck. I rubbed it with my good hand, hoping I didn't turn completely red.

Ryan walked toward us and found a spot between Maddie and me. He greeted all of us, holding out his hand to meet Cade, and then Ben. He teased him good-naturedly as they shook hands. "Are you THE Ben? These ladies' favorite guy?"

Ben wasted no time striking a Superman pose. He nodded confidently. "Absolutely I am." That cracked everyone up for a moment.

Then Maddie pointed to Cade and said, "We have a firefighter now too. Look at us, just drowning in heroes." We all looked at Cade, oohing.

He smiled humbly. "It's a job."

Maddie badgered him a little, "A job where you use your big muscles to carry beautiful, concussed women across intersections like a scene from a movie?" I wasn't expecting *that.* I blushed and looked at the ground.

Cade looked at me. "There are definitely perks."

"Aw." The whole group joined in. Maddie fanned her face. She loved a sweet moment. I, on the other hand, grew even more self-conscious, my face now beet red. I took a breath to change the subject, but Ryan beat me to it.

"Hey, Mia, I brought you something," he said. He held out a Sharpie marker toward me. I was surprised.

"What is that for?" I asked.

Ryan pulled the lid off then gestured to my cast. "No one has signed your cast yet. If no one signs your cast, you're doing it wrong."

I raised my eyebrows. "Ah. I didn't know there were rules. This is my first broken bone."

Ryan gently took my arm and began to write his name on my cast. "Well, now you're official." He smiled at me. I couldn't breathe for a second.

Maddie jumped in, startling me, and said, "Me next!" She took the pen from Ryan. I turned toward her to let her sign. Slowly, I spun around in a complete circle until all of them had signed my cast.

I looked around. "Thanks for making me legit, you guys."

Right then, Anna and Gage arrived, saying hello to everyone. They both shook hands with Cade and welcomed him. Then they took turns signing my cast. Afterward, everyone else got food, and we all went to find a spot on one of the blankets the Martins set up for picnicking and watching the fireworks. We visited and laughed while people slowly made their way over, claiming their spots for the show.

I looked up and saw Pam waving to me from across the yard. I excused myself then walked over to hug her neck.

"How are you feeling, hon?" she asked.

"I'm great," I told her. "I'm back to work, getting settled in the routine. Once I can wash my own hair, I'll be back to 100%."

"I heard you met my friend Stella Lyles a couple weeks ago," Pam smiled, looking pleased. "She thought a lot of you."

I was touched. I smiled gratefully. "She's great! It was fun to get to know her a little bit. I'm glad we got to meet."

Pam looked past me to the group I had left. Ryan and Cade sat on adjacent blankets, chatting. "Who's that guy talking to Ryan?" she asked.

"His name is Cade. We work together," I answered her.

Pam looked surprised. "He's here with you? Like a date?"

I nodded reluctantly. "Yeah, a first date. But he's also looking for a church home, so it's good for him to get to know some people from church, see if he can find some community."

"Oh." Pam looked confused. I'd never heard her say just a single word. Thinking of her fainting spell a couple months before, I asked if she was okay. She nodded, waving me off. "Yes, of course. I just thought— Well, I need to get these brownies cut so everybody can enjoy dessert during the fireworks. You go sit, Mia. I'll be back."

Before I could say anything else, she headed to the house. I watched her walk away. Something seemed…odd. I couldn't put my finger on it. I walked back over to the blanket and sat down next to Cade. Ryan was on my other side. For a second, I could smell Ryan's cologne on the breeze. It was light and refreshing, just the tiniest bit sweet. It smelled so nice I couldn't help but breathe in a little deeper. Cade shifted next to me, leaning over to answer a question Maddie asked.

The fireworks began. Everyone oohed and ahhed over the beautiful display. The Martins' house backed up to a golf course, and the fireworks were very close. This close up, they filled the sky. I was in awe, just like I had been every year.

After a while, my neck started to cramp on the left side. I couldn't reach it because of my cast. I tried stretching to see if the movement would help. Cade asked if I was okay, and I told him it was just a cramp. Without hesitation, he switched to caregiver mode, massaging the left side of my neck with his big hands. It helped immediately. I turned slightly so he wasn't awkwardly reaching around me.

My eyes happened to meet Ryan's. He smiled a small, tight smile then looked away, back at the fireworks. I sighed, feeling the familiar warmth swell in my chest while also self-conscious that Ryan was watching Cade touch my neck. Tension tickled at my mind. I had a sudden, strong urge to scoot closer to Ryan and explain, but I stayed put.

I wondered if Ryan had ever dated anyone around here. He hadn't mentioned anyone, but that didn't mean he didn't date. How would I feel if I saw him out with a girl? I didn't want to think about that scenario—at all. *What if...?*

No, I thought. *Thinking about that will not accomplish anything.* I took a breath. I looked at the fireworks, indulging in one silent thought: *I wish Anna was wrong.* I shifted away from Cade and thanked him for helping me with the neck cramp.

The fireworks ended, then everyone stood to help clean up. We folded blankets and took the dishes inside. Some other people were already washing dishes, so I left them to it then went out to find Cade. When I got back to my friends, Ryan was gone. Cade and Maddie were talking. He made her laugh. My heart warmed at the sight.

We all turned toward the gate to walk to our cars and head home. I hugged my friends goodbye while the guys all shook hands. Cade and I walked back to his truck, and he opened the door for me. I stepped up and sat down, buckling in. He got in, started the engine, and we were off.

We talked about the fireworks and the party all the way to my apartment building. I was thankful for such a successful evening. Cade parked the truck and turned to me. "I had a great time tonight. Thanks for inviting me."

"Thanks for taking me out! I had a great time too." I smiled.

Cade looked at me. "Mia, you are really fun. I enjoy you a lot. But I get the impression someone else beat me to the punch."

I froze for a second then sighed. I didn't know what to say.

"It's okay," Cade said. "I had a great time. I liked everybody. I'd like to be part of the group. I just don't want to step on anybody's toes. And I don't think it's a good idea to start something here," he said, gesturing between us, "when there is clearly...something. That wouldn't be good for anyone."

I covered my eyes with my hands. The heavy cast scratched my face, so I put it back down. I sighed.

"There's nothing with anyone. I'm just...messed up," I told him. Cade laughed.

"Oh, it's like that?" He chuckled and raised his eyebrows. "Mia, let me assure you, as someone who respects you and thinks you're great, there's *something* with someone. And it is *obvious*. That's all I'll say about it."

I sighed. "I wish I was...different."

Cade looked surprised. "What? Why? You're great the way you are! I don't know what's going on in your head, but you'll figure it out. Life is funny like that. It always works out."

I looked at Cade, encouraged. "True."

He grinned. "I've learned a little bit along the way."

With that last bit of wisdom, we both climbed out of the truck, and he walked me to the door. Cade hugged me, and smiled. "I had a lot of fun. Thanks for going out with me. I'm excited to be friends with you, Mia Browning."

I shot some finger guns at him and said, "Back at ya." He laughed as he walked down the stairs. I opened the door and waved goodbye to him then went inside.

Chapter 34

I woke up early on Saturday and decided to see if Anna and Gage were going to the farmer's market. They were, so they swung by to pick me up on their way. The band was back together. For the first couple of years here in Dallas, it had mostly been the three of us. I never got tired of Anna and Gage. I was grateful to still have them as a huge part of my life.

Gage looked at all the different names on my cast. "Did you do okay with the heat last night?" he asked.

"Yeah," I answered, looking it over. "I don't think it got too sweaty. It's not extra itchy today or anything. Only another week or so, and I'll be done with it!" I couldn't help but smile at the idea. The cast was small in the long run, but it was an annoyance. Covering it up for every shower was a hassle and it took forever to wiggle it through the sleeve of my scrubs on work days. Most of all, I was excited to be able to sleep without having to position the cast so carefully. I'd had a few harsh awakenings of the smacking myself variety, and that was no fun.

Gage pulled me from my thoughts with a big smile. "Then it's time. No more excuses. You are coming to my softball game tomorrow night, sis."

I enthusiastically agreed. "That sounds great! I can't wait to see y'all play!"

Anna put one hand on her hip and joked, "Maybe Mia can bring you guys some luck. This losing streak is getting pathetic."

Gage winced. "It's sad but true. We are bad. Really bad. But it's still fun! And we're gonna keep showing up—for FUN!"

"What an inspiring pep talk!" I was impressed. " Are you coaching this ragtag bunch?"

Gage shook his head, but Anna answered, "He ought to be coaching, but Stupid Preston insisted on doing the coaching."

I was surprised. "Why?"

Gage seemed to think it was reasonable. He shrugged. "Preston played in college. He has experience."

Anna rolled her eyes.

"Well, I'm excited to see y'all play!" I repeated.

It was really hot at the farmer's market. I bought an iced tea to sip as we wandered around. I gradually filled my canvas bag with gorgeous veggies: tomatoes, cucumber, squash, corn, and okra. I even bought a cantaloupe. My good arm felt like it was on the verge of breaking under the weight of all the produce, but we made it back to the car without incident.

Anna and Gage took me home then stayed long enough for Anna to wash my hair, so my curls were fresh for church on Sunday. I felt rested, relaxed. I put together a big bowl of fresh veggies for dinner. It was simple but delicious. I turned on a baseball game to watch while I ate. May as well re-acclimate to baseball words if I was going to a softball game the next evening. The Rangers were up by one. I watched for a while then went on to bed.

Sunday morning came bright and early. I was ready when Sarah picked me up for church. We arrived in time to avoid a glare from Ms. Alma and took our posts at the door. We were handing out bulletins as people walked in when Ryan's mom, Stella, arrived with Pam and John. I waved to her. She came over to give me a big hug. It was great to see her. We chatted for a minute before they all went in to take their seats. I promised her I'd come by soon to visit and see her flowers.

Church was wonderful, such an encouraging reminder of God's faithfulness and good plan for our lives. I left feeling uplifted. As usual, Ryan did a beautiful job leading worship, but he hadn't looked at me once. Usually, he'd smile or wave. I felt weirdly bereft leaving the sanctuary. I tried to shake off the feeling that he acted weird from the stage. I was probably reading too much into it. My thoughts were interrupted when I spotted Gage and Anna across the foyer. Cade was talking with them. I was glad he came back.

I wanted to go over and chat, but I was looking for Maddie. Sarah was leaving to go to the lake with Ben for the afternoon, so I needed Maddie to give me a ride to lunch. *This is getting old*, I thought to myself. I was desperately ready to buy a new car. The insurance company check had finally come in the mail yesterday. I needed to have my independence back. I found Maddie, and luckily, she was happy to give me a ride. We chatted about cars on the way to lunch, and we were still talking about them when we sat down in the restaurant.

Cade was already there, so Maddie sat next to him. He heard us discussing cars, so he began weighing in. I had done a little research so far, but I wasn't certain of what I wanted. We were chatting about interest rates and the best percentages when Ryan walked in. He sat down in the available chair, next to me.

"Hey," I greeted him. "Worship was beautiful. I saw your mom."

"Yeah? That's good," he replied, distracted.

"Are you going to be at the softball game tonight?" I asked, trying again.

"Yup, I'll be there," he answered.

"I'm finally going to the game!" I exclaimed with a quick shimmy. "I'm excited!"

He huffed a laugh. "Well, it's only fair to tell you to keep your expectations low. We don't win, but we have other good qualities."

I nodded. "I've heard some stories. I don't care. I'm still excited. Do you have any big moves I should be on the lookout for?"

He shook his head. "Definitely not. But maybe Cade will. He's joining the team. I just got a text."

We both looked over at Cade, who was still talking with Maddie.

"Cade, you're joining the softball team?" I asked.

Cade looked up, a friendly smile on his face. "Yes, ma'am. I'll be there with bells on."

Ryan said, "Maybe you can help turn things around."

Cade laughed, "I'm willing to try."

We all ate together, paid, and left. Ryan asked if I had a ride home. I told him Maddie was going to take me. He looked at me for a second, like he was absorbing what I'd said. He nodded, waved goodbye, and walked to his car.

About halfway to my place, Maddie said, "I want to ask you something." She sounded serious.

"What is it?" I asked.

Maddie stopped at a red light and turned to me. "Would you feel uncomfortable or offended if I asked out Cade?"

My heart lifted. "YES!" I did a victorious fist pump. "I knew it!" I looked at Maddie. She looked crestfallen. I realized what I'd said. "Oh, no! I meant no, I don't mind at all. I said yes, because I wanted to set y'all up at the Martins' the other night! Maddie, please believe me, I want you to go out with Cade. I think you'd be a great match!"

She looked relieved. "Oh, thank goodness." We both laughed with relief. "Maybe I'll see if he wants to go get a snow cone after the game or something," Maddie said.

I nodded. "Sounds good to me!" I was super excited and proud of Maddie. She dropped me off with a promise to let me know what Cade said. I went up the stairs to my apartment. I decided to take a little Sunday nap.

When I woke up, it was time to get ready for the game. I changed into shorts and a t-shirt then attempted to put my hair up one-handed. It was a disaster. *This cast really is for the birds,* I thought. I pulled a hair elastic onto my good wrist. I'd ask Anna to put it up for me at the game. Maddie texted a couple minutes later, saying she was downstairs, ready to go. I grabbed my purse and headed out.

We arrived at the ball field as the sun was setting. A cool breeze blew, redeeming the hot, humid day. Maddie and I found Anna seated in the stands. All the guys were in the field, warming up. They passed the ball from person to person then back around again. When the umpire blew his whistle, both teams headed to their dugouts.

We were batting first. Gage was up. Anna and I cheered obnoxiously as soon as he started walking to the plate. Gage smiled at us, rolling his eyes, then got into position. He let the first ball go by. The umpire called a strike.

This set Anna off. "Come on, ump! You need glasses! The ball was clearly outside!" I shook my head as other spectators turned to look at Anna. This was why Anna was a problem at sporting events. She'd never played, but she was so competitive it was ridiculous. I laughed to myself, knowing we may be in for a long night.

A girl a couple rows ahead of us turned around and stuck out her hand toward me. "You must be Mia! I'm Presley." I shook her hand.

"It's nice to meet you," I told her. Presley smiled. This must be Preston's new girlfriend. We chatted through the usual things: job, church, etc. I kept one eye on the game.

Cade had just gone up to bat. He swung, then we all heard a loud crack. Everyone stood up, clapping, hoping the ball went over the fence. Cade took off running, his long stride eating up the baseline. The ball made it over the fence, and Cade ran all around the bases to the roar of our cheering.

Maddie was next to me, yelling her head off. Anna turned to me and said, "That's the first home run of the whole season for our team! Cade's first at-bat, and he's already a hero!" We cheered with everyone else. The game continued. Ryan got on base, then Preston did. But Youth Guy Chris struck out. Everyone shook their heads and just yelled, "Bro."

As the game progressed, our team actually held their own, entering the final inning up by one. A guy named Teague was on base when Ryan hit a home run. We all jumped up, yelling and cheering. He gave an excited little jump before he dropped the bat and ran the bases. It was adorable.

We all looked at each other, saying, "Aww." Ryan's excitement was nothing compared to the rest of the team's, though. The guys were so happy to finally win a game that they all jumped up and down, cheering. When Ryan ran to home base, the whole team was there, enveloping him in a huge group hug. The girls and I all agreed that it was kinda cute how sports turned big, burly men into cuddly teddy bears. Anna gathered her stuff then gestured to Maddie and me to walk down to the field.

When we got over there, Gage picked up Anna, spinning her around. She cheered, hanging on to him.

Gage looked down at me and said, "Mia, I can't decide if Cade is our good luck charm or if you are!"

I laughed. "I'm sure it was Cade."

An arm snaked across my shoulders, pulling me against a set of ribs. Startled, I looked over and up to see Preston had wrapped his arm around me.

"I haven't seen you in a while, Mia! Thanks for coming!"

I hugged him with my good arm, then stepped away. "Congratulations on the win, Preston! Y'all played great!"

A pair of arms wrapped around him from behind, then Presley's head popped out from behind Preston's elbow. "Congratulations, babe!"

Preston looked down, turning to wrap an arm around her. "Babe! We won!" He picked her up and spun her around. I laughed, glad for each of them to have found their babe. I turned to look for my friends. Maddie was talking to Cade. Gage and Anna were gathering his stuff in the dugout. I started walking in that direction and caught up with Ryan.

"Congratulations!" I said.

He smiled, his eyes brilliant blue. "Thanks!"

"How does it feel to win one?" I asked.

"Better than losing, for sure," he said.

We got to the dugout, then Gage turned toward us. "We're headed out for celebratory ice cream, y'all! Everyone's coming! We'll see you there!"

Anna looked at me. "Do you have a ride, Mia?"

I replied, "Yes, I'm riding with Maddie. I'll see y'all there." They walked away.

Ryan started gathering his things then looked at me. "Are you sure you're riding with Maddie?" he asked. He gestured to the parking lot. "I think she just got in Cade's truck."

"Oh no! I forgot they were going out. Ugh. I wasn't paying attention," I said.

"You can ride with me," he offered.

"That would be great. Thanks, Ryan."

"Anytime," he responded.

We walked to Ryan's car in the parking lot. We kept the conversation going, but I had to acknowledge an awkward quietness, which hadn't occurred in a long time. I felt very aware of the last time we were around ice cream together. I had thought about that moment more often than I should. *Could he tell?* I wondered. *Had he thought of it since it happened?* Self-consciousness crept across my skin, making me blush.

When we got in the car, with the air conditioner blowing full blast, I asked him, "Are you doing okay?"

"Yeah, why?"

"You seem quiet," I pointed out.

Ryan sighed and ran his fingers through his hair, which made it stick up on that side. "I'm sorry. It's been a weird week. Obviously, counseling and processing. Also, my mom had a rough week, but she's good now. I'm just tired from all that and working this morning, plus the game just now. I did hit a home run after all."

Whew! I was relieved. Joking around was much more normal. "That home run *was* extra-hard work," I agreed. "I'm sorry about your mom. I'm glad she's okay."

We chatted the rest of the way about the church service earlier, but something was still off. I could feel it.

We arrived at the ice cream shop. As we walked up the sidewalk together, I pushed past the remaining awkwardness. "Okay, the moment has arrived," I announced. I held an imaginary microphone in his direction. "What ice cream will you choose?" I asked dramatically.

Ryan did not play along right away but yawned and stretched as he walked. His shirt started to ride up. I immediately looked away. *Nope.* I was definitely not going *there*. I'd probably start crying or something and make things even weirder.

Finally, he answered. "I'm feeling something chocolatey tonight."

I nodded, affirming his decision. "I like it. Chocolate makes every celebration better."

"What about you?" he asked.

I was considering a couple of options. "For a celebration, I think rocky road. It has a little bit of everything." He nodded, affirming my choice. He opened the door for me, the bell above jingling as we walked in to join the rest of the team. Everyone was talking excitedly in the line for ice cream, re-living every minute of the game. Maddie and Cade arrived after us, and the replay began again.

After I finished my cone, I got up to go to the restroom while everyone was discussing the other team's strategy. When I finished and was walking back to the group, Preston met me at the end of the hallway.

"Hey, Mia, can I ask you something?" he asked, looking uncomfortable.

My heart sank, but I pushed the feeling down. "Sure, what's up?"

Preston got to the point. "Does Ryan know?"

"Does Ryan know what?" I asked.

Preston sighed. "Ryan is a minister, Mia. Your past matters for a guy like him, like maybe even for his *job*. If you're going to date each other, Ryan needs to know."

I stood there for a second, deciding what to correct first, but before I could answer, we were interrupted by Ryan himself.

"Ryan needs to know what?" he asked pleasantly, looking Preston in the eye.

Preston looked down, putting his hands in his pockets. He shuffled his feet. "That's not my story to tell."

I looked back and forth between them, feeling helpless. This would not accomplish anything good, or so I thought.

Ryan took a breath then spoke reasonably. "Preston, I think I understand what you're getting at. I *do* know. I have actually been involved in that situation since the very beginning."

Preston was good at math. His reaction was almost instant. If I didn't know better, I'd think Preston's eyes were going to fall out of his head while they shifted between Ryan and me. I stayed quiet, fascinated, while Ryan went on, speaking kindly and calmly.

"If you have a problem with that, or questions, or if you'd like to hear more about God's faithfulness to me, I'd be glad to talk with you anytime. If you're feeling judgmental toward Mia, then you are welcome to judge me too. I know how it is, Preston. It's a little too easy to get comfortable judging situations when they're none of our business. I've been there. I'm happy to talk with you more if you ever want to."

There was no breath in my lungs.

I'd seen a lot of surprising things with Ryan, but I never dreamed he would stand up for me. Even more, stand *beside* me. For him, or anyone, to correct another man about something like *this* with such gentle strength and humility was inconceivable. My heart melted. In an instant, the weight of all the disappointments, the cutting remarks, the immediate breakups, and hurt I'd experienced over the years didn't vanish, but it grew much lighter.

Preston swallowed. "You're right, bro. I was wrong. I'm sorry." He turned to me. "He's right, Mia. I did judge you. I'm sorry. It's none of my business."

Wow. I would've expected Preston to be defensive, but I could see he had a lot of respect for Ryan. And despite my disappointing experience, he was a good man with a kind heart. I nodded. "Thank you, Preston. Of course I forgive you."

Ryan shook Preston's hand. "Thank you for apologizing. I appreciate it. No hard feelings here."

I walked back to my seat next to Maddie. I needed to process the last few minutes, but this wasn't the place. I put it in the back of my mind for now. I would think about it later. Ryan came back from the bathroom then sat beside me. His eyes looked bright, as if he was feeling a lot, too, but stuffing it down.

When everyone began getting ready to go, I asked Ryan if I should hitch a ride with someone else, in case he wanted some time to himself. He looked at me, his eyes pinning me to the spot. "No, of course not. I can take you home." I thanked him then followed him out the door and into the darkness.

In the car, as we pulled out of the parking lot, I told Ryan, "I won't need rides much longer. The insurance check came in the mail, so I'm going with Gage and Anna next weekend to test drive cars."

He smiled. "I'm sure you're excited to get your independence back, but I'm happy to drive you around anytime."

"Thanks," I told him.

I squirmed in my seat. I was so tempted to ignore what happened back there, but it wouldn't be good to let it fester, that would just breed anxiety. "Do you want to talk about what happened with Preston?"

Ryan considered this. I could see him moving through it in his mind. "I don't know, it seems pretty straightforward. I guess that has happened for you more than once?"

I looked at him, raising my eyebrows. "Well, this time was different because a heroic friend stood up for me. I can assure you, it was a first."

"Well, it was that or punch him," Ryan joked.

"Whoa!" I laughed in surprise.

He grinned, shaking his head. Then his smile faded. He gripped the steering wheel, crushing it in his hands. "Mia, I'm sorry. I can't imagine what you've been through, dealing with people and their...thoughtless words."

It was a balm to my bruised heart. I hadn't considered how it would feel to have my experience acknowledged by a man. I was amazed at his empathy. But I didn't want to rehash a bunch of pain. I kept it simple. "It's been tough at times. Every Christian I've dated has dumped me as soon as he found out what I did—including Preston."

His eyes widened. He shook his head, like he was trying to understand. "Maybe I should've punched him after all. I apologize for my species. Sometimes we are just grossly disappointing."

I couldn't help but laugh. "Well, thank you."

We arrived at my apartment. Ryan parked then turned to look at me in the dim light. He looked very serious. I wasn't sure what he was about to say.

"Mia, you are an incredible woman. I look at you, and I see so much more than your past. You bear God's image. You are precious, to Him and to me."

Well, I wasn't prepared for him to say anything like that. One second, I'd been fine; the next, I was undone. My eyes filled. I shook my head. "Gosh, Ryan. Thank you." Needing a distraction to keep myself from sobbing, I said, "You are seriously made for ministry."

He laughed, looking at me earnestly. "I mean every word, Mia."

Through watery eyes, I nodded. "God has given me even more healing and goodness through your friendship, Ryan. You are precious to me too. Thank you."

I reached across the console to hug him. He hugged me back. I thanked him for the ride and got out of the car. After such a crazy evening, I was surprised at how light I felt going up the stairs. *God really can redeem anything*, I realized yet again.

Chapter 35

I worked the next day, Monday. When I got home, I was worn out and very ready to get my cast off later in the week. Thursday could not come soon enough.

Tuesday, I was off work. I woke up early, refreshed. I checked my weather app. It wasn't too terribly hot outside yet. I was two days out from getting my cast off. I was so ready to run. But I knew I'd regret getting all sweaty, because then the cast would be miserable. I let myself go for a long walk. I got an iced coffee at the coffee shop then walked around my neighborhood.

There were cute shops in the area near my apartment, and the rest of the neighborhood was filled with cute older homes, most of them bungalow-style with big front porches. The neighborhood was well-kept, the big, old trees offering welcome shade. I was meandering along the sidewalk, enjoying the landscaping and cute houses. I had just passed an older couple walking a poodle when someone called my name.

"Mia!"

I stopped, turning to look. Over to my left, across the street, sat the cutest bungalow with beautiful Stella Lyles seated on the porch, waving at me. She seemed to be enjoying the shade in a wooden rocking chair. She was wearing her cooling vest. Looking both ways, I crossed the street then walked up the sidewalk to her house.

"Well, hi, sweet girl!" Stella exclaimed. She stood, ready to come greet me with a hug. "What brings you over here?" she asked. She steadied herself, holding onto the handrail as she carefully walked down the steps. She wrapped her arms around me and squeezed.

I returned her hug, as surprised as she was. "I live nearby. I'm just out for a walk. I didn't know you lived this close!"

She gestured to the yard. "Yes, this is home now. Ryan's getting some mulch out back. He should be back here in a minute."

I looked around, seeing several flats of flowers on the freshly-cut grass beside the front walk. A wide swath of flower beds ran along the front of the house on both sides of the concrete. A noise caught my attention. I nearly dropped my coffee when a sweaty, shirtless Ryan came around the corner, carrying a huge bag of mulch over his left shoulder.

Oh my.

I was not prepared for anything like this. My entire body flushed, my face reddening. My mouth went dry, and my knees felt weak. *Where to look?* I focused on his hairline. It seemed safest. I took a calming breath.

A shadow on his shoulder caught my eye. Was that a tattoo? *Holy cow.* The design covered his left deltoid. I couldn't see the details from where I was standing. I got distracted by the muscles flexing under his smooth skin as he balanced the heavy bag then set it on the ground by the flower bed.

Ryan straightened to his full height before he noticed me. He smiled. "Mia! Hey! What are you doing here?"

"Um..." I stammered pathetically.

I turned my head to look at Stella, who was smiling like she'd just won the lottery. Was she reading into this? Oh no. *Focus, Mia.*

"Just out walking," I finally answered him. "I didn't know y'all lived so close."

"We should have had you over before now," Stella said, giving Ryan a pointed look. She turned to me. "I'm glad you're here, Mia! The heat killed my flowers, so Ryan is placing these new seedlings and mulch for me. Then we're going to have some breakfast! You must join us. There's plenty!"

I started to shake my head. "Oh no, thank you. I don't want to intrude."

Stella wouldn't take no for an answer. "It's no imposition at all, dear girl! The more the merrier! I see you have coffee. I'll bring you a glass of ice water!"

She clapped her hands then carefully climbed the steps and headed inside. The matter was settled.

I looked around helplessly. Ryan wiped his gloved hands on his shorts and got to work on the seedlings in the tray. He held a small garden spade in one hand. His shoulders flexed as he dug in, moved the dirt, and gently placed the seedling in the hole. Then he moved on to the next one. I felt ridiculous, standing there doing nothing but ogling him.

"Can I do anything to help?" I asked him. He paused then looked up, smiling.

"Thank you for offering, but our gardening minions need two working arms. It's a requirement," he joked.

I sighed, frustrated. I was sick of this cast.

"It's okay, Mia," he said. "Why don't you keep my mom company while I do this, then we'll all have breakfast? She'd love the visit, if you have time. It's hard for her since she can't be the one doing this. It will be a good distraction for her."

"Okay." I nodded. I didn't need to be told twice. I didn't mind yardwork, but I was happy to have a chance to visit with Stella. I walked up the porch steps. Right as I got to the top, the door opened, and Stella came out with two glasses of ice water. She slowly walked over to me.

"Here we are. Come sit with me, Mia. I'm so glad you're here!" I took the glasses from her and set them down on a small table between the two chairs. Stella sat in one rocking chair, offering me the other.

"Tell me all about you. What's been going on lately?" she asked. Before I could answer, she looked over at Ryan. "Honey," she called, "be sure you don't plant those too far apart. I want it to look nice and full."

I turned to look, and my gaze collided with Ryan's, like he'd already been looking at me. He wore a little half-smile on his face. He met my eyes for a split second, then he blinked. He smiled at Stella. "I know, Mom. I'm doing it right, I promise."

I smiled at him, my heart melting. Not many people were so patient. Ryan was such a good guy. I was happy he and Stella had each other.

Stella and I chatted while Ryan steadily worked to get all the seedlings planted. Once the last seedling was in the ground, he laid the mulch in between all the plants, then raked it smooth. He watered the new plants with a professional-looking sprayer, a cheerful rainbow appearing briefly in the spray.

I put a lot of effort into keeping my eyes glued to Stella, so I wasn't prepared when Ryan came up the steps, pulling the gloves off his hands. His muscles bunched with the movement. He was all sweaty, with dirt smudging his arms and chest. He smiled at his mom. I took the opportunity to take a closer look at the tattoo. It was a picture of a lion coming through clouds and rays of light. It was beautiful.

"All done," he told her. Stella got up to go inspect the results. She stood on the porch, leaning over the rail, checking both sides.

"Thank you, honey." She smiled, turning around to pick up our water glasses. "I'm going to finish up breakfast. You've got time for a shower right quick."

Then she was walking inside, and we were left there, alone, on the porch. Standing with Ryan on the porch felt intimate, somehow. Warmth prickled across my skin. I was grateful I could blame the heat. Ryan looked at me.

"Thanks for coming by." He smiled. "Mom loves having visitors. I hope we're not keeping you from anything important."

I shook my head and stood. "Oh, it's no problem. This was a happy surprise. I love seeing y'all."

I got distracted by a smudge of dirt on his chin. It made me smile. Finally, an imperfection!

"What?" he asked, puzzled.

I pointed. "You've got some dirt, just right there."

He rubbed his chin. "There?" He must have had dirt on his fingers, because he only made it worse.

I nodded, laughing a little. Before I knew what he was doing, he reached out and dabbed some dirt on my cheek. "There you go. Now we're even," He said with a big grin.

"Ryan!" I laughed, dodging a split second too late. I rubbed hard at my cheek. I could tell he'd gotten me good.

I reached out to get him back, but he grabbed my hand at the last second. He held on and pulled me close to smudge dirt on my other cheek. I was down one arm, but I didn't give up. I twisted out of his light grip, but he wrapped one hand around my waist, trapping my back against his chest. We both gasped for air, laughing.

I reached up for one last try, and he caught my hand again. Too late. I'd smeared a tiny bit of dirt on his other cheek.

"Gotcha!" I cried with a triumphant shimmy.

We laughed together, and he released me. I stood back and smiled up at him. The moment drew out, neither of us moving. I shook myself and shifted my focus to his shoulder.

"I like your ink," I told him, taking in the tiny details, now that we were standing so close. The impulse to reach out and touch it was strong, but that was a bad idea.

He smirked and looked at it as if he'd forgotten it was there. "Thanks. I got it after I got baptized."

I nodded. It always felt good to learn more of his story, even a little detail like this. The moment stretched out, becoming unbearable. It was time to go inside. He leaned over and grabbed the door handle.

"Here, I'll show you where you can get cleaned up," he offered. He pulled the screen door open and gestured for me to walk in first.

A wonderful, sweet aroma greeted me as soon as we stepped through the doorway. Stella must be baking something. We walked into a bright, welcoming living room with white walls. A packed bookshelf lined the back wall. *That's no surprise,* I thought fondly. Ryan was usually reading something.

A navy couch sat under a window along the far wall with a pair of comfortable-looking leather recliners angled across from it. A lamp stood in the corner, and a homey basket of blankets rested on a rug positioned nicely between the recliners. Light streamed in through the big picture window facing the street, adding a cheerfulness to the room.

"I like your house," I told him, looking around. "It's very *you*."

"Thanks," Ryan answered. "It's a work in progress."

A wide opening to the left framed the dining room and a cheerful kitchen beyond. We walked across the living room toward a hallway. Light trickled in from a couple of doorways along the hall. Ryan stopped, leaning against the wall trim. He took a closer look at my face.

"Wow, I got you better than I thought. First door on the left; it's all yours." He smiled playfully, his eyes twinkling.

I smiled up at him, about to walk past, but something changed. Time stopped. In slow motion, it seemed the space narrowed. He was inches away, his chest and shoulders still bare, warm from the sun.

I was suspended, glued to that very spot, caught in his gaze. Ryan looked at my mouth. We moved closer to each other, the movement the most natural thing in the world. His hand gently grasped my hip, and heat spread across my skin. He brought up his other hand, his thumb brushing along my jaw. *Closer*. I could feel my stomach start to tremble, gravitating toward him.

I tried to make my brain work. I should be overthinking this, but I couldn't think of a single reason not to be right here. I could barely think at all. His eyes searched my face, then his forehead came down to rest on mine. His lips hovered right there, both of us waiting, savoring.

Our chests pressed against each other. My hands came up, of their own accord, to grasp his bare waist. We were breathing the same air. He was so close, and it felt so good. This was exactly where I wanted to be. It was where I *belonged*.

My heart was pounding. I couldn't move. Until I did. I tightened my grip on his waist and lifted my chin, closing the distance. I pressed my lips to his, a perfect fit.

Crash! The sound came from the kitchen. My eyes flew open. I jumped away from him. A split second of indecision crossed his face, then Ryan turned and walked past me toward the kitchen. He disappeared around the corner.

"Mom? You okay?" he called.

I heard Stella. "Oh, yes, just clumsy. I put a bowl too close to the edge, and it fell in the sink. Nothing to worry about."

Whew! I took a breath. I looked around, rubbing my lips with my fingertips. Before Ryan could come back, I quietly ran into the bathroom, shutting the door behind me. I took a deep breath, trying to slow down my heart rate. I covered my eyes, counting through my breaths. *One, two, three, four, five.*

Exhaling one more time, I looked around. I was in a small, clean bathroom with white walls and a frilly white shower curtain. A navy rug ran across the tile floor. I turned to check my reflection in the mirror.

He had, indeed, gotten me good. Dirt smudged my cheeks and trailed along my jawline, where he touched my face. *Nope, not thinking about that*. I wet my good hand, then rubbed it over my cheeks until all the dirt was rinsed off. I patted my face dry with the fluffy hand towel and looked at myself in the mirror. I willed my body to calm down. Every inch of my skin felt like fireworks.

What have I done?

I stood there, counting breaths, unsure what to do next. Should I leave? What could I say to Stella? What should I say to Ryan? What was he thinking? This was just a blip. An accident. Probably. We'd been spending a lot of time together, processing everything. The moment had snuck up on me. Our shared past was emotional, and this was just an overflow of all that.

It's simple, I told myself. *It was just an impulse. An accident. It won't happen again. Ryan and I are friends, and kissing ruins friendships. It won't happen again. It was just a moment. Don't give it another thought.*

I took a deep breath and gathered my courage. I opened the door. I walked down the hallway toward the living room and turned, walking into the kitchen. Stella was there alone. Ryan must have been in the shower. For a second, I was tempted to walk out the front door and leave, but Stella turned to me.

"Mia, could I ask you to put this bowl of fruit on the table for me, dear?"

I automatically reached out, accepting the bowl and took it to the table. I went back and asked what else I could help with. Stella smiled and asked me to move the muffins from the tin to a basket she'd already lined with a tea towel.

The muffins smelled amazing. I hadn't eaten yet, so I was starving. *Maybe that was the problem*, I thought. *Maybe I was just hungry*. Maybe when I got too hungry, I kissed men who were off-limits.

Seems reasonable to me, I told myself. Because *I* had been the one to kiss *him*. I needed to admit the truth to myself. It was me who closed the final gap. *Good grief*, I sighed inwardly. I wanted to hide my face in my hands, but what good would that do?

I was halfway finished with the muffins when Ryan came into the kitchen, fully clothed in a t-shirt and basketball shorts, his feet bare. His hair was wet from the shower, and he smelled like a dream. *I should have left*, I thought, my cheeks warming again. Goosebumps prickled across my skin. This was too much, too close, and way too comfortable. Attraction had always been there, but now awareness skyrocketed from an informed-and-controlled eight to a raging inferno: *fifteen*.

But it was too late now. Breakfast was ready. We all sat down at the table in the kitchen nook, like normal people who were not about to spontaneously combust. I looked around, hoping for a distraction. A window with gauzy, white curtains let in the pretty light. It danced across the blue tablecloth.

We sat down, and I looked up, making eye contact with Ryan. He smiled serenely and passed me the dish of scrambled eggs. We filled our plates, then Stella prayed for the meal before we dug in.

The food was great. Ryan asked me what I had going on in the week ahead. I told him I'd be working Tuesday, Wednesday, and Friday. Then Stella reminded him she needed him to prune the roses in the backyard before this afternoon, which led to a discussion of all the flowers Stella was growing in the back. The conversation flowed comfortably.

Once we all finished, we cleared the table. Stella started loading the dishwasher, but when I tried to help, she waved me off. It was mid-morning. I needed to get going.

"It's already hot out there. I can give you a ride home, Mia," Ryan offered. "Let me get some shoes on, then I'll be ready."

I wanted to protest, but I worried Stella would be suspicious. Plus, if I walked home, my cast would get all sweaty and itchy. *Stupid cast.* Bracing myself, I nodded, thanking him. Stella hugged me tightly and thanked me again for stopping by. She told me to come visit anytime.

Ryan and I walked out the kitchen door, which led to the garage, and got in his car. As soon as we were out of the garage and on the road, I turned to him. "Ryan, I shouldn't have kissed you. Your friendship is so important to me, and I would never do anything to jeopardize that. I don't know what happened. I guess I just...lost my mind for a second. I'm sorry. It won't happen again, I promise." I fiddled with my cast, afraid of what he might say.

Ryan took his eyes off the road for a second and looked at me. I couldn't read his face. "You have nothing to apologize for, Mia. I mean, I started it. It wasn't just you; it was me too." He slowed the car and turned into my apartment complex. All this time, he literally lived three blocks away. Ryan stopped the car by my building. He turned to me, about to say something, but he paused.

I waited a second, but nothing happened. "Thanks for the ride," I murmured. "And thank you for understanding about what happened earlier. I meant what I said, Ryan. You are important to me."

I paused, fully expecting him to reciprocate or at least agree. But he said nothing. He looked at me, his eyes bright with something I couldn't discern. Several seconds went by, and still he said nothing.

"Are you okay?" I asked, concerned.

He nodded, looking a little *off*. I couldn't put my finger on it. "Yeah, I'm good."

Hmm. Okay. Maybe he needed some time. I thanked him for the ride and told him I'd see him later. I got out of the car, feeling unsure about how that had gone. Should I apologize again? I wasn't sure. I didn't want to make a big deal out of it.

Think about something else, I commanded myself as I climbed the stairs and let myself into my apartment. I had a lot to do today. I needed to go to the store, but first I needed to make a list. Planning my shopping list on the notes app on my phone, I walked into the kitchen to fill a glass with water. I had just taken a sip when there was a knock at the door.

Chapter 36

I went to the door and peered through the peephole. Ryan stood there on the landing. I opened the door. He stepped forward into the middle of the doorway. Surprised, I silently moved aside, gesturing for him to come in. He walked past me into the living area. He turned to look at me, his eyes radiant, like blue fire. He was clearly agitated, but he stood, rooted to the spot, and spoke confidently.

"Mia, I need to take a step back. I don't want to be friends. I can't. I'm sorry." His voice broke, but he kept going, gesturing with his hands. "I fell in love with you a long time ago, and now it's so much more. We've both grown and changed. You're even more beautiful and so full of life. You're fun, and smart, and kind. I love your sassy wit and your pure heart."

He paused to take a breath and continued, "I think about you all the time. You love Jesus, and you love others. I can barely get through the song sometimes during church, worshiping God with you, thinking about everything He's done. You're amazing! My mother adores you. You're just the best."

His smile grew more radiant with every word. He ran his hand through his hair and gestured with his hands. He had more to say.

"I understand you may not feel the same way or want to be with me. Maybe it's too much. We have this history, and it's hard. You may not even think of me that way. Heck, you were out with another guy a couple of weeks ago. And I want you to have everything that's good for you. Truly. But I can't do *this*."

He motioned between us.

"I can't be friends, Mia. I want more—way too much. I want to honor your pain and what you've been through. We both still have healing to do, and I want to heal *with* you.

"This isn't an ultimatum. Of course we don't have to *do* anything or *be* anything. I never want to ask you for anything you don't want to give.

I'm saying I can't be *close* friends with you, Mia. Spending time with you, knowing your heart...I need to take a step back. Because I want it *all*."

His voice broke. He paused and swallowed. "Everything in me wants the whole world with you, forever. I want to serve you, and love you, and *kiss* you for the rest of my life. And I don't know if you would ever even want to try. I'm not sure it's fair to ask. But I need us to have different boundaries."

Words failed me. I was stunned. Of all the things I had ever been afraid he might say, I never dreamed he would say *any* of this. I had so many questions. I didn't know where to begin. How long had he felt this way?

My heart felt so warm and full, I thought I might explode, but I was also frozen with fear. My mind flitted from question to question like an unruly honeybee and settled into the what-ifs. What if we tried, and I wasn't enough? My dating choices haunted me. What if I was too broken, even for him? What if I hurt him? What if I lost him? All of it overwhelmed me. But Ryan wasn't finished.

"I'm going out of town to Nashville for a couple of weeks. This artist I used to work with is making a new album, and he asked me to come play for him. It's great money, and I miss the drums, so I'm gonna go do that. Then, a friend of mine is getting married there the weekend after next, so I'll stay for the wedding.

"I think it will be good for us—for me—to have some space for a while. I'm flying out this afternoon, and I'll be back the Monday after next. When I get home, maybe we could talk, if you want. I know this is a lot. It's not fair to just dump it all on you."

He looked at the ceiling, rubbing his hands over his eyes. "I'm totally word vomiting again." He took a deep breath and let it out. "I'm sorry for dumping all this on you and leaving. I don't expect anything from you. I'll see you in a couple of weeks."

I was still standing by the door, frozen. He walked to me and gently laid his hand on my cheek. He stroked my cheekbone with his thumb once, then he walked out, closing the door quietly behind him.

I stood there for a second, absorbing everything that had just happened. My cheek was warm where he touched it. I wasn't sure what to think or what to do. Should I go after him? Was I *ready* to go after him? So much of what Ryan said was wonderful, more than I ever could have dreamed. So much more, in fact, that I had honestly convinced myself something like this was an impossibility. I felt confused. I wasn't sure what to do.

Did I *want* to be with Ryan? I hadn't considered it as a possible choice. The last couple of months had been wonderful, with a few confusing moments. Of course I was drawn to Ryan like a magnet. He was beautiful, inside and out. Friendship with Ryan was easy and enjoyable.

Relationships had been such a strange experience for me. It took a long time to heal, and for a while, my past just seemed like too much to overcome. At times, I thought I was just too broken. But with Ryan, this unequivocal joy filled my heart. With Ryan, I lit up like a bonfire. All of me.

I loved our friendship. It was so much better than I ever could have hoped. Laughing and having fun with Ryan was easy, but he was a safe place for deeper, emotional things too.

Something tickled my face. Reaching up, I realized I was crying. This was a lot to process. Ryan had said he'd fallen in love with *me*. He wanted it all with *me*. *Wow*. I felt honored.

Part of me wanted to run over to his house and jump into his arms immediately. But part of me wondered, *was this too good to be true?* He was such a good, strong, truthful man. I didn't deserve him.

The shadow of my parents hovered in my mind for a second. The feelings of being unworthy of love were insidious; I didn't always recognize them. But Ryan wasn't my parents. He knew me. Accepted me. He *loved* me. He clearly thought I deserved him. Shouldn't that count for something?

The love of Jesus brought freedom. That love had set me free. I'd forgotten that. I shook my head, wiping my tears. I needed to reject the lie. With a clear mind, I considered Ryan and our friendship. There was no doubt in my mind that Ryan valued me. And I valued him. I was safe to love him. I took a deep breath. This was a lot to absorb.

I looked down and realized I was still holding my phone. The tasks of the week crowded into my thoughts. I had a lot to do in the coming days: getting a car, having my cast removed, not to mention work. But all I wanted was to sit and analyze this little bomb Ryan had dropped. I wasn't sure where to begin.

I texted Anna, Maddie, and Sarah an SOS. I needed my girls around me. They all answered pretty quickly, and we made a plan. We would convene right after work for an early dinner at my apartment.

I spent some time with the Lord, reading the Psalms and praying. I called Brooke and got her last appointment for that evening. Luckily, she'd had a cancellation and could see me. I hadn't been to see her since my accident. Then I called an Uber and went to the grocery store. I bought food to make for dinner with the girls plus food for the week. Ryan was at the back of my mind the whole time.

Thinking about everything that had transpired over these last couple of months filled my heart with joy. I was so grateful for him. I pictured his October sky eyes, his scruff, and his gentle, callused hands. I couldn't help but smile.

Then I remembered my dating experiences. My heart sank a little. What if I couldn't do it? What if I ruined it? What if I said yes, then I was terrible at dating him, much less loving him? I felt frustrated with myself. I hurt Ryan years ago, and now I had hurt him again with my assumptions. I didn't want to hurt him ever again. He was too important.

I needed to think carefully about this. He deserved for me to be completely certain of what I wanted. I wanted to cry at the idea of failing at this, something that felt so natural when I was nineteen. I was afraid of being a disappointment now, for both of us.

This back and forth was exhausting.

I got an Uber home. Once I was there, I put away the groceries. I seriously considered calling Ryan. He was one of the people I wanted to talk to about this the most. I valued his thoughts. He was a safe person for me. I trusted him. *Wow.* I sat in this realization for a few minutes. Ryan was safe for me. I repeat, in the best way, *wow.*

Anna, Sarah, and Maddie descended at 5:15 on the dot. Seeing as it was still 105° in the shade, I set out a variety of chilled salads on the counter: pasta salad, chicken salad, garden salad, and fruit salad, with an assortment of crackers ready to go.

We all loaded up our plates, then sat around the living room coffee table, eating. Sarah got us going. "Okay, Mia, what's up? What's the SOS?"

They all looked at me, ready to listen. I wasn't sure where to begin, so I just went with the simplest version. "Ryan told me he's in love with me."

I was sure they would all be shocked. Maybe not Anna, since she'd put her cards on the table a few weeks ago, but Sarah and Maddie for sure. So, I was the surprised one when Sarah exclaimed, "It's about time!"

For a moment, I wasn't sure I'd heard her correctly. Anna and Maddie were looking at her, nodding their heads in agreement.

"Sorry, I didn't understand what you said," I told Sarah.

Sarah smiled at me, full of hope. "I said it's about time, Mia. That man has been hanging on your every word since we rode the bus to camp! I watched it happen!"

Dumbfounded, I just stared at her. I looked at Anna and Maddie. They both nodded. Maddie was daintily loading chicken salad onto a cracker with her fork. She smirked. "Cade told me about the Fourth of July. He knew instantly he was invading another man's territory. He backed off quickly!"

"Oooh, yes!" Anna clapped her hands. She was clearly thrilled. "Did y'all kiss yet?"

I blushed bright red. "Anna!" I was about to say *of course not,* but then I remembered what happened earlier that morning. I covered my face with my hands, blushing scarlet. They all started squealing and shimmying.

"Tell us! Was it good? Oooh, was it GREAT?" Sarah howled.

I couldn't believe this. I called these friends for help with a crisis, and they were celebrating like Ryan and I were a foregone conclusion. Had I missed something all along?

"Y'all, I am really scared here. You know about my past. What if I can't do this?" My eyes filled with tears. The fear felt more real than anything else could. Failure seemed inevitable.

Anna put down her fork and scooted around to my side of the coffee table. She hugged me. "Mia, what if you *can*? It is for *freedom* that we have been set free! What if you could believe that freedom and take hold of it? What if you and Ryan both move forward together and have something really special? What if I'm right, which I am, and you and Ryan are made for each other?"

Maddie nodded. "Y'all are going to be great together, Mia. He's perfect for you!"

I wiped my eyes. "What if I hurt him, or he wakes up one day and can't stand me? What if he resents me?"

Sarah held out her hands. "Sister, love comes with risk for everyone. There are no guarantees. No one knows what life is going to throw at them or how they're going to handle it. We make a promise, and we give our all, then every one of us has the same option: trust God to meet us where we are. We need Him to be with us to provide the rest. God promises us strength for *this* day. The future is not in *your* hands."

Maddie nodded. "Yup, that's all of us. Remember when we studied Exodus? The Israelites didn't get Wednesday's manna on Monday. You know that, Mia. I get what you're saying, and I understand your fears, but at some point, you've got to let go and let God."

Anna nodded. "And *dating* isn't a covenant. You don't have to marry anybody unless you want to. But if you will just let yourself try, I think it could be wonderful."

Sarah nodded in agreement. "And if he screws it up, we'll beat him up," she declared stoutly.

Maddie and Anna both nodded, unflinching. My heart warmed. I was friends with some seriously fierce women. I wouldn't have it any other way.

"Okay, I will think about it," I promised.

We finished our meal and continued chatting. I wasn't the only one with an update. Sarah and Ben were looking at rings.

"It's fast," she admitted. "But we've known each other for years. I love him. He's the one I want to be with, so we're going for it." We all cheered excitedly then piled up in a big hug of congratulations, rejoicing for our friend.

Maddie and Cade had been spending time together too, which made me very excited and proud to have set them up. "I'm taking credit for this one," I insisted, raising my hand in triumph.

Maddie laughed. "I'll take the win. Thank you, Mia!"

We all laughed, congratulating each other. Eventually, it was time for me to leave for my appointment with Brooke. Maddie let me borrow her car so I wouldn't be waiting for an Uber in the dark. Having a car again was going to be fabulous, I thought. When we headed out, all I could think was how grateful I felt for my friends.

Chapter 37

When I arrived at Brooke's office, she could tell I'd been crying. "What happened?" she asked. I told her everything. "Wow," she responded. I thought to myself, *we've said that word an awful lot in this office lately.*

"Yeah," I sighed. "It's a lot. Brooke, I'm so scared. I've been afraid of losing our friendship. I kept telling myself no, anytime I got close or got distracted. And what about everything from before?"

Brooke sighed. "Mia, I understand how the memories mess with you, but you're not a helpless kid anymore. You are a new person. So is he. What would happen if you let yourself enjoy those feelings? What are you afraid of?"

I thought for a minute. "I'm afraid of getting hurt. But I'm also afraid of hurting him. Dating has been such a weird thing for me all this time. I just…what if I'm not good at dating Ryan either? What if I don't have the right love to give?" I paused.

Brooke nodded, understanding. "I get where you are coming from, with all of that. Those fears are understandable. But can I ask you to consider the other side of the coin? What if you're good at dating Ryan? What if he's good at dating you? What if you're good together? What do you have to lose, Mia?

"You've been protective of this friendship, and now he's said he doesn't want friendship. He wants more. He wants a life with YOU! It sounds like he's all in. You're out of excuses. And you're not special: this is the same decision all people who love someone have to make, for better or worse. Take a second, and forget what you think you deserve. None of us deserves freedom, but Jesus has set us free. It's time to decide what you *want*, then go for it."

I sat there, wrapping the hem of my shirt around my fingers in a zigzag pattern. My heart was pounding at the idea. I felt overheated and at the same time, chilled. I spent so long pushing down what I wanted when it came to Ryan because all of it felt like too much. To even let myself think about the things I wanted, with full honesty, felt like I was about to unleash a fire hose on my life, full blast. I was terrified. If I let myself want, I would lose control.

But the dam had already broken. I couldn't deny it anymore. I wanted him, in every way. I wanted his love, his focus and attention. I wanted to partner with him, to help with his mom, go grocery shopping together, and run together. I wanted to heal with him and grow even more. I wanted to be close with him, in every way. I wanted to raise children with him, go to counseling with him, and love him every minute of the day. I wanted to grow old with him. When I thought about walking through life, holding someone's hand, I wanted it to be Ryan's. For all of it.

I said it all out loud to Brooke. She nodded. "Thank you for telling me. I'm happy for you, Mia! And I'm glad you're being honest with yourself. So, now what? What will you do?"

I told her Ryan was gone for two weeks in Nashville. "I'll wait for him to come back. He said he needed space. I want to give him that. Then we can talk—assuming he doesn't change his mind between now and then."

Brooke rolled her eyes. "He won't. He's smart, Mia. He knows what he has in you."

I left Brooke's office feeling better. For the first time, I felt excited for the future. When I got home, I took a hot shower, then I went to bed. I prayed for wisdom, for peace, and for God's careful protection over both of us while Ryan was gone. I tossed and turned for a while, but sleep eventually found me.

Wednesday dawned, hot and humid. I went to work. My mind felt stuck in a loop. *Ryan, Ryan, Ryan.* Over and over. I had a hard time thinking about anything else. I was excited to be in love with him, but all the fears battled for attention in my brain. I was glad the ER was busy, so I was forced to focus on work.

In the evening, I went over to Anna and Gage's house for dinner. I told Gage what Ryan said the day before. Anna hadn't shared it with him yet, but hearing it again, she got all excited, as if it was new information. She jumped up and down. "YES! I knew it! I *knew* he loved you!"

Anna grabbed hold of me. She hugged the life out of me, pressing my cast painfully against my ribs.

I laughed and wiggled free. "We'll see. He's gone for two weeks to Nashville, so nothing is for sure."

Anna finished up the taco fixings while I poured lemonade into glasses filled with ice. Gage snuck a bite of shredded cheese and smiled at me.

"I'm glad you finally came around, Mia. It's been so obvious since the night he was here for game night. I saw how he looked at you." Then Gage's face turned very stern. "But now Ryan is my boy. My teammate. Now I have to ask you, Mia, what are your intentions?"

Anna grinned widely and fluttered her eyelashes at Gage. "My baby's so cute when he's acting all serious."

I laughed at Anna, but then I turned serious too. "To be honest, I'm not a hundred percent sure, Gage. Ryan said he doesn't want to be friends, which was my plan. I'm still scared of getting hurt or hurting him. But I think I'm ready to try dating him, which is terrifying, given my history."

Anna and Gage remembered seeing me at peak anxiety before a few dates. They understood how difficult that area of my life had been over the years.

Gage shook his head. "It's not going to be like that, Mia. Ryan is a good man. You are a wonderful woman. You're perfect for each other." He seemed completely assured. His confidence bolstered mine.

"Thank you for encouraging me, Gage." I hugged him.

"I've got your back," he declared, then proceeded to stuff three chips into his mouth at once.

I wrinkled my nose in distaste, shaking my head at his terrible manners. Channeling my best Youth Guy Chris impression, I looked at him, raised one eyebrow, and said, "Bro." Then he laughed so hard crumbs flew out of his mouth, landing on my shirt. So, that backfired. Ugh.

Chapter 38

Thursday, Anna took me to the orthopedist to get my cast off. *Finally!* When they unrolled the sock material, Anna could hardly bear to look. To be fair, my arm was disgusting, covered in flakes of dead skin. I thought it might take an entire tub of moisturizer to get it back to normal. After the doctor showed me some exercises to strengthen my wrist, we were free to go.

Once Anna dropped me off, I immediately jumped in the shower.. It took three rounds of exfoliator to get all the dead skin off. Afterward, I slathered moisturizer all over the fresh, pink skin. It felt amazing to be free from the heavy cast. I was so thankful. I hadn't expected a learning curve for using my own arm again, but while washing my hair, I accidentally hit myself in the face a couple times. My shoulder was used to lifting a heavier arm. I hoped I could adapt quickly. It wouldn't be very professional to hit myself in the face in front of a patient—worse, one of my co-workers.

I was working in the ER Friday. It was busy. I was assessing new patients as quickly as possible, very glad to have two working arms. I moved from one room into the next, looking up to greet the patient, and came face to face with Stella Lyles and Pam Martin. Pam beat me to it.

"Mia! I'm so glad it's you!" She turned to Stella. "Mia is a great nurse, Stella." I looked around for Ryan reflexively before remembering he was in Nashville. My heart gave a little lurch. *I miss him*, I thought. I turned to my friends, focusing on Stella. I needed to figure out what was going on.

"What happened?" I asked.

"Stella here has MS. She was working in the garden and got overheated," Pam explained.

Stella shook her head, exasperated. "I'm fine, Mia. This is just sweet Pam being cautious. My temperature got elevated, and my vision got a little blurry. That's all."

"*And* I saw you stumble a little getting to the door. I'm not going to take any chances, Stella. I promised Ryan," Pam pointed out, crossing her arms. Stella rolled her eyes, like a much younger woman.

Well, I thought, w*e've got our work cut out for us here*. I moved over to Stella to begin assessing her. Her temperature was only elevated a couple of degrees, so it was already coming down from the number Pam originally said. It was the same story with her blood pressure. I told them the doctor would be in shortly then left to assess the next patient.

A few minutes later, I saw the doctor go into the room. I followed him in. He looked Stella over carefully, reminding her of the importance of staying out of the heat. She rolled her eyes with frustration.

The doctor said she could go home but only if she promised to make wise choices and protect her health. She huffed petulantly, but made the promise. Smiling at her, I told her I'd get her discharge paperwork ready as soon as possible. I returned quickly. Stella was on the phone.

"No, honey, please don't come back. I'm fine!" She looked at me, and her eyes lit up. "Here, talk to Mia. She'll tell you. You stay put. I'm fine." Stella held the phone out to me, her blue eyes imploring me. It must have been Ryan. I took a breath, steeling myself to hear his deep voice after almost a week.

"Hello?"

"Mia? Is my mom okay? I can come home. I'm looking up flights. How bad is it?" He sounded panicky, but it was so good to hear his voice I couldn't help but smile.

"Hey," I said warmly. "She's fine. Pam was just being cautious, and the doctor is sending her home. It's okay. I promise."

"Oh." He exhaled, audibly relaxing. "Thank goodness. Do you think she'll be okay a little longer, then? I have a few more days left on this album, but I can come home Thursday night."

That was tempting. Hearing his voice made me miss him even more. It was all I could do not to say y*es, come home right now. Come home to* me. But he said he needed this space, and I wanted to honor his request.

Plus, his friend's wedding wasn't until Saturday, and he'd gone all the way to Nashville.

"Don't change your plans," I told him. "Stella is in good hands with Pam, and I can help too, if they need it. Everything is good here. You take your space and have fun at the wedding. We'll see you when you get back."

He thanked me, then things turned a little awkward. Holding in words like *I miss you, I want you, I love you* was harder than I thought. We said a quick goodbye. I sighed, looking down at the phone. Remembering Pam and Stella, I looked up, and they were both smiling like Cheshire cats.

Pam wiped a tear from her eyes and looked at Stella, shaking her head, placing a hand over her heart. "Oh, Stella, she's got it bad."

Stella laughed and nodded, agreeing. Pam stood and hugged me. "Honey, I'm so happy for you."

I felt confused and suddenly very self-conscious. "What?" I wiggled away, not looking Pam in the eye. I handed Stella's phone back to her.

"You and Ryan," Pam drawled, very satisfied with herself. She and Stella high-fived. Stella reached for my hand. I obediently put mine in hers.

"I couldn't ask for a better woman for my precious boy." She looked up at the ceiling, clasping both her hands around the one of mine she was holding. "Thank you, God!"

That did me in. Tears filled my eyes. I couldn't pretend not to know what they were talking about, but I was so thankful Stella felt this way that I couldn't hold it in. Tears rolled down my cheeks.

"Well, nothing's official," I blubbered. "He doesn't want to be friends. I don't deserve him, but I'm not sure I could help myself," I cried. Stella pursed her lips, tilted her head compassionately, and reached for me. I buried my head on her shoulder. She ran her fingers over my hair and patted my back. When I stood up, wiping my face, Stella spoke reassuringly.

"It's going to be okay. You'll figure it out together. My boy loves you, Mia, and I'm elated to see you love him too."

Pam wrapped her arms around me in a motherly embrace. I held on to her for a long time. It had been a long time since I'd been wrapped in that motherly, unconditional love, and here I was, positively drowning in it with both of them. I was overwhelmed.

"There's just so much," I said. "It's not simple."

Pam nodded. "I know, honey. You've told me your story, and Ryan told me he'd known you long ago. I figured y'all were talking about the same time frame, and I put it together. Mia, God's not surprised by this, or anything, ever. He can redeem anything. He can *do* anything. He's good through it *all*.

"You have this chance for happiness with a man who loves you! I see how he looks at you. It's the same way my Johnny looked at me when we were young, and it hasn't changed in thirty years. It's only grown deeper and richer. You grab ahold of him, and you don't let go, for anything. Don't be afraid. Be happy."

Stella nodded. "I couldn't have said it better myself."

I smiled through the tears. "Thank you both. I love you." We all hugged and finished crying, then Pam and Stella got ready to go. I got Stella's number and told her I'd check on her the next day. She said she was going to stay with Pam and John until Ryan came home, just so no one worried. I was glad to hear it. I was sure Ryan would be too. We made plans for me to go over Monday night for dinner, then they left.

I finished my shift and headed home, full of thanks and very tempted to call Ryan. Hearing his voice left a tingle in my spine I couldn't get rid of. It made me miss him even more. By the time I got home, I was exhausted, and my feet were killing me. I ate a quick dinner then fell asleep, reliving my conversation with Ryan, the memory of his voice soothing my busy brain into rest.

Saturday was an important day because it was finally time to gain back my independence. I was determined to buy a car. Gage and Anna wanted to go with me, and we had the whole day to run around, test-driving the options I'd settled on. I'd narrowed it down to three.

Gage told me he was excited to try his hand at haggling, but Anna shut that down immediately. He started to pout, but I met Gage's eyes in the rearview mirror. "I'll allow it but only if absolutely necessary," I told him firmly. Gage seemed satisfied and turned the music up. We sang along to the radio on the way to the first dealership then got out of the car, happy and excited.

By seven o'clock on Saturday night, we were no longer happy and excited. Tired and a little grumpy, we finally made a deal. I drove a new midsize sedan off the lot with minimal anxiety. Anna and Gage took me out for fajitas to celebrate. I was grateful to have a car again, and I loved everything about this one—the soft leather interior, the new car smell. It was a little over budget, but I was able to get a good percentage on the financing, and the check from the insurance for my other car made a sizable dent in the bottom line.

Relishing feeling like an adult again, I drove home, parking my new car in my reserved space. It felt great. I wanted to call Ryan to tell him about it, but I made myself wait. *One week down, one more to go*, I thought to myself, missing my friend, the man who had become such an important part of my life and heart.

Sunday was one of those days where everything just felt *off*. The piano player subbed as the worship leader. Even if I hadn't been in love with him, I had grown so spoiled to Ryan leading worship during the service that a new person just seemed wrong. It was fine, but I missed Ryan. Everything made me miss him that day. Church, lunch, even the softball game.

It seemed since I'd admitted my feelings to myself, I was now destined to be one of those needy women who wanted to be with her man all the time. I laughed at myself. I was sure we would both want our own space sometimes, but over the summer, he'd become a huge part of my life. Now, he was missing from everything I did and everywhere I went. I couldn't wait for him to come home. I was counting down the minutes.

The following week positively dragged by. Monday evening was the highlight. I went to dinner at the Martins', and it was lovely. Pam and John made steaks, claiming they wanted to keep Stella's iron up. Stella laughed at them, saying she was glad to be the excuse for good food anytime. We all laughed through dinner, talking about life and John's current, highly anxious remodeling client.

Once we finished eating, Pam and John insisted on taking a ride in my new car. John asked to drive it and took us straight to the ice cream shop. None of us were going to argue with that. We cheerfully walked in for a scoop, the bell on the door ringing with welcome. Seeing the ice cream made me miss Ryan so much my skin tingled. This distance and waiting certainly seemed to be making my heart grow fonder. Stella leaned over and said, "Mia, you look flushed. You may need two scoops." I smiled then asked her what she was planning to order.

"Anything without mint," she answered. "Ryan and I got surprise-minted by an ice cream once. Neither of us can stand it now." I hadn't re-alized there was a story there. She told me it happened at a birthday party when Ryan was young. The host had brought out strawberry cake with ice cream. Assuming the ice cream was vanilla flavored, everyone at the party dug in, but it turned out to be a homemade mint sherbet, strong enough to burn their mouths. They had understandably feared mint-flavored desserts ever since.

"I can handle brushing my teeth and all," Stella pointed out. "Mint BELONGS there. But not with birthday cake. Gross! I've always been suspicious of ice cream ever since."

I could understand how something like that could happen. Life was full of surprises—some of them nice, some of them downright nasty. We played it safe and each ordered strawberry. It was far down the line, away from the mint chocolate chip.

We sat down to enjoy our ice cream and visit a while. Crunching on the last of my waffle cone, I noticed the ice cream shop employees were washing their utensils, wiping down counters. It was closing time.

I took the Martins and Stella back to the house then prepared to head home for the night. I went to hug Stella goodbye, but she had something else to say. "You know, Mia, Ryan is usually in the studio every waking hour on these trips. But he has called to check on me every day this past week. I don't think he would mind if I told you…he doesn't have a date for the wedding on Saturday in Nashville. Weddings are no fun if you don't have anyone to dance with. I just happen to have the invitation here, in case you're feeling up for a road trip in that new car of yours."

She winked and pulled out a white square full of words written in elegant script. She handed it to me, patting my hand. Warmth spread through me, not only at the idea of seeing Ryan sooner but also that Stella would find such a special way to give her blessing. This was a gift. I hugged her tightly and said, "Thank you." I headed home, formulating a plan, growing more excited by the moment.

I worked Tuesday, Wednesday, and Friday. Lots of patients, lots of paperwork, and lots of running around, helping people. By Friday night, I was wiped out. I was glad I packed on Thursday for the weekend. I'd chosen a flowy blue dress with brown leather wedges for the wedding. I was so excited I could barely sleep, but I needed rest. The wedding was at 5:00 pm the following day. I would need to leave bright and early to make it on time.

Chapter 39

I was up before the sun on Saturday morning then headed out as soon as possible. I was glad I remembered to download some playlists, podcasts, and audiobooks to my phone so I had plenty to listen to on the long drive.

Traffic flowed well all the way to Memphis. Lines of cars stretched for what felt like miles. We sat and sat. I wiggled in my seat, frustrated. Time was ticking down. I was going to be cutting it close.

Sitting in traffic, I prayed I would make it on time. I wanted to see him so badly. I listened to an audiobook to pass the time, then finally, an ambulance rushed past on the shoulder of the road, lights flashing. I prayed for the people involved.

Traffic slowly unwound, everyone pausing to view the wreckage. I knew better than to look; it was too soon. I didn't want to be dealing with any more anxiety than I already was. I drove and drove, careful not to start speeding like crazy as I got closer. My heart sped up when I finally exited off the highway. Almost there.

The traffic in Memphis slowed me down too much—the wedding was about to start. I needed to change clothes and get ready. I accepted my fate. Waiting until the reception gave me a little bit of extra time to clean up and get my hair and makeup how I wanted it. I went ahead and checked into the hotel room I'd reserved near the wedding venue. I was yearning to see Ryan, but if I was going to make *The Big Declaration* to the love of my life, I wanted to look my best.

I took a quick shower to wash away the road trip. I sprayed perfume on my skin and dabbed makeup carefully onto my face. I swept lipstick across my lips, pressed, and blotted. I scrunched my curls into some sense of order, hoping for the best. I shimmied into my blue dress, drawing the straps up over my arms then zipping it up my ribs.

I was lamenting the stark tan lines on my left arm when I remembered Ryan hadn't seen my arm without the cast yet. Two weeks was a long time. I began to feel a flutter of nerves. *What if I'm too late? What if he's changed his mind, and he says no? Maybe he's met someone else. What if he loves it here in Nashville so much he's decided to move back?*

I closed my eyes. *No, Mia.* I took a breath, reminding myself of the truest thing. I was safe in the hand of God, and everything happens in His perfect timing. If Ryan didn't want me anymore, I would survive it. I would keep going.

But I didn't want to miss the chance to love him and be loved by him, because of fear. That would be so dumb. I fastened my wedges, solved the complicated puzzle of fitting my wallet, keys, phone, and lipstick into my tiny clutch, grabbed my room key, and headed out. The invitation was in the passenger seat of my car. It was too late to make it to the wedding; the reception would have to do.

I pulled up to a beautiful building nearby. The parking lot was full, but eventually, I found a spot in the far corner. I took a moment to push my hair behind my ear and pressed my lips together. I gathered my courage, entered the building, and walked into the first party I could find. I quickly realized I had mistakenly walked into a bar mitzvah. I went right back out, apologizing to some confused partygoers.

Sighing, I walked through the building, looking for the wedding reception. I found it at the far end of the building, outside in a beautiful garden area. The walk helped clear my head, and when I found the reception, I was able to go in, confident and ready.

People milled around. Over the hum of people and the fans blowing cool air, I could hear a live band playing over in the corner. I stood, looking for Ryan amid the crowd. I didn't see him at first, so I wandered around a bit. I passed the dance floor, which was already full of people dancing, laughing, and celebrating.

Finally, I spied him, talking to a couple of older men in line at the bar. He looked so incredibly handsome in his gray linen suit that I almost couldn't move. His face was clean shaven, and his hair was carefully styled. He looked content and happy, if a little tired. He was smiling and laughed at something one of them said.

I felt a little awkward interrupting, but I also couldn't have helped myself if I tried. I gathered my courage, every bit of it I could muster. *Lord, help me do this*. I straightened my spine and walked toward my future. I grew more certain with every step. Holding onto my clutch for dear life, I tapped his shoulder. He turned.

"Excuse me," I said. "I was wondering if you'd like to dance."

It was all I could say. I looked into those blue eyes as they lit up, and I was lost. He smiled. I could see his shoulders loosen, joy filling his expression.

"Mia." He marveled at me, like he couldn't believe I was real. "I'd love to." He looked over at the men he'd been talking to. "Excuse me, guys."

Beaming, he took my hand, and we walked to the dance floor. He twirled me around and took me in his arms. "I can't believe you're here. I have been wishing for you every second," he rumbled softly into my ear. He pulled back to look at my face. Before he could say another word, I looked into those beautiful blue eyes and told the truth.

"I couldn't wait any longer. I had to see you. I—" I lost my breath and paused for a second to get it back. "I love you, Ryan. I do. I *have*. I'm sorry I pushed you away. I was so scared. I *am* so scared—still."

We swayed to the music. He held me tight. He smiled, his eyes going *full-blast blue*. "I'm glad to hear that. I love you too. And I'm scared too."

I smiled back at him as a peaceful warmth spread through me. It was right to come here, to be with him. It was perfect. He touched my face then wrapped his arms around me, still dancing, and kissed my forehead.

"We can take it slow," he said. "I'm not going to propose right this minute." The music changed, but we stayed where we were, holding onto each other. He kept talking. "I want to be with you, Mia. Whatever that means, whatever you need, today. We can cross the next bridge when we come to it."

I wanted to be totally honest, to let him know what he was getting, from the beginning.

"Ryan, dating has been a disaster for me. I don't know if I can do it well, even with you," I confessed.

He looked at me, full of confidence. "Let's enjoy the journey. We'll figure it out together." He closed his eyes then brought his face down by my temple. I wrapped my arms around him, holding him as tight as I could.

The world disappeared. Everything around us was a melodic blur. His breath warmed my hair as his hand ran across my back then settled on my waist. He tilted his head, the breeze shifting his hair. "How are you here? How did you find me?"

"I got a new car! And your mom gave me the invitation and suggested I attend as your plus-one." I smiled sheepishly. "Stella is totally in our business." That made him laugh.

"I'm okay with that, to an extent. To quote a wise woman I know, 'boundaries are good for everyone,'" Ryan said and smiled. He grew serious. "I'm glad I get to love you, Mia Browning. I'm honored to have the chance."

My heart exploded some more. This man. This sweet, good, new man. *How can it be? How have you done this, Lord?* I could hardly believe it. But here we were. I looked at him and made myself a promise. I said it aloud as best I could. "You have my heart, Ryan Blackstone Lyles."

He placed his forehead on mine. "And you have mine, Mia Browning," he murmured. He looked into my eyes and caressed my cheekbone with his thumb. "You're so beautiful." He pressed his lips to mine gently, and we were kissing. I was kissing Ryan.

Pure. Joy. Flames erupted from my heart, sweeping over my skin, racing all through my torso. I ran my hands up his shoulders and around his neck. I breathed him in, and he held me tight, pulling me even closer. Understanding bloomed: it wouldn't matter how much time passed. Whether I was nineteen, twenty-nine, or even ninety-nine, Ryan's kiss brought my whole being to life—body, heart, mind, and soul.

Just when the whole room disappeared and I was only aware of Ryan, he pulled back a little, breathing hard. He blinked, like he was finding his balance again.

"Wow." He smiled.

Wow was right. One kiss, and I lit up like a Christmas tree. He was practically glowing too. *Wow, indeed.* We continued dancing, holding each other close, while my heart rate slowed to a reasonable pace. I guess I shouldn't have been surprised. But *wow*.

I needed to ground myself, or I was going to float away on a steamy hot air balloon and never return to reality. I asked how things had gone in Nashville. Ryan told me about playing drums in the studio. He said he enjoyed it, but it was nice to do it occasionally rather than for a living.

I told Ryan about Gage's haggling antics with the salesperson over my new car, and we both laughed. Then I told him about his mom and Pam in the ER, how excited they'd been about us loving each other.

"I'm pretty excited about it myself," he said, smiling down at me. I blushed, overwhelmed with all of it. To think, fear could have kept me from this moment with him, maybe for always. I looked into Ryan's blue eyes, thanking God for giving me courage, promising myself I would embrace life instead of running away or hiding from it. Ryan pulled me close again, then we danced the night away.

Later, after I met lots of people who really loved and missed Ryan, and the happy couple drove away in a fancy sports car, Ryan walked me to my car in the parking lot. He'd ridden with a friend to the wedding, and now he was the one needing a ride. He held my hand as we walked. I relished every second of his touch. We approached my car, and he congratulated me again, knowing my independence was important to me. He raised our hands, spinning me right into his arms to continue dancing.

"When do you work next week?" he asked. I took a second to think about it. Work seemed like another world entirely. I was very focused on swaying to an imaginary song with this man in my arms.

"I work Tuesday, Wednesday, and Friday," I answered, laying my head on his shoulder. His hands wrapped around my waist, holding me close, keeping us on the beat. I wrapped my hand behind his neck, swaying with him, relishing the moment.

"Are you planning to drive back right away? Or maybe you'd like to stay tomorrow? I could show you around Nashville. No pressure either way," he offered.

I didn't need any time to decide. "I'd love to," I answered him. Then it was my turn to invite him somewhere.

"How would you feel about canceling your plane ticket then driving back with me on Monday?"

He pretended to weigh his options. "Hmm, two boring hours in a seat next to a stranger, or a nice long road trip sharing snacks and music with the woman I love? No contest. Sign me up. I'll even help with the driving, if you like."

He took my hand in his, twirled me around, then pulled me close again. We kept dancing, slowly swaying. My feet hurt, but I couldn't give up this moment, cuddled so closely with him. Then he dipped me, and I shrieked a laugh. He pulled me up, back into his strong arms.

"I like this imaginary song," I told him, looking into his blue eyes, knowing I belonged right here. I was filled with gratitude and feeling reflective. This was a new love, but it felt safe, and good, and right. Enduring. I'd never been this certain of anything. Ryan was my home. I knew him, and he knew me. I teared up, looking at him. "Thank you for this," I whispered, overwhelmed in the best way.

Ryan looked at me. "Thank *you*, Mia."

I squeezed his hand in mine. "We could stand here all night in this parking lot, thanking each other, if you want, but these shoes are killing me. How about some sleep, then maybe we could grab coffee in the morning, and go from there?"

He smiled. "Sounds good to me. Let's go."

I nodded. Ryan kissed me slowly and sweetly, then with a quiet growl, he pulled me closer and kissed me so passionately I thought I'd explode. We came up for air and both laughed self-consciously. *Wow.*

Desires I'd previously thought might be dead were rising up in me, alive and well. I wasn't the only one. Ryan took a deep breath and a step back. He took my hand then kissed my knuckles. I laid my palm on his cheek, relishing the moment. Love and awe for this man filled my heart all over again.

We tacitly agreed it was time to move on to a different task, like driving. He opened my car door for me, making sure I was settled before closing the door. Feeling completely cheesy, I blew him a kiss as he walked around to the passenger side and got in. I couldn't help myself.

I'd inadvertently booked my room at the same hotel where he was staying, so that was convenient. While we drove back to the hotel, Ryan told me about all the places he loved in Nashville. I was excited to see some of them the following day.

When we arrived, we walked inside, my hand in his. We walked through the lobby to the elevators. Ryan wrapped his hand around my waist while we waited. He turned, looking into my eyes. "Thank you for coming all this way. I was overjoyed to turn around and see you standing there. Did I mention you look beautiful?"

"Back atcha," I said, laying my head on his shoulder. The elevator bell dinged softly as we stepped in. It was just the two of us. When the doors closed, I wrapped my arms around his waist and held on tight, kissing him and breathing him in. We reached my floor way too quickly. I wasn't ready to let go of him, but it was time.

Ryan's room was on a different floor. Meeting my eyes, he said, "I'm going to say goodnight here, if it's okay with you. I think it would be wise."

I understood, and my heart melted some more. Going home alone was a line I had drawn years ago, but it was typically left up to me to say it. Gratitude warmed my heart. I nodded, looking into his eyes. I couldn't help but smile.

"Wisdom is good. Thank you for a wonderful evening. Goodnight." I kissed him and stepped off the elevator. He smiled, his eyes sparkling as he lifted his hand in a little wave as the doors closed. Walking down the hallway, I couldn't help myself. I spun in a little circle, absolutely giddy. *Wow!* This was the best night of my life. *Thank you, Lord*, I prayed as I let myself into my room and closed the door.

I slept great then rose early to meet Ryan in the lobby the next morning for coffee. He was standing by a tall potted plant, looking so handsome he was practically glowing. His shirt matched his eyes, which made my knees feel weak just looking at him. The coffee he was holding in each hand made him look even better. *I can't believe he's mine,* I thought. Ryan handed me my coffee and kissed me on the cheek.

"Mornin'!" he greeted me.

Those blue eyes pulled me right in. A sense of belonging and joy filled my heart. I thought back. Just weeks ago, the idea of saying yes to this felt terrifying. Now, I was here, with him, and there was literally nowhere else I'd rather be. Of course, it wouldn't always be perfect. We were two human beings. But he was absolutely worth trying for, and thank God, so was I.

I thought of Anna's words. *Do it afraid.* To have a great love, I would have to embrace all the possibilities, take the chance. I could see that now.

Today, we would head out and explore the city together. Ryan would show me his old haunts and take me to eat at his favorite restaurant. To-morrow, we would go home and live our lives, in love with each other.

Against all odds, it was exactly right. I was incredibly grateful and excited to have the chance to build a life with Ryan. After everything, it seemed like it should have been impossible, but I wasn't afraid anymore. We would try, we would put in the work, and we would keep going. We'd trust God to meet us, to fill the gaps. He was faithful. We could count on Him.

With a heart overflowing with joy, I embraced Ryan Blackstone Lyles, the man I would love until my dying breath. The man who loved me in return. He took my hand as we walked out into the sunshine, ready to face the day. *Thank you, Lord.*

Epilogue

One year later

Anna, Gage, and I stood by the bar with a decent view of the stage across the crowded club. The band sounded great, and the room was filled with revelers, dancing, talking, and celebrating. The bass guitar strummed, and I felt the vibration through my entire body. It had been a long time since I'd been in a club, dancing to live music. It smelled the same as I remembered.

Right before the beat dropped, I looked across the room, sinking into those blue eyes. My heart clenched, taking in my drummer, my husband of three months. Ryan was seated behind the drum set, wearing a black t-shirt and looking so good I thought my skin might burst into flames. He winked at me, smiling, and I melted. I raised my glass and shimmied in response. For a moment, I couldn't take my eyes off him as he moved, keeping the beat pulsing through the song.

We were in Nashville for Ryan to play on an album in the studio. The band invited him to come play at the club with them too, claiming that playing in the club kept them *loose*, whatever that meant. Ryan agreed, and here we were, enjoying a night out, reminiscent of long ago, but so much better, in every way.

Anna's baby bump was just starting to show, and Gage kept a protective hand over it, in case the music scared the baby. Anna and I smiled at each other, mutually melting over how sweet it was. Gage was already a puddle over this baby, and we were all excited to see it. We'd find out whether it was a boy or girl next week! I couldn't wait to start buying him or her gifts from Aunt Mia and Uncle Ryan.

Anna, Gage, and I danced through the whole set. At the end, the crowd gradually thinned. Gage took Anna back to the hotel, saying they'd see us in the morning. She went to bed early these days. While the band cleaned up and the bartender swept, different band members came up to thank me for being there and sharing my husband with them for the evening. I appreciated that, but I knew he'd loved every minute.

Finally, Ryan was walking over to me, all sweaty, smiling ear to ear. He'd looked at me the same way on our wedding day, three months ago.

I remembered walking down the aisle on my dad's arm as "The Doxology" played.

Praise God, from whom all blessings flow,
Praise Him, all creatures here below.
Praise Him above, ye Heavenly host,
Praise Father, Son, and Holy Ghost. Amen.

It took all I had to keep myself from running down that aisle to join Ryan, to promise each other the rest of our lives. My favorite memory was seeing him smile, full of freedom and joy, knowing the same smile was on my face. I would never tire of this goodness, this precious man. My eyes teared up a little, just thinking about everything God had done to get us here and all the good ahead.

I was brought back to the present as my husband approached. He was sweaty, his eyes so blue they practically glowed. A joyful warmth spread through me, just looking at him. "Hi," he greeted me happily before he picked me up and spun me around. "You ready to go home?"

I laughed, wrapping my arms around his waist once he set me down. I laid my head on his shoulder. His arms came around me, and I snuggled in closer. "I am home."

He smiled at my cheesiness and said, "Love you." He took my hand then walked beside me. We headed out into the night, together. *Thank you, God.*

Discussion Questions

1. What encouraged your heart as you read this story?

2. What did you want more of, once you turned the final page?

3. Was there a character you could relate to, or see yourself in? Why?

4. What part of the story did you want to go back and read again? What part made you laugh?

5. Mia has a wonderful group of friends, and even mentors in her life. Where have you found community? How have those relationships impacted your life?

6. The Martins are mentors for Mia. She even calls Pam a *church mother.* Do you have friendships with people you look up to and learn from? And on the flip side: Everyone is looking up to someone. Do you have relationships with people who are looking up to you? How can you be intentional in both kinds of relationships?

7. The Church is God's Family, a city on a hill, shining brightly in a dark world. Take a few moments to reflect and consider how your local church is shining bright with the Light of Jesus in your area. How are you taking part in that, or how can you, if you are not currently serving?

8. What did you think of the scene in the ice cream shop with Preston? Have you felt judged by others before? Have you been the one doing the judging? How did that situation make you think?

9. Forgiveness plays a big part in Mia's healing—forgiving her parents, Ryan, and also herself, sometimes over and over. How does forgiveness work? How do we achieve it? How has forgiveness brought you freedom in your own life?

10. What attributes of God's character did you see on display throughout the story? (For example: His faithfulness, sovereignty, mercy, etc.)

11. How do you see God currently working in your own story?

12. Sometimes people and their experiences can be more complicated than social media or television would lead us to believe. If you have sinned and needed grace, and have been met with the love of Jesus, you know how vulnerable and precious that experience can be. Who around you is in need of love or encouragement today? Take a moment to pray and ask God to give you eyes to see, and a heart to love them.

13. If you could write the next five years of Mia's life, what would happen?

Acknowledgements

Oh goodness, where to begin? When I started this little venture, I did it just to see if I could. Then I wasn't sure if I should keep trying, or let it go. My friends Martha, Sarah, and my own precious mama read it for me and all gave a resounding *YES!* That encouragement was a huge gift to me, and it is the reason you are holding this book at all. Thank you for that encouragement, dear ones. I guess we truly never know what God is going to do with our mustard seed or mite!

To Lindsay Stadter, your beta read skills were enormously helpful! Thank you x 1,000!

To the Pettys and Snells, thank you for the work you do at Hope Women's Center (www.myhope.org)! I have thought of their work many times throughout the writing of this book. I admire the mission and loving kindness of that ministry, and all the ways they love and help the women and men who go there.

To Ann and Elizabeth, thank you for helping me to be brave, and for teaching me so much about grace and All The Things, all the time.

To all my friends who read the early versions of the book and gave helpful feedback and encouragement, thank you. Your friendships are one of God's very best gifts to me on this earth, and I am so grateful! You are the reason it was so important to me to give Mia strong female friendships. Every woman should have such fierce truth-tellers to love her!

To the incredibly gracious women who shared their experiences with me, thank you. You shared something heartbreaking, raw, and difficult, and you did it with so much grace and hope. Your stories are proof that Jesus truly changes *everything*! Praise Him! I am so grateful for each of you and the story He is writing with your lives!

Sweet Ashley, thank you for your professional help and guidance on the therapy portions of this story. Your expertise was invaluable!

To my kind editor Jenn Lockwood, thank you for your good work! You were easy to work with and such an encouragement to me! Thank you!

To Ceilidh Shaffer, thank you so much for this amazing cover art! You are incredibly talented and gracious!

I heard someone say that sometimes we just need the right person to believe in us. For me, one September morning last year, that person happened to be Jan Watkins, my church mother, Bible teacher, and friend. Thank you for keeping the main thing the main thing, and for speaking words of life at every turn.

To all the friends and family who have been so supportive and excited for me, thank you! It's meant so much to have you ask me about the book and show your excitement and support!

To my precious family, thank you so much! Thank you for your support, your enthusiasm, your patience, and all your love! Loving you is my favorite part of life.

Printed in the USA
CPSIA information can be obtained
at www.ICGtesting.com
CBHW070911250924
14863CB00055B/1183

9 798991 136112